The Patriot Game

Also by John de St. Jorre

THE NIGERIAN CIVIL WAR

John de St. Jorre and Brian Shakespeare

———

The Patriot Game

HODDER AND STOUGHTON
LONDON SYDNEY AUCKLAND TORONTO

The characters in this book are entirely imaginary and bear no relation to any living person.

For Besfy and Cassiopeia

Contents

Glossary

SAS: Special Air Service (semi-clandestine, operational unit of the British Army)

SIS/MI6: Secret Intelligence Service (British Secret Service)

MI5: British Security Service (responsible for internal security of UK and colonies)

SB: Special Branch ('The Branch') (Counter-intelligence wing of the police)

RUC: Royal Ulster Constabulary (Police force of Northern Ireland)

CIA: Central Intelligence Agency of USA

FBI: Federal Bureau of Investigation of USA

'The Met': Metropolitan Police Force of London

Gardai: Police force of the Irish Republic

IRA: The Irish Republican Army—an illegal organisation in both parts of Ireland

The Provos: Provisional wing of the IRA formed in 1969 after split

The Officials: the other wing of the IRA

'Taig': Perjorative name for Catholics

'Prod': Perjorative name for Protestants

'Joe': an agent

Prologue

"The passion for destruction is also a creative passion."
                                                    Michael Bakunin

THE AFTERNOON DRAGGED SLOWLY by for the three men sitting
in the small front room in a terraced house in Ballymena. At
five o'clock Rory stubbed out his cigarette in an overflowing
ashtray and stood up.

"It's time," he said.

The youngest of the trio went to the back of the house and
spoke to the owner's wife. She gave him a key and pointed to a
shed at the bottom of the garden. Ten minutes later he returned
to the front room cradling the Thompsons in his arms. He had
already put his shoulder holster on and tucked the Walther
into it. Clips of ammunition were passed round and as they
gave their weapons a final check they heard the sound of a
vehicle drawing up outside. Rory pulled back the blinds and
peered out. He turned back to the others who had cleared the
tea-mugs off the table and were having a final look at a large-
scale street map of the town.

"Right on time," he said. "OK?"

They nodded, the younger one grinning nervously. Rory and the boy took the Thompsons, holding them by the stocks pointing downwards along the line of the thigh underneath their overcoats. The second man, grizzled and older than the others, went out into the street. He talked to the driver of the small van which had drawn up outside. He took the keys and got into the driver's seat. The driver waved goodbye and hurried off down the road with the springy step of a man who has just left a dentist's surgery.

The front door of the house opened. Rory and his young companion slipped quickly into the seat beside the driver, with Rory on the outside. The back of the van was a jumble of builders' tools, ropes, paint pots, a couple of large steel boxes and an untidy heap of empty sacks.

"Let's go," said Rory.

The van pulled away from the kerb and headed towards the centre of the town. It was 5.30 p.m. There was the bustling, slightly festive air that small towns acquire late on Friday afternoon with the prospect of the weekend close at hand. It was a blustery, chill day. Although the rain had held off, the heavy clouds showed signs of bringing daylight to a premature end.

The grizzled man drove fast, but with care, and within fifteen minutes they were cruising down Conroy Street. "There it is!" the young gunman whispered. He pointed to the line of stationary cars on the left side of the road. The yellow Zephyr was parked almost opposite the side alley. There was no one in it.

The van turned sharp left at the next street and then left again. Just before it reached the end of the narrow alley it pulled into the kerb and stopped. Rory and the young man got out and walked along the pavement to the alley entrance. Rory turned the corner and began walking up it while the other moved on to the next intersection. Offices and shops were beginning to close.

The driver of the van had pulled out a newspaper and, spreading it over the steering-wheel, appeared to be reading. After a couple of minutes, however, he bundled it up and climbed out of the vehicle, the paper still in his hand. The young man had reappeared at the far end of the street. Then he vanished again. A couple of quick strides brought the driver into the entrance of the alley. He paused, looked along it for a second, and carried on walking. As he did so he raised the newspaper momentarily into the air and then let his arm drop into a natural swing.

Twilight was fading fast as a fair-haired man in his early forties stepped out of his office on the other side of the block. Solidly-built, with an unmistakable air of confidence and authority, he began to walk to the junction with Conroy Street. Just behind him and to his right strode a uniformed policeman. On the other side, a few yards further from him, was another man. He was dressed in civilian clothes, but bore the same wary look. As this curious trio were about to turn into Conroy Street, a young woman coming in the opposite direction put out her hand and smiled warmly. "How are you, Minister? It's nice to see you again. And how's Cathleen getting along, it can't be long now, can it?" She laughed gaily and chattered on. The Minister smiled back at her, said a few words and walked on. A few other passers-by also recognised their Member of Parliament and smiled their greetings. The Ballymena Town Hall clock struck six.

If the Minister or his police escort had turned to look back as they drew abreast of the Minister's parked car, they would have seen a young athletic-looking man in a long overcoat with a high collar coming round the corner behind them. Or they might have noticed a tough-looking man striding down the narrow alleyway towards them. They saw neither because by this time they were hurrying ahead to reach their car. It was parked some way in front of the Minister's, who had already begun to fumble for the keys of the yellow Zephyr.

The events during the next thirty seconds happened with such speed that they were to defy a rational reconstruction. Even eyewitnesses in the street could barely piece together what happened. As the Minister unlocked the car door and slid into the driving seat, the young man increased his pace almost to a run, linked up with the stocky gunman emerging from the shadow of the alley and together they drew level with the Zephyr. The big, ugly sub-machine guns were in their hands, spitting flame at the man behind the wheel of the car. A stuttering roar came from the Thompsons as the heavy bullets smacked into the metal door and the Minister slumped forward on to the steering column, crimson gouts of blood pumping from wounds in his jaw, neck and chest.

The gunmen swung round as if yoked together. They raced down the alley, their feet pounding on the cobbles. Seconds later a small, nondescript van shot across the opening at the far end, rocked to a halt and was off again.

Back in Conroy Street women stood transfixed, screaming. The Minister lay motionless, his shattered head propped up against the steering-wheel as his life dripped steadily away into an expanding pool on the floor of the car. The police escort, caught unawares, had already turned the next corner and were still out of sight.

James Grogan looked at his watch. 6.15 p.m. The Andersonstown district of Belfast was full of the smell of warm food, thousands of busy women cooking their families' suppers. He had the radio on. A news flash should come at any moment. But the telephone rang first. It was the IRA contact in Ballymena. "Your horse made it, Jimmy," the man said, elation in his voice, "but only by a neck." He laughed and rang off. Grogan put the receiver down with a sigh. They'd done it. Good lads, good lads, They shouldn't have any trouble getting clear. Rory and the boy were to be taken across the border after dropping off the guns. The older man would go back to Londonderry.

Then the flash came through. Grogan sat quietly for a long time, not a shadow of an expression on his thin face. It couldn't be true. Nobody could survive four bullets in those parts of the body at *that* range! Jesus, those bloody cowboys with their pump guns. All that planning and they still couldn't pull it off.

The next full bulletin and television news confirmed it. The Minister, by a miracle, had survived and might pull through.

The following morning, the newspapers were full of the assassination attempt.

FOUR WOUNDS, BUT OUT OF DANGER. MINISTER SHOT DOWN IN MURDER ATTEMPT, trumpeted a Belfast paper.

"Last night the Minister's condition was stated to be 'comparatively good and improved'. He underwent an operation in Ballymena hospital before being removed to Belfast. The Minister's mother, who dashed to her son's bedside after the emergency operation, was quoted as saying: 'So far as I can find out he may live.' Surgeons at the Belfast hospital where the Minister is being treated, said his escape had been 'a miracle'. Chances of survival from such a point-blank machine-gun attack had been about 100–1."

"Internment, 'Bloody Sunday', road-cratering and recent British legislation were given as reasons for the assassination bid," another newspaper said.

Rory should have left those bloody archaic Thompsons in the museum where they belonged. But as usual, they had ignored his advice and done it their own way. Grogan felt Dublin had deliberately tied one arm behind his back. He should have led the unit. He'd put it to them straight the next time he saw them. He was their best man, they knew it and he knew it. And he was sick of having his advice ignored.

PART I

The Decision

"Because I helped to wind the clock
I come to hear it strike."
W. B. Yeats

I

JAMES GROGAN PICKED UP the cigarette papers and tin of tobacco on the kiosk counter and crossed the crowded pavement. As he bent down to open the door of his car a sudden gust plucked at him, wrapping his coat tightly round his body, and an unseen hand smacked him solidly against the wing of the car.

For a fraction of a second before the roar of the explosion there was a terrible tranquillity. Then pandemonium broke loose. The blast engulfed the street, rippling down its length, sucking out windows as if they were rice-paper and hurling people to the ground. The crash of splintering glass and crumbling brickwork mingled with a swelling cacophony of shouts and screams. Men and women were running in the direction of the explosion which seemed to have come from the central shopping place a hundred yards or so down the street. As they streamed past their eyes were glazed but something in the way they moved betrayed a primitive excitement.

Bruised and a little shaken, Grogan jumped into his car and began to drive slowly with the crowd. He had gone no more than fifty yards when he came up against a hastily-erected police cordon around the Lotus café. The bomb appeared to have exploded in the ground floor tea-room, though Grogan found it difficult to see what had actually happened. He tried to reverse but was blocked on all sides by the crowd. He climbed out and, taller than most Irishmen, peered over the heads of the densely-packed mass. The smoke and dust were beginning to settle and reveal the carnage. Bodies—and bits of them—littered the floor and pavement. Women were still screaming and a child, thrown out it seemed through the main door by the force of the blast, sat howling disconsolately in a pool of blood, shattered crockery and fragments of glass. A Red Cross man pulling at someone half buried under the rubble suddenly lurched backwards in a sickening movement which left him ashen and holding the victim's arm—and nothing else. There was a choking sound of vomiting and the crowd sagged as several people plunged to the ground. Grogan saw two old men crying and hugging each other. A voice keyed high in hysteria, moaned: "Oh no, oh no, oh no . . ."

Grogan turned away, his face tense, and fought his way back to the car. This time he managed to back out and turn. He remained in first gear as he drove back the way he had come. An ambulance, its bell ringing furiously, spun past him as he turned left off York Street into Donegall Street. As the clamour receded he was struck by the absolute, almost terrifying normality of the rest of the city. Even in the next block the single-minded shoppers seemed to be unaware of the holocaust. They're getting used to it, he thought. Secretly they believe it can't happen to them. It's a thousand to one chance: it will always be someone else. He suddenly saw again that famous press picture of an elegant French woman skirting the body of an Arab lying like a sack of spilt coal on a main thoroughfare in Algiers at the height of the OAS terror. Belfast was closer to that than many people realised.

Clear of the centre of the city he increased speed with a vicious jab on the accelerator and the Fiat leapt forward towards the open country. An hour or so later having branched west on the Dungannon road and with more than half the distance to the border covered, Grogan stopped the car, wound down the driver's window and rolled himself a cigarette. He sat smoking quietly, drawing the tobacco deep down into his lungs and watched the shadows of the cumulus clouds race each other over the warm countryside. Then he started the car up again and switched on the radio to catch the Northern Ireland news. It was full of the café bombing:

" . . . At least three women and two children died in an explosion in the Lotus Café in York Street today. One hundred and thirty-four people were wounded, many of them seriously. The blast, caused by thirty pounds of gelignite, ripped through the ground floor of the popular restaurant at twenty past three this afternoon at the height of the weekend shopping period. Police cordoned off the area and army bomb-disposal squads stood by in case of a second explosion. One of the dead women had just recovered from serious injuries sustained in a bombing incident six months ago. The Prime Minister has condemned the incident, calling it 'an appallingly brutal and callous act'. In an unprecedented statement from the Royal Victoria Hospital where the victims were taken, a senior house surgeon said: 'In the course of the last two hours surgeons at this hospital have amputated forty limbs. The worse cases include a young woman who has lost both legs, both arms and an eye, another who has had one leg and two arms amputated, a child now without legs, two more young women each of whom have lost a leg and an arm, another child . . .' "

Grogan turned the radio off with a sharp flick of his wrist. Women, children . . . women, children. What about the bloody men, he thought bitterly as he sped through County Fermanagh. What about the bloody men?

The light was fading as he approached the border post, Grogan allowed the car to run down gently, forty — thirty — twenty miles an hour. The last hundred yards were covered so slowly that the small group of officials and soldiers were watching him attentively when he finally braked, a few inches from the horizontal white boom. A little way back he had passed the signpost SLIGO 20 MILES which, still framed in his mind, was like a wooden epitaph for his father. All that, he reflected, had been at the end of the futile border campaign more than a decade ago when he had been away from Ireland. He was in Aden then and he'd felt guilty. But there was nothing he could have done. Now he wanted to find out more.

The sun suddenly broke through the low-lying cloud and a

fresh breeze blew straight up the road from the South. Grogan had no reason to expect any trouble at the border. That, he thought ironically, was more likely to come when he reached Dublin. He had come a long way round from Belfast to pay tribute to his dead father. He scanned the reception party with a professional's eye—just a few border guards reinforced by a mobile British army patrol. Their Saracen and Land-Rover were parked away from the road, not bothering with the partial camouflage provided by the trees and bushes nearby. The soldiers were the Devonshire and Dorsets. A good infantry regiment but no more than that.

Grogan leaned through the car window. His voice held hardly a trace of the original Irish accent.

"I'm heading for Westport, County Mayo. Any chance of making it by eight o'clock?"

"Sure you can," one of the border guards replied pleasantly.

As they checked his car and papers, the soldiers began to lose interest though they kept their weapons at the ready. With the lack of nostalgia that he had only recently acquired in the North, he thought of the last time he had been in British uniform. If these young soldiers with their beardless faces could have looked into his past they wouldn't be lounging under the trees. He felt, in spite of himself, that glow of satisfaction which comes from having mastered a special set of skills. The marriage of theory and practice had been a harmonious one. His father could have benefited from that union in those very hills, green, undulating but so devoid of cover, ten years ago.

The boom arching upwards in front of him sliced through his reverie and he drove off as gently as he had arrived, down the deserted road into the Republic. He had crossed a lot of borders, but the contrast presented by this one was always striking. On the Northern side the fields were laid out like small parcels; fences and clipped hedges primly delineated limits of ownership. In the South the landscape stretched out expansively, less disciplined by the hands of its cultivators. He felt the petty meannesses of the North slide away and a sudden elation as a bend in the road revealed a panorama of the Sligo mountains. He could smell the sea. At the next crossroads he slowed the car to study the signposts. He swung the Fiat sharply

over to the left-hand fork, leaving the sign WESTPORT 63 MILES
on his right, and headed inland.

The splintering crash resounded through the house and tore
Grogan from the deep coil of sleep. Gruff voices and shouted
orders came from below. The metallic crunch of rounds being
slotted home into SLRs jerked him into a heart-thumping con-
sciousness. Was it this house or the one next-door? Already out
of bed and pulling on his clothes with quick decisive movements,
Grogan was not the kind of man who might wait to find out.
Old Mrs. McCafferty rushed into the room, her hair in curlers
and her nightdress, patched and tattered, streaming behind her.
   "Out, Jimmy—down the back way, the gate's open at the
end of the yard!"
   Another thundering crash shook the frail terraced house.
   "Holy Mary Mother of God, there goes my feckin' front
door!" The old woman, toothless and shaking in the cold,
damned the British soldiers to hell and pushed Grogan through
the passage. The raw night air of Derry bit into his lungs as he
slipped out of the cabbage patch behind the house. The door
was well-oiled and made no sound as it swung open. He turned
sharp left into the covered alley which led down away from
the Bogside to the river. Not a good place to be cornered but
they had told him that it was unknown to the army. He vaulted
over the low guard rail that sealed off the passage from a
vacant plot and, crouching low to keep his silhouette below the
top of the fence, moved easily towards the far wall. In the distance he heard some muffled shouts and a Land-Rover gathering speed. A dog barked. Tracker? Steady, not too much
imagination now. Treat it like the exercise it so closely re-
sembled, but play it cool and for real. The night mist was thicker
here in the open space; thick and protective. His hands reached
up for the top of the brickwork, his muscles tightened and he
began to pull himself upwards in a strong, fluid movement.
But something was wrong, his fingers were slipping, the wall
was advancing on him . . . the mist had turned into a murky
fog, the dog into a dense pall of smoke . . . he was falling, falling,
falling . . .

Grogan woke bathed in sweat, his hands gripping the brass uprights of the familiar bed in Dublin. A warm lump beside him stirred gently. Christ, that had been too close for comfort! Was he developing powers of total recall, he wondered? But why did it always end at the worst moment? He'd got away, hadn't he? And he'd not put a foot wrong either — except for that bloody wall tumbling down on him.

The curtain over the window in the snug bedroom above Mairin's antique shop flapped loosely in the early morning breeze. Fruit and vegetable lorries were already pounding across O'Connell Bridge. The salty breath of the sea, carried into the heart of the city by the Liffey which flowered almost under the windowsill, dried Grogan's damp face. There were always physical stage-props for dreams, good or bad, he reflected drowsily: the Foyle, the Liffey . . . Derry, Dublin. The tension had gone like a departing ghost, and his body sank back into the soft down of the bed.

"Are you all right?" The voice was muffled. In addition to her many attributes Mairin could count the ability to breathe where most people would suffocate, Grogan thought.

"I'm fine," he said. "Just reliving a little of an active past."

The warm bundle of bedclothes moved slowly but purposefully. He could feel her hair, that fine red mane, brush across his belly. A soft wetness moved over him. The warm odours of the bed and the euphoria which the safety of the South always brought released a surge of sensuality. He pulled back the covers and reached down to stroke the nape of Mairin's neck. There were freckles just below the hairline and on top of her heavy white breasts which swung in a slow deliberate circle over his groin.

"Hallo," she said, smiling her crooked smile.

"Hallo yourself, what are we going to do today?"

"Something you like and I like." She swung round, surprisingly agile for such a solid girl, straddled him and impaled herself all in one movement. It took his breath away — it always did. She smiled again and grasped his shoulders. He put his arms around her waist and pulled her down. "There's something to be said for Women's Lib after all," he grinned.

She began to move on him, again slowly and with that curious deliberation which was so characteristic of her. "Don't blaspheme, you male chauvinist Bog Irishman. And pay attention. I love you."

Later they lay peacefully in a classic but quite unconscious pose on the big brass bed. Her long fiery red hair spread across his chest like water-grass, her head tucked against his chin. Grogan, lean and saturnine, held her loosely in his arms, affectionate, amused, just a little patronising. Sixteen years older than her, they had first met at a Sinn Fein gathering in Trinity College where she was studying political science. And he was still more conscious of the generation gap—and the educational void—between them than she was. She often teased him about his age but it did not really mean anything to her; her emotional commitment to him reduced problems of this kind to rubble. For him it was more complex: he'd never had trouble getting girls—of any age—but Mairin was the first girl he had met who possessed such a fine blend of brain, body and temperament. At times he felt intimidated by her, especially when his stock of tough worldly wisdom ran against her varied education, sheer intelligence and sharp intensity of feeling. He was a country boy from Kerry, who had left school at fourteen; what could he do about that? But while she made him feel deprived she also made him proud—to be with her and to be seen to be with her. He wasn't, it must be clear by now, he felt, just another thick ex-soldier or mindless IRA gunman.

"Was it bad up there this time?" She stirred against him.

"Not too good. We don't have the men half the time and even when we do, they're the wrong ones. Fifteen-year-old drop-outs with fire in their bellies and rice pudding in their skulls."

"At least they try," she said. "That's more than you can say for the fat cats down here, commuting to and from the Scampi Belt and talking high and mighty about the glorious unity of our native island." She turned sideways and looked straight at him.

"Oh, they try all right. But where does a bomb in a crowded café get you? They often blow themselves up before they do anybody else any fucking harm. As for discipline or a sense of security or working together as a unit—forget it. You might as well try and win the World Cup with a team of dustmen."

A gust of wind ruffled the curtains. Grogan, feeling the return of an old bitterness shifted down into the bed and pulled the covers over them. The book which he had been reading the night before had fallen onto the floor, its title-page uppermost. Downstairs a door banged. It must be Mairin's sister opening up the shop, he thought. Bloody Christ, how to fight a war without properly trained and equipped troops. He'd tried to teach them but they didn't want to know. In the North, to believe in the cause was enough. As if passion could blow up a Saracen, or a sense of history knock off a British soldier.

"The army are getting more information than they should do these days," he said. "They're not stupid like you think, you know. I know my old pals. I almost ran into some of the old bastards the other night." He laughed.

"What did you do in the British army, Jimmy?" Her head was pressed against his chest.

"I was long-service, good-conduct, non-officer material; a foot-slogger, the salt or the scum of the earth. I fucked about in what were the farther-flung corners of the Empire for twelve bleeding years. I did my duty, kept my nose clean and became, as they say in the recruiting posters, a professional. That meant I could fire a rifle without breaking my collar-bone, stick a knife in someone without getting snarled up in his rib-cage, leap out of the sky at six thousand feet and come down in one piece, lick the company commander's boots without spewing up on them, screw his wife, discreetly, thus preserving her sanity and his honour, keep on the right side of the sergeant-major and out of the scrawny arms of the queer padre and at the end of it still emerge as 'a useful member of society'." He looked down at her and laughed.

She didn't like that laugh. It held no amusement.

"But you still haven't told me what you really did in the army," she said, suddenly annoyed.

"Look, I was a mercenary 'fighting for monetary gain on behalf of a foreign power'. But I was a bloody good one. And to prove it, after serving with our old friends the paras—the butchers of Derry—I put down for the SAS."

"Which means?"

"Special Air Service, it's Britain's best-kept non-secret. The crack unit of the British army. You name it, we did it—behind the lines, counter-insurgency, bodyguarding, rubbing out, special operations—all in a day's work. Nothing political, you understand, no hard feelings: just a bunch of good-hearted heavies; soldiering at its best, peak of fitness, all the skills, great comradeship and all that crap." Grogan smiled.

"But you enjoyed it, didn't you, Jimmy?"

"Yes, I suppose I did," he admitted. "But then I was younger, the sap still rising, and it was so good to be liberated from this mournful, damp little island with its pinched faces and clerical straitjacket. You've no idea, Mairin, what it used to be like to come from the country, to be poor, to be trapped in our Celtic past which all those well-heeled romantics from the comfort of their Ballsbridge villas rave on about. You burnt your bra and I crossed the Irish sea. It was just marvellous to get out and be free. And then as soon as you get that you begin to look for another home, another allegiance, even another millstone round your neck. And I found it, curiously enough, in the British army, particularly in the SAS. But that's all a long time ago," he added a little defensively.

She leant over and kissed him, on the forehead brushing his dark hair back, and then full on the lips.

"Like some tea?"

"Love some."

She climbed out of bed, put on an old dressing-gown and went across to close the window. The breeze had stiffened and Grogan, lying in the pool of warm fragrance left by her young body, could hear the seagulls shrieking over the Liffey. A tug hooted somewhere down the river. The army *had* done something for him. It had instilled the ethos of the fighting man. He'd never been able to put this into adequate words, though he'd tried more than once when Mairin pressed him. Instinctively, he knew now what made men fight—and be proud of it —from time immemorial. He knew it was right for him. That it *was* him. With this knowledge, he still didn't know what he wanted to do with his life but the colour tones were distinct— fear, excitement, achievement.

He turned over in bed and took a letter out of the drawer of the bedside table. Addressed to him, it bore the datestamp FAIRFORD, GLOUCESTERSHIRE. The contents were brief and to the point. The signature was the unmistakable scrawl of his old friend. CONCORDE was going well, Padraig said. He thought it wiser to talk to Grogan rather than write about his queries. Was there any chance of Grogan coming over to England soon?

Grogan slid the letter under the pillow as Mairin returned with the tea.

2

THE SPECIAL BRANCH OFFICES in Claremont Street, Belfast, are less accessible than the CID sections. A large grille door manned by a security guard shows that the Branch performs a different function from the rest of the police force. Regarded by the men and women who work for it as an élite, it is looked upon with some awe by the uniformed branches. Once inside the zone, however, there are the levelling institutional smells of formaldehyde and carbolic, stale cigarette smoke and sweat. As elsewhere in the station the shiny walls, a pallid shade of green, are fingermarked and in need of repainting. The shabby offices are overfurnished and underheated. Steel tables, spring-backed chairs, filing cabinets, plastic lampshades and tin wastepaper baskets seem to have been thrown together without rhyme or reason, as cluttered as an auction room before a sale. But they produce a distinctive flavour. Past the guard, through the grille, the underlying tension shared by all police stations deepens.

Sitting in his inner office Chief Superintendent Charles Christie was disturbed. Things had not been going well recently. He had the uncomfortable feeling that time and events were slipping through his grasp. A team of Scotland Yard 'special advisers' had arrived the week before. Christie had been given strict instructions to co-operate fully but there was already no doubt in his mind that 'co-operation' was the thin end of the wedge.

Christie had been born in Belfast fifty years ago. He had lived here nearly all his life. A Scots Protestant in origin, he held strong Unionist views. He did not regard the present troubles as a religious problem, though his enemy was almost exclusively a Catholic one, but as a straightforward question of politics: Unionists and Loyalists against Republicans and Terrorists. Christie had built his career in the RUC slowly and on the whole unspectacularly. A big man, his physical courage and strength had served him well and he had been awarded the Police Medal for bravery eleven years ago. Not long afterwards he had been transferred to Special Branch. When the civil rights movement began to gain momentum in 1969 Christie was rewarded for his dedication by being placed in charge of the newly-reorganised IRA section. This was the toughest task, of all and, he had to admit, he had so far failed to come up with the goods. Put very simply, this was the penetration of the IRA in the Belfast area.

Now he had to cope with the newcomers, Barnes and Franks. He had heard of Chief Superintendent Barnes, who had served in Kenya and Aden after early, tough years in Palestine and who was known as a ruthless operator. A cool, remote man of about his own age. Not the same kind of temperament, though.

When they had first talked Barnes asked right away to look over the Special Branch files. Christie had felt a twinge of vulnerability as he handed them over. After all, they represented the total effort of his section and he was only too conscious of the gaps to be filled. Barnes and Franks had spent most of the day going over the files, thick with well-thumbed and annotated papers in expandable hard-covers, each one titled with an agent's number. For security reasons the names were held separate from the files.

"I can see your section has been putting in a lot of hard work," Barnes had said. "You've really had to start again since '69, haven't you?"

Christie had felt reassured.

"Yes. Most of the IRA cases were put on ice after the border campaign broke up. It wasn't till the bastards showed up again, masquerading as part of the civil rights movement that we were allowed to have a crack at them. Then we had to sort them out from the long-hairs and the commies. By the time we'd done that they were nearly all new faces. A lot of them twenty-five and under. Many old timers just didn't come back into the movement. Now we've got kids of eighteen and nineteen as IRA officers."

"Isn't that because the army lifted the top rank and they're the only replacements?" Barnes asked.

"That's the situation now," said Christie. "But even at the start quite a lot of the old, known IRA men just didn't come forward. They'd done their bit and settled into a quieter life. Of course, they still provide shelter for men on the run. But the real gunmen are a new generation."

"What about internment?" put in Franks.

"It's put nine hundred men out of action, but only about a hundred are hard-core. The trouble is, it's made the Catholic ghettos really pull together. The support of the IRA's fantastic there now. But we've had a go at fourteen of the hard cases in Long Kesh and we've squeezed out a fair bit of information."

Christie grinned. Barnes could imagine the Ulsterman's interrogation methods.

"What about your regular sources?"

"You've seen the files," replied Christie. "It's become very difficult. Most of the Catholic community are terrified out of their wits. Tarring and feathering, red-leading and shooting, the IRA have really intimidated them. The small-time low-level informers have pretty well dried up, and we haven't got a big fish on the inside yet."

"Well, looking at the files there are some definite possibilities," Barnes had said. "The 31121 case, for example, is interesting. Have you tried putting pressure on him?"

"It's not as easy as that," Christie had felt at a disadvantage, though he did not quite know why. "He's a cunning old sod. As a matter of fact, I'm seeing him soon. It's difficult to know what's in it for him, unless it's a bit of insurance on both sides. If you ask him a direct question, he gets vague. He only likes talking when he's warmed up. Then he'll let things drop, but always between the lines, if you see what I mean. It's difficult to pin him down to details, and he dries up if you try."

"That's the kind of business we're in," said Barnes, looking at Franks. "I wonder if we could work out a way to get him more on the hook?"

It did not sound quite like a question to Christie. He was beginning to feel angry.

"Well, if you have any ideas, I'd be glad to hear them. Personally, I was never for handling his type with kid gloves." Christie instinctively realised he might be treading a dangerous path. "But he's the kind you have to chat up to get anything from."

They had discussed a few more cases and now, as Christie mulled over their conversation, he still felt aggrieved. He could not quite pin it down, but he had the feeling that Barnes, in his detached way, had been getting at him. Christie had no inferiority complex and approached most problems with the classic attitude of the army sergeant-major: "You play ball with me and . . ." After all, he thought to himself, we're on the same side. At least we're supposed to be.

Suddenly his telephone rang. He listened for a few moments, flushed with irritation and banged down the receiver. He picked it up again, dialled an internal number and got through to Barnes. For the first time with the Englishman he felt on home ground.

"The sods have blown up Murphy's Bar in the Falls Road. You'd better come and have a look for yourselves." He did not mention casualties.

As Barnes hurried down the corridor he felt the familiar tension, a surge of finely-balanced excitement and fear rising in him. The daily challenge of his job was satisfying but often meant little more than the tactful manipulation of his superiors, which he enjoyed, and the delegation of responsibility. It was the big job, the special assignment like this Irish business, that really stretched him.

Physical danger was something else. It was rare these days, with colonial wars a fading memory, to find Special Branch stepping into the firing line. The occasional arrest of a sub-versive or an Angry Brigade activist rarely meant carrying a gun. And yet here he was in the UK in the 1970s, in the midst of a full-blown counter-insurgency operation with bombs going off in the night, internment camps and barbed wire, daily arrests and 'positive' interrogations, and that uncomfortable sensation that comes from being an identified and highly vulnerable target. A fear that sits patiently at your shoulder and does not go away. 'Emergencies' were what the British called these situations. We have a marvellous talent, he reflected, for understatement. As if Malaya, Kenya and now Ulster were on the banal level of a municipal power-cut.

As always, he thought, the sharp end is the most exciting thing. The years hadn't altered this: his reactions were still those of a younger man, a tightening in the stomach, an increased awareness. He remembered the exact sensation when years ago he had stood in front of the smoking pile that minutes before had been the King David Hotel in Jerusalem. He should have died with the rest, suffocated by plaster and dust or smashed to a pulp by falling masonry, when the hotel, then the British police and army headquarters, blossomed into the blue Jerusalem sky. But he had slipped out for coffee and a breath of fresh air ten minutes before the hotel went up. Palestine, he thought, lovely, sunny, blue-skied, dusty, hate-filled, murderous Palestine! Barnes's round, unlined face showed no sign of tension as he stepped out into the dank Belfast streets.

Soldiers of the Royal Green Jackets and a platoon of the Parachute Regiment had already cordoned off the scene of the explosion by the time the Special Branch men arrived. A Saracen, followed by a larger armoured troop-carrying vehicle known as a 'pig', gears crunching and transmission whining, closed up behind the cordoned-off area. Fresh troops in full riot kit, shields, transparent visors, and flak-jackets, tumbled out. An officer, young and over-incisive, barked a string of orders. It was raining again. Somewhere in the distance an ambulance siren moaned. A fair-sized crowd—there's always a bloody crowd, thought Barnes—had collected and was pressing against the cordon trying to see what had happened.

There wasn't much left to see. The little corner pub had

collapsed like a house of cards. The walls had fallen inwards, dissolving into rubble and burying everything inside with a terrible finality. Strips of mock brocade wallpaper flapped in the damp breeze. A brass bed, hurled upwards and twisted by the blast, swung crazily from the only beam that remained in something like its original place. The rain, suddenly intensifying, was turning the dust into grey porridge. A team of St. John Ambulance men, helped by policemen and soldiers, plucked and pulled at the rubble. There was a sudden piercing cry from the debris. A shiver ran through the onlookers and they moved as if by a prearranged signal, inwards and forwards, inert yet expectant, against the soldiers. Every now and then the cordon swayed, sagged and opened to allow stretcher-bearers through. They quickly returned with blood-soaked bundles, lifeless and meaningless, under sodden blankets.

Christie, with the air of a man who is used to being recognised and obeyed, shouldered his way through the crowd. A uniformed inspector in the RUC took him by the arm and gave him a terse account of the incident. A gelignite bomb had gone off a little after noon, just as the lunchtime drinkers were coming in for their first jar of the day. There had, it appeared, been no suspicious visitors earlier. No men in belted raincoats and wide-brimmed trilbies, the archetypal IRA bombers verging on self-parody who had been involved in other incidents. Nor had there been any warning. Murphy's had been a Catholic bar, Barnes reflected, in the heart of a Catholic ghetto. Could this then have been an accident? A staging place for some of that highly volatile 'gelly' the Provisionals were forced to use these days. Or was it a spectacular reprisal, a Mafia-like stroke of vengeance against poor Murphy, his family and friends? Or perhaps—an even nastier thought—the long-awaited Protestant backlash had begun?

"The Provos again," said Christie firmly, looking Barnes straight in the eyes.

"Ah . . . yes," replied Barnes noncommittally.

"Very similar to the explosion at McGurk's. That one destroyed the bar completely and killed fifteen people. Either it's a reprisal against squealers or it could have been an accident . . . Stupid, murdering bastards!" Christie spat out.

Barnes caught Franks's eye and winked, a curiously lizard-like motion.

"Nothing much we can do here. I suppose we'd better go back to those files," he said.

Franks nodded. He didn't like Christie's manner nor his assumptions. But he hadn't seen anything as bad as this since the Lowry massacre during the Mau Mau troubles.

As they turned to go two things happened almost simultaneously. A terrible groan, muffled and barely human, came out of the centre of what had been Murphy's Bar. Then a shot rang out. The crowd, a living thing, broke and ran.

"Sniper!" Christie bellowed, hurling himself down behind the police car.

Confused yells and shouts drowned the cries of the unknown and suddenly forgotten victim in Murphy's ruin. A woman screamed. Soldiers were racing in all directions at once. Two more shots, heavier, more menacing, cracked in quick succession in the leaden air. Three chunky 'paras' smashed their way through what remained of the crowd and flung themselves down behind a low wall which had survived the explosion. More troops arrived as if from nowhere and took up defensive positions facing a row of houses fifty yards down the street which ran away diagonally from the wrecked pub. A lone and immensely brave St. John Ambulance man continued to tear at the rubble as a deadly crossfire established itself between the gunmen and the soldiers. The young officer's voice, high-pitched now, could be heard again. In the distance, during a lull in the shooting, came the monotonous rhythm of clanging dustbin lids, that curiously offensive hymn of hate of the Catholic women of Belfast.

Barnes found himself at the far end of the wall at the corner of the street. He had got there, he noted with pleasure, purely by instinct and he was pretty sure he had seen where the sniper's fire was coming from. He leant over to the paratrooper nearest to him.

"They're firing from the fifth house down. The one with the red door," he said, pointing cautiously over the wall.

The soldier, a ginger-haired youngster with a flat immobile face, looked at him coldly.

"Get the fuck out of here," he hissed.

Barnes, for a fleeting second, was stunned. Then he understood. He choked down a rebuke and ran back to the car. In civilian clothes anyone could be the enemy. There was no colour of the skin, slant of the eyes or curve of the nose to distinguish sides in this man's war. You were fighting on home ground. It was like the bloody Wars of the Roses! Forget Palestine and all that, if he could. This was civil war in British suburbia.

The shooting had died down. Four paras were edging their way slowly down the far side of the street. A Saracen ground along the road that ran parallel, its six massive wheels pulverizing the thin asphalt crust. Journalists had surrounded the army officer and a couple of photographers were trying to coax new angles out of Murphy's pyre. The relief workers were back at the smouldering rubble pulling out the corpse of the man who had cried out. There's something crazy and unreal about all this, Barnes thought. Like making a film: "Stand by, Lights, Action, Cut." But here in Belfast, after the take, another human being is dead. Or rather two human beings, he corrected himself, as an ambulance drew up across the road near the low wall and he caught sight of the waxen face of an astonishingly young soldier, a mere child, prone on a stretcher.

He looked around for Franks. The viciousness of the Ulster crisis struck him with a new force. But he'd been up against tough opponents before. This was a different kind of war, fought under different rules. But in the long haul, he thought, the Irish usually defeat themselves. It's just a matter of the length of the rope.

During his first three months in Dublin, Humphrey James reflected, quite a lot had happened. That much of it was unpleasant came as no real surprise to him for he had a pretty fatalistic view of life, especially where the office was concerned. Not so long ago he had been comfortably settled in the SIS headquarters in London working in the Economic Department, his main task the congenial one of maintaining his organisation's links to the City and banking world. This had involved a fair amount of lushing up contacts, which in turn had meant a more than generous entertainment allowance. James, a man with an eye for the main chance, had kept not too far in the back of his mind the idea that these connections could be useful in ten years or so when he would be thinking of retiring. Several of his colleagues recently had retired early on full pension to fill comfortable banking niches as 'foreign affairs consultants', 'EEC specialists' and the like. After all, years of service abroad, a couple of foreign languages, and an understanding of what makes people tick must be worth something to a merchant bank, he thought.

James looked through the venetian blinds on the window of his makeshift office at the heavy rain clouds building up on the skyline. He remembered how suddenly he had been called in by the Deputy Chief and after the usual guff about the crucial importance of the new job and how he was particularly suited for it he'd been, as the service euphemistically put it, 'offered' Dublin. He was to set up a new station and his cover would be First Secretary Commercial, which would enable him to get out of the Embassy and move around the local community. His brief was to find sources to penetrate the IRA. But, as the Deputy had explained, the really important task was to get the INTERFACE case going. It had been an extraordinary development, an agent of that importance walking in off the street. James knew that the slightest mishandling on his part could be fatal. Only a few senior people in Head Office knew about the case, but they would be watching him very closely indeed. All the same, James's first reaction had been annoyance. He had never been to Ireland in his life and all those tourist advertisements for green fields and space had left him cold. He would have preferred something a bit more exotic. Ireland was not really 'abroad' and in his view the Irish were a pretty dull lot. In addition to being uprooted from a pleasant job, the post presented James with another source of irritation. It was not the first time that some highly predictable crisis had developed as a result of which he was suddenly called upon to pack his bags, leap on to a plane and build up an intelligence network from scratch. Other colleagues went from one well-established, smooth-running, fully-operative post to another, but he had twice before found himself a John the Baptist. All right, he had responded to the challenge before, but why the hell was the office so often caught short without any assets and totally un-prepared in a crisis area? Even as he asked himself he knew the answer. Fundamentally, it was lack of money and resources; but possibly even more important, the way priorities worked within the service and the organisation's lack of pull inside the government machine. He knew only too well that other powerful Whitehall departments like the Treasury and the Foreign and Commonwealth Office, although happy to be the recipient of intelligence when their own interests were at stake, had an inherent distaste for spying and, more, of those in-volved in it. Which meant in practice that people like himself, and the service in general, were treated in a subtly but dis-tinctly different way from other government servants. Like a different kind of animal. Well maybe we are, he thought. Or maybe we become so.

In any case he could not claim that his time in Dublin so far had not been full. He had started off by making his number with the rest of the Embassy staff enlisting their sympathy and support. Then he had begun to move around Dublin society, at first through his colleagues in the Embassy and then using his cover work as an *entrée*. Knowing people, building up con-tacts, were the essence of his work. He had spent weeks instal-ling a new safe zone protected by steel grilles, alarm systems and combination locks. All this had to be delivered from London and the installation completed by special technicians sent out from Head Office. He had set up new systems within the Em-bassy for separating off his work; channels for his coding, tele-graphing and diplomatic bag procedures. And after all that, the bloody Irish had burnt the place down. So now he was in this ramshackle temporary accommodation, which was insecure as hell and meant they had to limit all their papers, codes, equip-ment to what would go into one incendiary safe. This was nothing more than a large box fitted with a device which could reduce the contents to ashes and molten metal in a few minutes.

As he looked discontentedly around his new room, James caught a glimpse of his secretary through the half-open door. Poor old cow, he thought, not much of a life for her uprooted every couple of years and dumped God knows where without friends or family. He supposed that for her, like himself, the office became a substitute.

"Harriet!" he shouted and saw her jump. He knew she had been decoding a telegram that had come in at least an hour ago and he wondered what was taking so long.

"Would you bring me that correspondence from Belfast ending in Nicholas Stoughton's letter about Special Branch."

Stoughton was his opposite number in Belfast, operating under military cover as a major on the GOC's personal staff. James smiled as he remembered the cause of Nicholas's annoyance at their last meeting in London. Nicholas had been recruited into the service some years before in the Far East where he had been serving as a regular officer in one of the parachute regiments. As he had often remarked since: "I lost a vocation and found a well-paid job." The irony of his posting to Belfast was that since Ulster was an integral part of the United Kingdom he was not eligible for the generous foreign allowances which are normally given to SIS officers overseas and which largely subsidise their tours back at Head Office in London. Nicholas had complained bitterly, only to be told that this was a very special situation. Northern Ireland was properly the domain of MI5; SIS were there very much on sufferance; it could not be regarded in any sense as an overseas posting since it was on home ground. As the two had agreed at the time, it was the old story of the Finance Department playing both ends against the middle and always coming out top, though Nicholas had a cruder expression for it. At least, James thought, I'm getting my whack of allowances. They wouldn't dare to pull that one on me in the Republic.

Harriet came bustling in. She had balanced his morning coffee on top of the file he had asked for and she had the decoded telegram in her other hand. As the placed these in front of him some coffee slopped over the telegram and she scampered out to find a *Kleenex*. She dabbed ineffectually at it and smudged the text. James's eye skipped over the stained letter symbols indicating the addressees and came directly to the body of the text.

A. SPECIAL MEETING OF WORKING SUB-COMMITTEE (IRELAND) OF JOINT INTELLIGENCE COUNCIL (JIC) TO BE CALLED WITHIN 48 RPT 48 HOURS.

B. PURPOSE TO SUMMARISE INTELLIGENCE FROM ALL

SOURCES ON REPUBLIC'S ATTITUDE TO BOTH WINGS IRA
RPT IRA. ALSO ON KNOWN ASPECTS IRA RPT IRA OPERATIONAL
PLANNING.

    C. NEW CONTRIBUTIONS FROM ADDRESSEES URGENTLY
REQUIRED.

    D. FOR YOUR OWN INFORMATION ONLY: JIC WILL PREPARE
FULL POSITION PAPER FOR FORTHCOMING DISCUSSION AT
CABINET LEVEL OF POSSIBLE CHANGES IN HMG POLICY.

"Christ Almighty!" he exploded. "They don't want much,
do they?"

Harriet still stood there, all but visibly trembling, and he
thought better of asking why she had taken a whole hour to
decode such a short message or why she had buggered around
making a cup of coffee with this kind of flap building up. She
must have been on to a soft touch in her previous posting, and
knowing her boss there he could understand why. What she
needed was . . . He checked himself and dismissed Harriet with
a nod.

Automatically he glanced at the correspondence he had
asked for from Belfast. The last letter from Nicholas had given
a clear exposition of the problem from the Belfast end, with the
opposing if not actually warring factions of military intelligence, MI5, Scotland Yard advisers, local Special Branch and
his own service. At least Nicholas had a few obvious places to
turn to. Suddenly James felt very much on his own. The 'for
your own information only' rider meant that he could not even
discuss this development with his own Ambassador. He thought
carefully about the things he must do, got up to put on his overcoat, and as he left his office he told Harriet to expect him when
she saw him but in any event not to close up the office until he
got back.

his charm, guts and zest for living. But when the chips were down, he was no soldier. He had great heart, but not the training nor really the belly for it. Like many others, he was an amateur playing at soldiers because he believed in a cause. Or because his emotions were all bound up in it, which was not the same thing. But he was up against professionals and the result, sooner or later, was inevitable. The amazing thing Grogan thought, was that so many of them kept coming forward . . . Irish history provided plenty of examples of stepping into dead men's shoes.

The van turned into a familiar street and then through wooden gates, under a battered sign — MAGAN'S SERVICE STATION — into a gravelled yard. The gates swung shut behind them as Grogan drove into the shed at the end. Their weapons were quickly taken away. They washed thoroughly, changed their clothes and went upstairs to old Tom Magan's sitting room. He poured them each a stiff whiskey and turned on the radio.

They waited a long time, almost two hours, for the special news bulletin. There was a great deal of exuberant speculation, mixed with some misgivings from the others. Grogan listened, but did not join in. It had been his first real taste of action in a long while. Finally the news came. Grogan listened to the bland narrative that always seems so artificial to those who have participated in the events.

". . . four British soldiers killed, including a lieutenant, and three more wounded. In a running fight after leaving one of their dead in the ambush house, two IRA gunmen were shot and killed by a detachment from the Parachute Regiment which had moved up quickly in support of the ambushed convoy. The gunmen, it is thought, were trying to reach a getaway vehicle parked a hundred yards from the scene of the shooting. A security cordon was placed around the area within minutes of the incident — but several more gunmen managed to get away. An intensive search is now . . ."

So that was that. You could call it a kind of victory.

6

"I KNOW, I KNOW," Kelly was saying a little wearily, "but we can't keep a day-to-day check on everything that's going on up there." He shifted the telephone receiver round to the other ear. Perhaps that would make MacStiofain's complaint a little more bearable. "I understand you wanting to go to Derry again, though I can't say I like it. Bogside and Creggan may be 'no-go' for the British army, but the RUC still have a few feelers out there. And then there's the border."

Kelly looked out over the grey roofs of Dublin, glistening from the morning rain. Why were all revolutionary leaders so bloody inflexible, he pondered. MacStiofain was a dedicated man.The cause was his entire life, so much so that it was sometimes hard to get through to him about the daily nuts and bolts of the job. That's where the trouble usually began. Kelly swung his legs across the side of the armchair while he told Mac-Stiofain he would double his efforts to keep closer track of their operations and tighten the disciplinary rein. The Provos' chief-of-staff would, he knew, go to Derry whatever he said.

He put the receiver down and turned back to the thick-set man in the chair opposite him.

"You see our problem," he said.

"Yes." The other man paused. "Do you want me to be absolutely frank?"

"What else would I want you to be?" Kelly said quietly.

"Well now, you know how it is, there are a lot of rumours going around. I don't want to be the cause of any ill-feeling or anything like that."

"I'm sure you don't," Kelly said encouragingly. He looked more closely at O'Flaherty. The man seemed to be ill at ease, unusual for him. Kelly knew he'd had a rough time in the North before his dramatic escape from Crumlin Road gaol. He looked down at O'Flaherty's broad and powerful hands. A little below the back of the right thumb there was a large, fresh scar, roughly triangular in shape. This was where, O'Flaherty had told them, the British paratroopers had inserted the long steel needles, pushing them through the flesh until they reached the bone. Then the scraping had begun. It was inside the brain rather than in his hand that O'Flaherty had felt the pain, Kelly remembered.

"I left Belfast the day before yesterday," the visitor began. "It took me more than twenty-four hours to get down. I can't take any chances these days, you know that." Kelly nodded. "Andersonstown and Ballymurphy were fine when I left. The boys are in good heart and that new load of gelignite was brought safely in to Andersonstown where we do most of the preparation now. Guns and ammo's OK too and, as for transport, we can pick up a van or car whenever we need one. Only two setbacks there: they got Tom Murphy and Patrick McConville from the Ballymurphy battalion, but you probably heard about that."

Kelly hadn't but nodded again.

"But the Ardoyne's different," O'Flaherty continued, "something wrong there."

"What do you mean?"

"Well, it's hard to put your finger on it, but nothing's gone right since that bloody man Grogan was signed on." The last sentence came in a rush.

Kelly said sharply, "He's a good man—what have you got against him?"

"I've got nothing against him, I just . . ."

"Wait a minute," Kelly cut in. "You were in the Border Campaign . . . Weren't you with his father when he died?"

There was silence. Kelly waited.

"I was," said O'Flaherty slowly, choosing his words as if he were threading his way through a minefield. "We crossed together—at least we started together. But it was a hell of a night, you know, wind, rain, hail—the lot. And they'd been tipped off, Christ knows who by. There were four of us: Paddy Henry, Cathal Ryan, myself and Grogan. He was old, you know, too feckin' old for that sort of game." He paused and rubbed the puckered flesh around the scar of his hand.

"Go on," Kelly said.

"There's not much more to it. We were skirting a small hill, having walked for bloody miles to avoid the roads. Henry was up in front because he knew the way, then Ryan and me and some way behind now, old Grogan. We were nearly there, a quarter of a mile at the outside. I turned round to see where the old man was, then we heard the first shot. Down we went. I can smell that turf today. A mole never went deeper. Then a feckin' fusillade opened up—they seemed to be shooting straight over us from our right. I heard a groan—a long way away it seemed, but behind us. We lay there so long I thought we'd turn to coal. But Ryan was the boss and said don't move. Finally we got up. The storm, if anything, had got worse which was great for us—but not for the old man who'd bought one."

"What did you do?"

"What could we do? He was bleeding like a stuck pig from a wound the size of my fist." O'Flaherty bunched his fingers into a massive knot. "We bound him up as best we could but now the heavens had opened. It was as much as the three of us could do to lift him up on to my shoulders and stagger on."

"And then?"

"Oh, we made it in the end. Slipping and sliding and falling about like drunken men. Somehow we reached the Belleek road and stopped a van. Frightened the life out of the old gombeen driving it. But he was obliging enough when Cathal demonstrated the bolt action of the Thompson to his wife."

"And the old man?"

"Dead as a doorstopper. Must have gone when we were still

struggling in that blasted bog. By the time we reached the hospital he was already stiffening up. The pity of it was, he wanted to cross in another place but Dublin wouldn't allow it."

O'Flaherty fell silent. The telling of the story, hauling back harsh memories from a fading past, seemed to have imposed a strain upon him. Then Kelly remembered something.

"Aren't you the only one left from that crossing?"

O'Flaherty looked startled.

"Why, yes, I suppose I am. Henry died in a car crash in '63 and Ryan was shot in Derry by the British last year," he said slowly, as if he didn't quite believe it himself. "I'd never thought of that before. Why do you ask?"

"It just occurred to me, that's all. What's the trouble with Jimmy Grogan?"

"Well, to start with, he's arrogant, a know-all and a bastard to work with. All right, so he's been in the British army and he's good with explosives but he's a latecomer here. And if he's the professional that he claims he is, the first thing he should know is how to obey orders."

"Isn't he doing that?" asked Kelly.

"Well, I've heard some complaints from the boys in the Ardoyne and I know the battalion commander isn't at all happy with him. It seems that Grogan has been doing pretty much as he pleases since he came back this time. I don't trust him either."

"Wait a minute," said Kelly sharply. "Incompatibility is one thing, but disloyalty is something else."

"Well, that may be pushing it a bit far," O'Flaherty conceded in a tone that was far from conciliatory. "But that SAS background of his stinks to me. You know we've heard quite a few rumours that the British are thinking of using SAS men against us as sort of urban counter-guerrillas, operating in civilian clothes in small units. They could even come down here and have a crack at people like you and MacStiofain."

"That's highly unlikely," said Kelly. "I think I know the British well enough by now. Their real trouble is that they rarely have the courage of their political convictions. You need to be a Celt to do something like that. Anyway, don't worry, I'll keep a close eye on Grogan. And thank you for telling me all this. You'd better stay around here for a bit. You're too hot for

6

the North. There may be one or two little jobs you can do for me down here."

Kelly smiled suddenly, got up and led O'Flaherty to the door. As the stocky gunman was about to step across the threshold, Kelly reached out and shook him by the hand. "Keep in touch," he said.

It had been another night of violence in Belfast. The city looked shell-shocked and exhausted as the first flickerings of dawn revealed a monotonous landscape of slate and stone with smoke curling upwards from a thousand chimneys. The grimy streets, many of them still littered with the debris of the Irishman's baffling religious war, slowly began to disgorge their foot-soldiers. Burnt tyres, stones, bits of twisted iron and nail-bomb fragments scarred the pavements. Children's shrill cries in that peculiar warbling Belfast accent echoed along the Victorian terraces as they scavenged for the British army's rubber bullets. A faint but unmistakable trace of the army's knee-sagging CS gas hung in the icy air.

Christie's powerful body looked as though it had been poured into the capstan chair at the head of the table in the conference room of the RUC headquarters.

"Gentlemen," he said, leaning forward slightly, "this is an interesting report" — He tapped the papers in front of him with a blunt forefinger — "But I'm afraid its main drift is wrong. As wrong as can be."

He looked around the polished table at Barnes and Franks and then at his own assistant. It had started to rain again and all they could hear through the heavily-barred windows was the sound of water sloshing into the drains. Somewhere in the remote distance there was a muffled explosion.

"It says, in essence, the Provos are going to carry the war across the water. Right? That they're going to alter their strategy entirely and attack targets in England. Well, I think that's a load of balls."

"What makes you so sure?" asked Franks.

"A new source of mine gave me the whole picture last night. He's a Belfast man and has his nose into the IRA around here.

This," Christie tapped the papers again, "is from MI6 in Dublin."

Franks exchanged a quick glance with Barnes. "What does *your* man have to say?" he asked.

"There's to be an intensification of the campaign of violence here and in Londonderry—also spreading to some of the smaller country towns which haven't been much affected so far. The idea is to mobilise maximum force and get a sort of *blitzkrieg* going."

"I thought we'd got that already," said Barnes, his mind on the shattered streets and scorched buildings that he drove past every day on his way to the police headquarters.

"We've seen nothing yet, he says." Christie laughed harshly. "The Provos' aim is to cause as much disruption as possible, probably by more bombing of urban centres during peak hours, that kind of thing. Totally indiscriminate."

"But what the hell's the point of that?" demanded Franks.

"Anarchy," said Christie with grim relish. "What they want more than anything else is to show that we are out of control; that the writ of Stormont no longer runs throughout this Province."

"They're already on the way to doing just that," Franks said.

"What do you mean?" Christie demanded, bristling.

"Bogside and Creggan, 'Free Derry'—Stormont's authority stops dead at the barricades, doesn't it?"

"Not if I had my way, it wouldn't," replied Christie menacingly.

"What *is* your way, exactly?" asked Barnes in an almost dreamy voice.

"Look," said Christie, pushing the papers in front of him to one side, "we've been playing this game by the wrong set of rules, too long. If only you people, and the whole of Whitehall, would face up to it: there aren't really any bloody rules at all when you're dealing with a bunch of Catholic fanatics like the IRA. It's the jungle—a green Irish jungle. You've got to descend to their bog level and treat them in the only way they'll ever understand."

"Which is?" asked Franks, knowing the answer.

"The boot. They work by violence, terror, ruthlessness. You have to match that in kind or you'll get nowhere. Oh, I know all about the moral issues — and the risks." He waved a meaty hand in the air. "Democracy may be one thing — but survival, my friends, is another."

Poor bastard, thought Barnes. Poor confused bastard. He suddenly saw Christie's dilemma clearly for the first time. Here he was, a senior cop who has come up the hard way. He was undoubtedly a proud and loyal servant of the Crown. But he was still an Irishman and working on his home ground. Not, as he once put it for Barnes' and Franks' benefit, in some 'coconut colony' like Kenya or Aden. The way of life he was struggling to preserve was his own. An Ulster Loyalist to the core, like most of them here, he could never seem to rid himself of a lurking suspicion that one day Whitehall would sell them all down the river to Dublin. And although Christie was, Barnes knew, not a believer in 'UDI' he sensed that the Ulsterman had more than once cast an envious eye in the direction of that successful secessionist, Rhodesia. But the real agony for Christie was that he belonged to an establishment which, with the situation steadily deteriorating, was being brought increasingly under the control of London. And there was no way out even though, in common with many Ulster Protestants, he disagreed almost as much with Whitehall as they did with their declared enemies in the IRA and Republic. His job, his wife and three children, his whole life-style ultimately depended on a government he neither liked nor trusted.

"All right," Franks was saying, "but do you really think you'll break the IRA like that?"

"There's no other way," replied Christie tersely. "We've got to turn the screw. More raids, arrests, rougher interrogations. For a start, we can squeeze more juice out of some of the top-level internees. For Christ's sake, after all these years we've finally got the weapon we wanted and needed. Internment. And what are we doing? Playing pussy-foot with it and letting soft-tongued, lily-livered English lawyers come in and criticise everything from brewing the tea to the bloody laundry arrangements."

"But this doesn't seem to be getting us anywhere," objected Franks, his voice rising. "I've got no time for Wilson but he was on the nail when he said 'internment is the recruiting sergeant of the IRA'. Just look at the figures. The whole story's there. And if you think your bully-boy methods are going to sort this out, you're very much mistaken. If there's one thing we've learnt," he nodded across to Barnes, "it's that a knee in the groin doesn't alter the course of history."

"And if there's one thing you English will never learn it's that this is Ireland and Ireland's different!" Christie's fist came crashing down on the polished surface of the table making the glasses of water skitter. His face was red and he had begun to sweat.

Franks said quietly: "That's what they all say—at the beginning. But, you know, you'll never win that way."

"Are you bloody well trying to tell me how . . ." The buzzer on the telephone at Christie's side burped twice, demanding attention. He scooped up the receiver and grunted.

"All right," he said, "send him in."

Somewhere in the belly of the building a metal door clanged and footsteps echoed along a distant corridor. There was an embarrassed silence in the conference room, Christie's aide, a nervous young detective, fiddled with his papers and quenched a non-existent thirst with the glass of water in front of him. There was a crisp knock on the door.

"Come in," said Christie.

A tall, good-looking British army officer walked in. His highly-polished brown shoes squeaked protestingly as he strode across to greet Christie.

"This is Major Dalrymple, Brigade Intelligence Officer attached to this headquarters," Christie announced.

"I've got something that will interest you this time," said the major, sitting down and pulling out a file from his briefcase. "We snatched a man early this morning in the Lower Falls area. Name of O'Hara, Kevin O'Hara. He's on the wanted list and we got a tip-off last night that he was passing through Belfast and staying with a cousin of his in Rockfort Street. The 1st Paras went for him at 3 a.m. Had a spot of bother getting in —the door had been specially reinforced, double Chubb locks, chains. Bit like breaking into the Tower of London, to tell you the truth."

The major paused for dramatic effect. It wasn't every day he held the centre of the stage in Special Branch headquarters.

"Then we had some trouble with the lady of the house, who

had a vocabulary that would make a Guards sergeant-major blush. But we got our man all right. He'd locked himself in the lavatory and was about to launch himself like Tarzan out of the window and across the rooftops when he was spotted. Bit of a struggle—tough chap—but nothing serious."

"Where is he now?" asked Christie.

"Down at Brigade, safely tucked away. Like to come and have a look at him?"

"Yes, I'll be down as soon as we've finished here. By the way, there was an explosion about half an hour ago. Sounded like somewhere on the east of town."

Dalyrymple adjusted the perfectly symmetrical knot to his tie and laughed.

"Oh that. Own goal, I'm afraid. A costly one too—one car, four Provos—all blown to kingdom come."

He got up, shook hands formally with everyone, and strode out, an immaculate, machine-tooled product of the British establishment, military division. This brand, Barnes reflected, has been so successful over the years that no one has seen any reason for changing it.

Christie looked at the others with a new satisfaction. The atmosphere was a little easier now. Though far from mollified the Ulsterman felt things were beginning to go his way.

"Look, Christie," Barnes said, "no one is trying to tell you how to run your show—least of all us interlopers. But are you really so sure the Provos aren't going to strike at England? Our SIS friends down in Dublin operate at a pretty sophisticated level and the IRA do have their top, policy-making men there."

"It's the Belfast tail that often wags the Dublin dog in this game," said Christie.

"But that doesn't stop Dublin initiating and carrying out operations elsewhere. Perhaps even without the local lads here knowing anything about it. Another thing, all the evidence we have suggests the Provos are already fully extended and feeling the pinch from internment. The wanted list shortens daily. And I don't see how you'll get anything worthwhile—whatever methods you choose to use—out of people *already* inside. Surely they're the last to know anything about the IRA's future plans."

Christie stood up suddenly. His face was red again, slightly mottled and beginning to glisten.

"You've got no confidence in us, that's as plain as can be. Not a shred of bloody confidence. Well, you do it your way and I'll do it mine. I've got my commissioner to answer to. He's got views on history too, you know, and I can tell you they're light years away from yours."

Christie swept up his papers, beckoned to his assistant, and strode out of the room without another word.

7

GROGAN TURNED OVER IN BED and looked at his watch. Eight twenty-five. He was awake at once. One of his boyhood heroes had been Lord Baden-Powell and he'd pored over the book in which that lean, ascetic old man (there had been a photograph he remembered well as a frontispiece) had recounted tales from Boer War days. Two things had caught the young Grogan's imagination. One was the author's account of how he assessed a man's character when he came across an empty shack out in the bush and looked through it—if there was a toothbrush, however worn, it indicated that the owner took some pride in his personal appearance. The second thing was Baden-Powell's description of his ability to concentrate his mind before going to sleep on the exact hour, minute even, he wished to wake. Grogan had practised this trick, quickly mastered it, and it had served him well since. Though this morning he was awake five minutes before the time he'd set himself. He was slipping. Well, all skills have to be maintained by constant practice, he thought.

Grogan pulled on his trousers and walked out to the small bathroom to shave. He had been billeted in this house for two days now—he changed location once or twice a week these days—and he knew that the old widower and his son would already have left for the building site. And happy to get employment these days, he thought, when anything up to half the men in some of the Catholic areas were out of work. They'd installed the bathroom themselves, a luxury in this part of town, but it sure as hell lacked the feminine touch. Grogan looked at the disordered collection of razors and rusting toilet articles on the shelf beside the cracked mirror. He didn't mind living out rough in the country, liked it even, but in between times he preferred things to be clean and neat.

While he shaved he went over in his mind events of the past few days. It was funny how, with him, a major decision often took some time. He would mull over things, his mind would worry away at all sorts of abstractions. and then quite suddenly he would know just what he was going to do.

He went back to the bedroom and reached into the smaller of the two canvas bags he'd carried with him throughout this trip. He dug out a pen and writing paper and set them on the small table beside the bed. He wrote on the envelope first, an address in Kilburn, London. Then he started the letter.

Dear Cathal,

I was down in Kerry a few days ago and they all send their regards. You're still well remembered for chasing the colleens, but there's no hard feelings there.

Mother, of course, is suddenly a lot older but she's sprightly enough and gets around. She's much quieter than I used to remember—I suppose she's finally come to terms with things, Father's death and all that. Batty was in fine form, with more than a few drinks in him most evenings and spinning out those old warrior's tales. They get taller every time in the telling. He particularly wished to be remembered to you. They're a great bunch, I must say. When I'm there I always wonder why I've stayed away so long. Just like you do, I expect.

Cathal, you'll remember we talked about the quarry project last time we met. Well, I've been having a few ideas up here and I think I'll take you up on the offer. If you can get something organised right away, that would be very good.

Don't write to me because I'll be moving around a bit and anyway the address you've got is out of date now.

One more thing, I'd be glad if you could look around for a place outside Kilburn. Too many familiar faces there—and nosey people.

Take care, I'll be in touch pretty soon.

Jimmy.

Grogan read over the letter and stamped the envelope. He finished dressing and went out.

Five minutes later he was driving his rented car across the so-called peace line that divided the Catholic ghetto from the Protestant area of the Shankhill Road. Taking this route into the city, Grogan had to pass a British army post close to Divis Street. This was usually a tense area, with the army between the two enclaves. This particular post, Grogan knew, had been sniped at only the day before from the tall block of the Divis Flats, a Catholic stronghold. Approaching the post, Grogan was obliged to slow down to less than ten miles an hour to pass over the series of ramps built into the road. These sharp ridges effectively prevented machine-gun and grenade attacks from fast-travelling cars. The post itself was a newly-built concrete block surrounded by sandbags and a high mesh of barbed wire, the total effect contrasting strangely with the suburban streets.

Today two soldiers from the Gloucester Regiment stood outside the post, SLRs sloping up to the sky and fingers ready on the trigger guards. The corporal peered at him through the windscreen, then waved him through without stopping the car. Sometimes they stopped you, sometimes they didn't . . . Grogan drove on into the main shopping area, pulling up near a bombed but still functioning post office to slip his letter into the outside box. As he walked back to the car he moved with the crowd of pedestrians, who, he noticed, were carefully skirting parked vehicles, sometimes even crossing the street to avoid them. Another facet of civil war in Belfast, he thought.

Grogan drove off again, heading down towards the station. He passed the towering Europa Hotel, where the international press stayed. Most of the British journalists, he knew, usually chose something less institutional and more homely, like the Royal Avenue. A small group of clergymen at the entrance of the Europa were submitting goodhumouredly to a half-hearted body check by the hotel security guard. The city was in a state of siege all right.

He parked in the courtyard of the station, next door to the Europa, and walked inside to find a telephone booth. A minute later he was through to the number in Dublin, the familiar soft, rich voice at the other end of the line.

"How're you keeping, then?" he said.

"You old crook!" Mairin replied. "I was wondering how long it would take you. I'm not always sitting here waiting for you to call."

"I know you're not. I suppose you were out all night again?"

"Wish I had been." She sounded as if she meant it. "I was too busy with Jade and Tula. The newsletter is due out tomorrow."

Grogan remembered them, a young couple who'd been at Trinity College with Mairin. They were now involved in producing some half-baked left-wing broadsheet. The names themselves were a generation gap for him.

"Look, I was thinking of taking you for a little holiday. Four or five days . . . working holiday kind of thing. Can you get away? I'll let you have the details by the weekend. I wanted to know if you were free before I made any arrangements."

There was a silence for a moment before Mairin replied. "Yes, I'm sure I could. I'd love to come, but what . . ."

Grogan interrupted. "Look, don't ask me any questions because I'm not sure yet about bookings and things. I'll be in touch with you again very soon, OK?"

"Yes, of course, love. Ring me when you know. I'll fix up to get away any time after Saturday. I love you, you know."

"I'll bear it in mind," said Grogan and hung up. He walked back to his car, feeling happier than he had done for some time. Things were beginning to work out. He had one more job to do before the morning was through.

Three quarters of an hour and two road-checks later, he was turning in at Tom Magan's garage. The army were really getting a grip on the city. At the last road-block a private had checked the boot and the bonnet.

"Where do you work?"

"I'm on holiday from London."

"Sooner you than me, mate. Funny place to choose."

"Well, I'm visiting relatives. They chose it."

His neutral accent, almost English, usually eased his way through this kind of situation.

Tom led him upstairs and he gratefully accepted a cup of coffee from the pot simmering on a hotplate in the sitting-room-cum-office. The coffee always tasted stewed, but it was the only breakfast he'd get this morning.

Grogan reflected that Magan was for the IRA what the British intelligence service would call a live letter box. He'd once spent a fortnight on a familiarisation course as part of some special training in the SAS — he remembered the windswept old barracks near the sea, remarkably modernised and comfortable once you were inside. He could visualise the magnetic blackboard with its seemingly endless list of words and abbreviations: LIVE LETTER BOX (LLB), DEAD LETTER BOX (DLB), CUT-OUT (CO), and the rest. There he'd learned (just a lot of jargon for what was really common sense, he thought) that the DLB was a place of concealment, a hole in the wall for instance, where you could leave messages. An LLB, on the other hand, was a live person, through whom communications passed. Except that, now he came to think of it, he'd been taught that the LLB should be as little involved as possible in the activities of the people working on either side of him.

Magan had become inextricably involved in what was going on as the facilities of his garage became increasingly indispensable. He was another of those staunch, old-style republicans who'd offered his services soon after the Provisionals had come into existence in the North. The fact that the Provos had arms and were prepared to use them in defence of the Catholic population pleased Magan. It was a change after all the left-wing talk from Dublin since the end of the border campaign. From the time Grogan first arrived in Belfast, Magan had been a key contact.

Magan had not been expecting him.

"I'm glad you dropped in today, Jimmy," he said. "There's some bad news. Kevin O'Hara's been lifted, those feckin' paras again. It seems he put up a hell of a fight. Smashed half the inside of his poor old cousin's house, God bless her, but the bastards got him down and put the boot in."

"I wouldn't like to be the man to pick Kevin in a fight," Grogan said.

"Nor I indeed. He took hold of a poker, and there's a couple in hospital now. But he took a hammering. They carried him out unconscious."

"When did it happen?" Grogan asked.

"The night before last. They took him away about three thirty in the morning."

"Well, I don't know what else he could give away, but he certainly knows me—and by the right name."

"Don't worry about Kevin O'Hara. He wouldn't talk if they cut the testicles off him. He's as tough as a bull's pissle, that man."

"The trouble is," Grogan said thoughtfully, "they've got more sophisticated methods, if they want to use them. I've seen some tough nuts crack, myself. They'll know Kevin was in the middle of things and they may be tempted to have a go at him."

The two men looked at each other. Grogan could see that the old man's faith in O'Hara was unshakeable. Perhaps he was right.

"Look, Tom," he said, "I'm going away for a few days. I've just heard from Kerry that my mother's sick. She's getting on, and they wouldn't get in touch with me if it wasn't serious. I'll drop off my car and catch the plane down—there's no point in delaying."

The old man leaned forward, laying a gnarled hand on Grogan's shoulder, his ruddy face full of sympathy.

"I'm sorry for your trouble, Jimmy," he said simply. "You're quite right. You get off straight away and I'll pass the word along that you're gone for a few days to Jack Kelly."

Grogan grunted. "Have you known him for a long time?" he asked.

"I was with him in the old days before I settled down. A deep man. He's dedicated his life to the movement." He paused. "Did you know he was a rival of your father's at one time, Jimmy?"

"No, I didn't. Was he in the North with him?"

"No, he was down in Dublin directing operations. I was working with him then. He planned the crossing that your father was on when he was killed. He was very cut up about it, I remember."

"He never told me about it," Grogan said sharply.

"He's not a talkative fellow, as you know. He's got a lot to think about these days. Maybe he forgot . . . Anyway, good luck on your trip. I hope to God your mother's all right."

The simple directness and lack of guile of the old man made Grogan feel ashamed. As he said goodbye he wondered if he would ever see him again.

PART II

The Preparation

"When the finger points at the moon, the idiot
looks at the finger."

Chinese proverb

8

CHARLES CHRISTIE WAS IN AN IRRITABLE MOOD as he strode into the Military Detention Centre on the outskirts of Belfast. Although twenty-four hours had elapsed since his row with the Scotland Yard men, their doubts about his methods and the implied criticism of his ability still rankled. He found himself torn between wanting to prove that they were wrong, in some spectacular way, and hoping like hell that they would simply climb on a plane and go back to London. But the way his luck was going these days, he reflected, neither was likely to happen.

He showed his pass at the main entrance of the Centre and asked to see Major Dalrymple. A corporal led him down a long passage into the heart of the building where the army's principal communications network for the Belfast area was located. He could hear the whine of radio transmitters as they passed the main ops room. Dalrymple's office, marked BDE. I.O., was close-by and the major rose to greet him.

"Glad to see you, Chief Superintendent," he said, pumping Christie's hand. "Our friend's in fine fettle today . . . well . . ." he corrected himself, "let's say, better shape than when you saw him yesterday."

"What does the doctor think?"

"Let me see," said the other, looking down at a piece of paper on his desk. "Facial cuts, bruises and lacerations are not serious, though his left eye is giving him trouble. Ribs badly bruised but none broken." The major looked up. "No, the only thing is that arm, fractured in two places, not one as we first thought. He'll live."

"They invariably do," said Christie sourly.

Dalyrymple's office was an immaculate, polished mirror of himself. A leather-backed blotter, a couple of ballpoint pens, an alabaster paperweight and three trays — IN, OUT and PENDING — with their meagre contents neatly stacked inside them, were all that adorned the mahogany desk. On a bookshelf stood a photograph of the major's Sandhurst passing-out parade and a small silver cup commemorating his prowess as a marksman at Bisley. On the wall opposite the bookshelf there was a large tactical map of Belfast and its suburbs, protected by a thick piece of talc and dotted with coloured pins.

"O'Hara *is* from the Ardoyne battalion, isn't he?" Dalyrymple asked looking at the map.

"Yes," Christie replied, "he admitted that much when I saw him yesterday and I've been checking up on him at the office. Born in Londonderry but family moved to Belfast. Known Republican sympathiser from his earliest days. Joined the Provos in '69. We picked him up a couple of times before internment but couldn't make anything stick. Missed him, you'll recall," Christie gave the major a steely look, "in the original sweep and he's been bloody elusive ever since."

"Will he know very much if he's been on the run?"

"Enough to make it worth our while," said Christie evenly. "I'm pretty damn sure he's an officer in the Ardoyne lot. Anyway, we'll soon find out. All right if I see him now?" he asked.

"Of course, Chief Superintendent, but . . ." he hesitated.

"Yes," said Christie rising from his chair.

"The question of custody . . ." the major's voice had lost its usual incisiveness.

"What about it?" Christie said brusquely.

"Well, O'Hara is technically our responsibility while he remains here . . . indeed until he's safely in Long Kesh. And I was just wondering . . ."

"For heaven's sake, out with it, man!" Christie snapped.

"It's simply that we have to carry the can if there are any complaints later, if you see what I mean." Dalyrymple examined the gold signet ring on the little finger of his left hand. "The Old Man is very concerned that we should keep our noses clean after the Compton Report and all that, you know."

Christie laughed shortly. "Look, major, you're not the only ones with those kind of problems. The press are down our throats half the time. And I've got a boss with a sense of public relations, too. Don't worry," he said in a tone he may have meant to be soothing but to Dalyrymple sounded patronising, "the army's new to this game, but we've been playing it for a long, long time. You can rely on me."

Dalyrymple looked relieved and accompanied him to the door.

"My orderly will take you down to the cells," he said.

Christie asked the major to send his police assistant down to him when he arrived and followed the corporal to the lift. They went down two floors to the lower basement which looked as though it had been converted from a warehouse storeroom. There were several old packing-cases, strips of metal bindings and bent nails lying around. The air held a dank and musty smell as if the central-heating system had somehow passed that floor by. A uniformed military policeman, red cap, white cross-belts and an automatic in his holster, unlocked a steel-mesh door and let them into the security zone.

"Chief Superintendent Christie of the RUC Special Branch," the corporal announced. "O'Hara," he added simply.

"This way, sir," the MP said.

The other cells in the wing were empty. The MP stopped at No. 4 and looked through the Judas spy-hole in the door.

"He's asleep, sir. Do you want to go in?" The military policeman was about to insert a key into the lock when Christie put a hand on his arm.

"Wait a minute; let me have a look at him first."

Christie pressed his eye against the aperture and looked into the cell. The view through the hole was curious, like looking through a fish-eye lens. The edges of the small room with its high, barred window, were slightly out of focus strengthening the clarity and the impact of the centre with its narrow bed against the far wall. O'Hara was sprawled across the coarse army blanket, his head half off the pillow as if he had fallen asleep the moment his body had touched the bed. He was a man of medium height, strongly built, with particularly powerful-looking legs. His light brown hair, with its pronounced widow's peak, was tousled and there were patches of dried blood over his temples. His left eye was badly swollen and bits of sticking plaster concealed part of his face. His right arm had been bound and strapped firmly across the chest. O'Hara's rhythmic snoring, harsh and vaguely obscene, was the only sound to be heard in the block.

"I want to be alone with him," said Christie.

"Very good, sir. Ring if you want me, the bell's on the left as you go in." They were almost talking in whispers now.

Christie continued staring into the cell as the footsteps of the two soldiers echoed down the corridor. Then he took the key the military policeman had handed him, opened the cell-door quietly and stepped inside. O'Hara slept on, mumbling something unintelligible in his sleep. Christie carefully re-locked the door and pocketed the key. He bent down, picked up a dirty mess-tin from the table beside the bed and with a back-handed movement banged it hard against the wall.

"All right, O'Hara, enough of that—where do you think you are, in the bloody Europa!" he roared.

O'Hara clumsily sat upright, supporting himself on the bed with his good arm. His left eye remained almost totally closed.

"Who are you?" he asked, his voice slurred.

"Never you mind. I'm here to have a chat and it's entirely up to you whether it's a pleasant little chat . . . or a very nasty little chat. Entirely up to you, you understand?"

O'Hara nodded. He was fully awake now. He licked his cracked lips and touched his swollen eye delicately with his fingers.

"Jesus, these bloody paras," he muttered more to himself than to Christie. "You haven't got a cigarette have you? Or a glass of water?" he asked.

"All in good time, my friend," said Christie. He picked up the only chair in the room, turned it round so that its back was facing O'Hara and straddled it.

"OK," he said. "Let's begin. You are Kevin O'Hara, aged twenty-seven, third son of Patrick and Moira O'Hara of the Bogside, erstwhile bricklayer's mate, more recently an unemployed layabout and parasite of the State. You joined the IRA —an illegal organisation—in September 1969, were promoted sergeant in the Provisionals' Ardoyne battalion in May '70 and at some later date, which I cannot now recall but doesn't much matter, made the rank of lieutenant. A position of responsibility in an organisation which doesn't know the meaning of the word. Correct me if I'm wrong."

O'Hara nodded again. He only seemed partly aware of what was going on. At least that was the impression he gave.

"Now it's your turn, O'Hara," said Christie remorselessly. "I want to hear your voice."

"How long are they going to keep me here? I want to see a lawyer, I've got a right . . ."

"You've got no bloody rights," Christie roared. "You and your kind gave up your rights when you blew innocent women and children to bits in the centre of the city. See here, O'Hara," he leant forward over the chair and waved his fist at him, "don't try and string me along. I'm no soft-centred Englishman so don't pull any of those Taig tricks on me."

"I can't tell you anything because I don't know anything," said O'Hara, speaking slowly and with difficulty.

"Balls," said Christie. "The only thing you don't know is how easy you've had it so far. Even the army are getting chicken-hearted these days. A few months ago you wouldn't have been snoring your head off but up against a wall leaning on your fingertips with a hood over your head. Don't get carried away because they've stopped that now. I'm still around and you know who I am, don't you?"

O'Hara didn't answer but stared sullenly at the big Ulsterman. He did know, from photographs he'd been shown.

"When is this new terror campaign going to start? You've had a special directive from Dublin, haven't you?"

O'Hara remained silent.

"What is Flynn up to—is he still your courier?" O'Hara's good eye registered a flicker of recognition. Christie pounced. "Out with it, man, you know who I'm talking about." But still O'Hara refused to speak.

"Don't con me, O'Hara," said Christie, his voice rising. "You know a few things all right and I'm going to get them out of you, if it's the last thing I do."

"You're wasting your time," the IRA man said, trying to prop himself up more comfortably on the hard bed. "I don't know anything—and if I did, I wouldn't tell the likes of you," he said in a sudden burst of defiance.

Christie stood up slowly. "I'll give you one more chance, one more chance and that's it. I want to know more about the political split in the Provos that happened recently in Dublin, I want to know more about where the gelignite comes from and I want to know about the shooting of the Minister. Right, on your feet . . . on your bloody feet!"

O'Hara struggled upright but as he cleared the bed he lost his balance and was about to topple over. Christie grabbed him by the arms, straightened him up and pushed him firmly against the cell wall. The IRA man gasped as Christie gripped his broken arm and his face turned ashen. The policeman took a couple of steps backwards and examined O'Hara who had brought his good arm across the injured one in a protective gesture.

"I'm going to help your memory, my friend," said Christie with a tight smile. "How's your kid brother getting along . . . young Dick, isn't it?"

O'Hara looked startled. "What about him? Don't mix him up in all this, he's clean and you know it."

"He's a bright boy, isn't he?" continued Christie in a conversational tone. "One of the brightest in his year. Won a few school prizes too, I seem to remember. Now, let me see, he must be seventeen now . . . due to take his 'A' levels this year, right? Should have no trouble getting into university, they say . . . so long as he passes his 'A' levels, of course."

"I told you, he's got nothing to do with all this," O'Hara said again, suddenly coming to life, "nothing at all."

"I am also to believe," said Christie, remorselessly, "that though a brilliant boy, he is, like many highly intelligent people, a little erratic, even unstable, you might say. Easily discouraged and short on stamina. If, therefore, he should by some mishap fail to pass—or even to take—his exams this summer, a promising academic career could be cut short, eh?"

"Look, Christie . . ." O'Hara took an involuntary, faltering step forward, his left hand out in a mute appeal.

"Aha . . . that's better, much better," said Christie, grinning.

"You can't do anything to that boy," said O'Hara, ignoring Christie's last remark.

"I wouldn't bet on that, my friend."

"Well, what . . ."

"Oh, nothing nasty or brutal. But a spell in Long Kesh or Magilligan wouldn't do the young lad any harm, I'm sure. You can become a 'graduate' there too—at least that's what your people call them, don't they?"

"You bastard . . ." O'Hara slumped onto the bed.

"Stand up!" Christie bellowed. "Who in Christ's name said you could sit down?" O'Hara lurched to his feet again and Christie moved towards him, a clasp-knife in his hand, its blade extended. O'Hara backed against the wall in alarm, crouching in a defensive stance.

"Stand up! Don't move . . . not a muscle or you'll be in real trouble."

Christie reached for the knot of O'Hara's bandages, inserted the blade of the knife under it and with a quick jerk cut it cleanly in two. The ends fell back and the tension in the tightly-bound wrappings across O'Hara's chest eased immediately. With a few deft movements, surprising in such a large man, Christie unwound the bandage which strapped O'Hara's arm to his chest. The IRA man seemed too stunned to move and stood with his arm crooked in the position it had been placed by the doctor. He stared at Christie. The injured arm, broken in two places above the elbow, had been temporarily set with a couple of splints and bound up.

Christie stood back. He closed the clasp-knife and surveyed his handiwork. "Now, will you answer my questions in a civil manner?"

O'Hara sagged against the wall. Then, painfully, he straightenened himself up and looked at Christie with a terrible hatred.

"Fuck off!"

Christie sucked in his breath with a hiss, took a step towards O'Hara, then with a mighty effort of will checked himself. He went to the door and opened it. As he was about to go out he turned to his prisoner. "Don't move and think hard . . . I'll give you a couple of hours."

He locked the door and walked down the corridor. His assistant was waiting at the entrance to the security zone. He was the young detective who had been with Christie in the conference room during the confrontation with Barnes and Franks. Christie handed him the key to O'Hara's cell. He told him to go along and give the IRA man "a bit of the old soft-shoulder treatment", then call him in an hour or so at Dalyrymple's office.

A little before noon, Christie knocked on the door of cell No. 4 and his assistant let him in. O'Hara was back on the bed, propped up against the pillow. The bandage Christie had taken off was rolled up loosely on the bedside table next to a half-empty mug of tea. There was a smell of cigarette smoke in the close air of the cell. Christie nodded to the detective who handed the key back and went out.

O'Hara, still holding his bad arm in its original crooked position, looked at the big policeman stonily. Christie said: "No more beating about the bush, O'Hara. It's time to talk— and watch your bloody language."

O'Hara said nothing.

"You're wasting your time, Christie."

Christie lunged forward, picked up the other man as if he were a child, and smacked him viciously against the far wall of the cell. He spun him round to face the wall and pulled his legs back, leaving O'Hara propped up by the fingers of his left hand. The IRA man groaned as pain shot through his fractured arm but there was no other sound in the cell except the heavy breathing of the two men. Christie reached up and pressed the bell at the side of the door.

"The Ballymena job—who shot the Minister?"

"I don't know," O'Hara croaked.

"Who planned it?"

"Don't know," he mumbled.

"Did they cross the border?"

Silence.

"Where does the gelignite come from? What have the Scots to do with it? The last lot came from Ayrshire, didn't it?"

Silence.

There was a knock at the door. Christie opened it, keeping a wary eye on O'Hara. He spoke briefly to his assistant ". . . and pull in young O'Hara, Richard O'Hara, while you're at it," he finished.

"You bastard, you filthy, stinking bastard . . . leave that kid alone . . ."

O'Hara, his face contorted with fury, heaved himself off the wall and came in low at Christie, his left fist swinging in towards the big man's stomach. Christie let him come and then with a vicious jerk upwards of his knee caught O'Hara full flush in the face, knocking his head up and sent a right crashing into his jaw. O'Hara's head snapped back like a dead chicken's and he catapulted over the bedside table onto the floor. Some of the sticking plaster had come off the lower part of his face. He was bleeding badly. Christie locked the cell door, strode across its narrow width, dragged O'Hara up by his shirt collar and pinned him against the wall with a massive hand around his throat. Christie started to beat a light tattoo on O'Hara's injured arm with his free hand. There was one lead he particularly wanted to follow up.

"You've got ex-SAS men with you haven't you?" he hissed in O'Hara's ear. "Haven't you?"

O'Hara shrieked as Christie's fist pounded his arm.

"No, no, no, no, no . . . I don't know."

"I want their names, their names, you hear," Christie's words had begun to match the rhythm of his blows. His other hand squeezed O'Hara's throat more tightly.

"For Christ's sake . . ." O'Hara gasped, his face beginning to bulge and turn purple.

"Names, bloody names, you murdering bastard . . ." Christie pounded on.

It was now or never, he knew. He heard O'Hara gasp, a hoarse, scraping noise from deep in his throat . . . "Who?" roared Christie. "BROGAN?" He gave the IRA man a really vicious crack across the bandaged arm . . . There it was again . . . ah, that was it—GROGAN.

He let go of O'Hara's throat. The man gasped for air and then suddenly vomited. His legs gave way under him and slid slowly down the wall onto the floor. His good arm began to move across his body in that protective way again but stopped half-way. His head fell heavily forward onto his chest.

Christie straightened up and stared down at him. A pig in his shit where he belongs, he thought. He tidied his clothes and pulled out a comb and ran it through his sparse hair.

Five minutes later he was back in Dalyrymple's office having told his assistant to get O'Hara cleaned and bandaged up. The young detective had looked paler than usual, he thought.

Barnes was quickly put on the line.

"Our Republican friend's come across," Christie said triumphantly, "with the name of Grogan. Ex-SAS and one of the Provos' big fish. I'm putting him on the wanted list right away. And there'll be more information where that came from. Once these boys start they'll go on for ever." Christie chuckled. "The Irish gift of the gab, you know." In his present mood he even felt a mild indulgence towards Barnes.

He thanked Dalyrymple for his help and walked down the corridor to the main entrance. He wanted to get back to the office quickly. Later he would have another go at friend O'Hara. He now felt elated, quite the reverse of his mood when he had entered the building three hours earlier.

As he was turning into the entrance hall an army officer in a white coat stopped him.

"Are you Chief Superintendent Christie?" the man asked.

"Yes, why?"

"I'm Colonel Wainwright. I am the senior medical officer in this brigade."

"Good morning, Colonel," said Christie formally. "What can I do for you?"

"All prisoners and detainees come under my charge here, Chief Superintendent," said the colonel coldly. "You ought to be bloody ashamed of yourself."

"I'm sorry, I don't quite . . ."

"You know exactly what I mean. As far as I'm concerned you and your kind are no better than the IRA: you're all on the same primitive, barbaric level. Good morning." The colonel strode away, his white coat billowing out behind him.

Christie opened his mouth to speak, then shut it like a trap.

It wasn't as if he did this every day. But there were times when you had to pay the enemy in his own coin. His job was to protect the innocent. He spun on his heel and marched out of the building.

9

THE CORPORATION BUS SWUNG PAST the Belfast Customs House and came to a stop on Donegall Quay with a sigh of air-brakes. The passengers clambered out, jostling one another with their suitcases. They began to straggle like a defeated army down the quayside towards the cross-channel steamer berths. Grogan picked up his bags and walked along with the rest. On the way from the Ardoyne the bus had passed the scene of the ambush where Gould had been killed by the British, to join the pantheon of Irish patriots. Today nothing remained to mark the clash except a lumpy ridge across the road and the bullet-scarred walls.

The Liverpool ferry was due to leave in half an hour. Grogan checked his ticket at the gangway and went on board. It was a crisp March morning. Many of the passengers, especially mothers with young children, already looked harassed and tired. Grogan found himself a space on the boat-deck. Keeping his bags by his side, he leant over the rail, watching an army patrol driving slowly about the quayside.

A hoarse blast from the steamer's siren sent the gulls wheeling and screaming above its masts as it inched away from the quay. As the ship moved down the Victoria Channel into Belfast Lough, Grogan looked back over the city. An unlovely place, he thought. He felt the deck lift under his feet as the ship struck the open sea. He turned his face away from Ireland and went down to the saloon on the lower deck for a drink. The room was full of noisy men, the air clogged with the stale smells of beer, smoke and leather. The keen, salty wind which roared around the ship never seemed to enter this protected enclave. Grogan took his glass over to a corner-table which was bolted down to the deck. He rummaged in a canvas bag, pulled out Muldoon's last letter and checked the address. As he put the letter back he felt into the bottom of the bag and touched the cold, oily steel of the Colt ·45.

There was a delay in docking at Liverpool but no other trouble. It was well past two o'clock in the morning when Grogan stepped off the train in London. He decided against telephoning Muldoon and caught a taxi, giving the driver the address in Kilburn. Ten minutes later the cab pulled into a mews and rattled over the cobblestones to a small builder's yard at the end of a narrow cul-de-sac. Two mews houses had been knocked into one. Over one of the garage doors was the sign in Gothic lettering, CATHAL MULDOON & SONS. A model of initiative and free enterprise. Grogan smiled in the dark as he paid off the driver. Muldoon had no sons, but he was a man of unfaltering optimism. Grogan rang the bell and waited. He was about to ring again when he heard heavy footsteps on the stairs. The next minute Muldoon, a rangy, long-chinned Celt, was peering out through bleary eyes.

"James," he said formally. Then he reached out and grasped Grogan's hand warmly. "Come in, come in — I didn't know when to expect you."

Muldoon's voice dropped to a whisper inside the house. His wife had been unwell and his daughters were fast asleep, he explained. But that was no reason why he and Grogan shouldn't have a few jars. They settled down in the sitting room above the garage and workshop and Muldoon dug out a bottle of Irish whiskey.

Muldoon was now fully awake. "It's good to see you. It really is." He clinked glasses with Grogan and took a hefty swig.

"And you, Cathal," replied Grogan. "I missed you the last time I came through. What's the trouble with Margaret, is she bad?"

"No, it's nothing much, a touch of the flu and generally run down. You know what a worrier she is. Tell me about your people."

"Tureencahill's certainly prosperous these days," Grogan said. "There are three factories there now. The factory's joined the priest and pub to complete the holy trinity. People talk about them in the same reverent breath."

Muldoon laughed as he refilled the glasses.

"How's Father O'Reagan?" he asked. "The old bugger must be past seventy now?"

"Don't worry," said Grogan, "he won't chase you out of town if you go back. He's made his peace with God and reckons you've made yours with the Devil."

Grogan and Muldoon grew up in Tureencahill. Inseparable during their schooldays, later they drifted apart. Grogan came to England to join the army while Muldoon went to sea in the merchant navy. Their paths had crossed from time to time, and they had stayed in touch over the years. While Grogan was still abroad with the SAS, Muldoon had settled down, establishing carpentry and building business first in Liverpool, now in London's 'little Ireland' of Kilburn.

"So what have you been up to, Jimmy," Muldoon said. "I didn't even know you'd left FIRMCOR until I got your letter."

"Bloody FIRMCOR! That was always a mistake," Grogan said. "Though to be fair, they were good to me. An executive job, travelling all over the country, good pay. I even managed to save a bit. It looked good when I came out of the army, but it was never right for me." He looked up at his friend and grinned. "Looking after payrolls and guarding insurance companies—it's not the same thing as the SAS, even at three times the pay. Funnily enough, it was one of the boys in FIRMCOR who put the IRA approach to me when it came. You know the touch—things are tough in the North, remember your father, we need your kind of experience to help train the lads . . . So I just decided to quit and have a look around."

"And how is it up there?" Muldoon asked.

"Bloody rough. Direct rule took us by surprise, but the whole thing's a mess anyway. Officials and Provos at each other's throats, the Catholics in the ghettoes running around like chickens with their heads off. I felt I had to give it a try and there was nothing I could do when my father was killed, being away in Aden. This was a chance to fill the gap."

Muldoon nodded sympathetically. "Your old man, he always wanted to make a Republican out of you, did he not?"

"You might say he forced it down my throat," Grogan laughed harshly. "It's funny the way fathers and sons never see eye to eye. Maybe it was just me. Anyway, I felt I'd had it in my teens—the old-style Republicans were getting no-where fast, and I wanted to get away and find my own feet. So I did."

"And now you're back in the middle of it," Muldoon said. "You might as well have stayed from the beginning."

"Not quite. I learned quite a few things while I was away. Enough to know that they're handling it badly now, whatever it was really like before. The Provos are incompetent, unpro-fessional—they're just trying to muddle through and that's not good enough. I tried to tell them what was wrong—even went to Dublin to do it. I put out a plan that would work much more effectively, but they couldn't see it. Go back to Belfast, they said. Carry on the good work." He shrugged. "Which means killing more women, maiming more children."

"And now?" Muldoon asked.

"I'm on my own now, with something very definite in mind. It's funny how the decisions in your life are made. All of a sudden, they've crept stealthily up on you and that's it. They're there." He paused. "But you, Cathal, I don't want to get you involved."

"Come on, Jimmy." Muldoon's voice was tense. "You're not to leave me out of this. If I've done precious little, you still know how I feel. I tell you what really got my goat. It wasn't only the business at Derry, it was the terrifying reactions of the average Englishmen here. You would have thought there would be a little understanding, a little feeling." Muldoon's long thin face was tense and slightly pale as he leant forward towards Grogan. "I tell you, it really stirred something in me. Here, let me show you something."

He got up and went to the sideboard. A picture of Christ

hung on the wall above it, with an outsize and very bloody sacred heart. Rays of light in heavy gold paint shone in all directions from the exposed heart. The picture reminded Grogan of Kerry in a way that little else could. Muldoon rifled through a drawer and pulled out a crumpled newspaper cutting.

"It's from *The Guardian*," he said. "A letter from a retired army officer to the commanding officer of the 1st Paras in Ulster. It was a couple of days after the Derry killings." Muldoon paused, then began reading: " 'As an ex-parachute brigade commander, I write to say how proud it made one feel to see the way, on television, in which your lads went into action against those blighters last Sunday. They looked splendid and, as usual, bang on the ball. It seems to me and many others that prompt retaliatory action such as this is long overdue. It will have, I've little doubt, a most salutary effect. Should have happened long since. I sincerely trust you successfully weather these thoroughly unjustified but seemingly inevitable brickbats and recriminations emanating mostly from those who either have no sense of law and order, duty or perspective or who are spineless.' "

The two friends looked at each other in a moment of cold understanding. "Bloody marvellous, isn't it?" said Grogan. "That's your British officer to a T."

Neither of them spoke for a moment. Then Muldoon asked, "When do we start?"

"Are you sure you want to get involved?"

"I've been living the quiet life long enough," Muldoon said. "Could do with a bit of action. What do you need?"

Grogan unwound his long legs, got up and went to the window. The first grey glimmering of dawn was showing through the thin curtains. He turned back to Muldoon.

"A flat, a van and five hundred pounds of gelignite."

Muldoon laughed, excited.

"Grand. You can stay here as long as you want, you know . . ."

"It wouldn't be safe, much as I'd like to."

"I've got another idea. I'm full of ideas at four o'clock in the morning," he said as he poured more drinks. "Look, I've been doing a conversion job on an old warehouse down near the river."

"By yourself?"

"Now . . . yes. I was working with a couple of other fellers.

They've finished their part and I'm tidying up. It's a nice place. We can set you up with a few sticks of furniture and there's even a telephone."

"Anyone else in the building?"

"Not yet . . . and there won't be for a month or so. There's been a hitch on the planning permission for the lower floors. I'm the only one with this." He pulled out a bunch of keys from his dressing-gown pocket and held up a bright new, shiny Yale key. "It's all yours," he said simply.

"Thanks," said Grogan. "Where did you say it was?"

"I didn't, but it's Southwark."

"Southwark?" Grogan sounded surprised.

"Yes, Southwark—what's wrong with that? Not the best address, perhaps, but quiet enough."

"Nothing's wrong with that, nothing at all," Grogan relaxed. "You're a great man, Muldoon. What did you find out about the quarries?"

"Well, it strikes me we can try the West Country—Dorset, Devon way. Or we can go further afield to Scotland. You'll need some help and I could do with a lungful or two of country air."

Muldoon fished some large-scale Ordnance Survey maps out of the sideboard drawer and the two men studied them. At last, Grogan looked up.

"I'd prefer Scotland, Cathal. It's more out of the way. The Scottish police are a separate force. There's likely to be more confusion up there when they hear of it. Some bloke blew himself up with a car-load of gelignite in the north-west a few weeks ago. There are also some Scottish nationalists around. And extremist, Protestant groups who're helping their friends in Ulster. The RUC picked up four men and a car-load of arms in Belfast docks recently from Scotland."

"Sounds fine. Let me take you over to the Southwark place tomorrow—I mean today," he said, looking at his watch with a smile. "Then, if it suits you, we could take off the following day. You haven't seen my latest toy, have you?"

Grogan shook his head. Muldoon was never without some kind of mechanical plaything. Miniature railway engines, musical instruments, old cars, once even, he remembered, an incredibly rusted penny-farthing.

8

"An old Citroën—the Big Six, they call it. You know the cars. The French cops used them in the thirties and forties. It's big, all right. Black, sleek and beautiful. We could go in that." His eyes glowed and he drained his glass.

It was broad daylight by the time Grogan fell asleep. Things had begun well. He was lucky to have a man like Muldoon at his side. He felt in a detached frame of mind, as if he was planning but someone else was *doing*, all the time. But he felt no qualms, no doubt or fear. The time to turn back had long since passed.

A noisy group was passing in the street below the Provisionals' Lower Kevin Street headquarters and raised a ragged cheer on their way to watch the traditional Commemoration Parade.

"It's great to be in Dublin on Easter Monday. Yeats *was* talking about the 1916 Easter rising in that poem about 'a terrible beauty was born', wasn't he?"

Tony Sullivan's soft, resonant American voice sounded out of place in the sparsely furnished office. His long hair, the loose denim uniform of his generation and the collection of rings on his fingers irritated Kelly. Sullivan leaned, arms outstretched, against the window frame and looked down into the street.

"He was," Kelly replied shortly. He had a busy schedule today, but his visitor was important enough to warrant some of his time. "I want to take you round to see a few things later this morning. It won't be the usual parade because Lynch isn't allowing the army to march. But it will give you the feel of things."

Sullivan turned to him, with the easy assurance of his youth and comfortable New York middle-class background. This was the first time he'd been to Ireland.

"I'd be very grateful if you'd fill me in on the historical background. My family left for the States eighty-odd years ago and I guess I'm pretty weak on the details."

"I'll be glad to," said Kelly. "But before we leave the office, just tell me how AID FOR IRELAND is handling the pressure from Washington to account to the money it's raising."

Sullivan was the youngest member of the IREAID Committee

working from a small store in the Kingsbridge section of the Bronx. In the past two years they had raised about two hundred and fifty thousand dollars. A sizeable sum of money, especially knowing that it mostly came from weekend dances, bucket collections, sales of IRA buttons and bar lotteries.

"It's very simple," Sullivan replied. "We were made to register, under the Foreign Agents Registration Act of 1938. We protested, on the grounds that we're raising money for a moral cause, we weren't, as the Act puts it, 'engaging in propaganda and other activities on behalf of foreign governments or political parties'. So . . . we have to make up accounts. But they're retrospective . . . you get the picture. It's all phoney, really."

Kelly frowned as one of the two telephones in front of him rang. He picked it up, listened for a moment and, putting his hand over the mouthpiece, spoke to Sullivan.

"I've just got a few calls to take care of, then we'll go out. Will you wait for me downstairs for five minutes?"

Sullivan left the room while Kelly took the call. It was from his opposite number in the Officials who very rarely rang him these days.

"What can I do for you, Liam?" Kelly listened for several minutes without interrupting, looking through the correspondence on his desk. When he spoke it was with deliberate calmness.

"Yes, I've registered your protest and I'll see it's passed along. But you know as well as I do that this kind of misunderstanding is bound to happen. I respect Cathal Goulding's position. But I have orders to follow. You can't expect us to check back with you every time an announcement is to be made to the press."

Kelly listened again, but this time cut in more quickly. He made no attempt to conceal his irritation.

"Yes, I know you're trying to hold the movement together. But I can suggest better ways of doing it than griping to me on the phone when something goes wrong. If you'd had the guts to stand up to . . ."

Kelly stopped as he realised the line had gone dead. Well, he'd done his best. He was more prepared than most of the Provos to maintain links to the Officials. He'd authorised a fair amount of local co-ordination in the North. But the only result was stupid, pointless argument over trivial misunderstandings. Kelly had known Liam Fogarty long before the split in 1969 and had never thought much of him. Just a political theorist with a distaste for action outside the polling booths, he had little or no knowledge of operational requirements.

Kelly shrugged. He dialled a number in the suburbs. This time O'Flaherty was in.

"I'd like a word with you, Paddy, after the Parade. Will you meet me in Flannery's bar at one o'clock and I'll stand you lunch?"

He held the receiver in his hand for a moment after O'Flaherty had hung up. He'd backed hunches many times before and learned to follow his intuition. This time he hoped he'd made a mistake about Grogan. He made several more calls before leaving the office.

Twenty minutes later Kelly and Sullivan were on the other side of the river and were walking in the direction of O'Connell Street, where the Parade always took place.

They made an odd pair, Kelly small and compact in a conservative suit alongside the tall, casually dressed, shambling American. Kelly pointed down Moore Street.

"That's the place where the first party of fighting men made their break after the post office went up in flames, looking for a place to set up a new headquarters. They were led by The O'Rahilly—that's an hereditary Irish title. He knew it was almost the end. The group came under heavy fire from a barricade and The O'Rahilly was hit twice. But he ran out into the street with a revolver blazing in each hand. He was cut down by a hundred British rifles."

Sullivan whistled. "Sound like Butch Cassidy and the Sundance Kid."

Kelly looked unimpressed.

"But that was a different epoch," Sullivan went on. "They got caught by the army in some South American republic . . . They made a movie out of it," he ended lamely. Kelly said nothing.

They turned into O'Connell Street at the corner where the General Post Office stands. The Parade, much smaller than usual, had already broken up and knots of people clustered around a speaker standing on the back of an open truck. They threaded through the edges of the crowd, Kelly pausing here and there to shake hands.

After listening for a while, they moved away. Kelly began to outline the events of the Easter Uprising.

"They set up the revolutionary headquarters in the Post Office, hoisted the Republican flag and just over there on those steps Padraig Pearse read out the Proclamation of the Irish Republic. That was on Easter Monday, 24 April, 1916. They held out for a week, outnumbered twenty to one. Twelve hundred men against the British army. The leaders knew they were going to their deaths, but they believed that only a blood sacrifice would establish the Republic."

Kelly slowed his pace for a moment and turned to the young American.

"You quoted Yeats back there in the office. Perhaps you know another poem of his about the decision those men made:

> There's nothing but our own red blood
> Can make a right Rose Tree."

Sullivan thought Kelly was beginning to sound aggressive.

"Of the seven men who signed the Proclamation the greatest were James Connolly and Padraig Pearse. The first was a socialist, the second a poet. They made an interesting pair, symbolising two traditions of Irish nationalism, the cause of labour and the Gaelic heritage." They were clear of the crowd now, walking through the centre of the city.

"The last battle was for King's Street. Five thousand British soldiers, with armoured cars and artillery, took more than a day to advance. There were only two hundred of our men still holding out. One British regiment, the South Staffs, swept through, bayoneting and shooting everyone in sight, including women and children sheltering in the cellars. Pearse decided to surrender to stop more atrocities. When they came to execute Connolly, who was badly wounded in the fighting and had gangrenous wounds, he had to be tied into a chair to be shot."

"Americans may have lost sight of the origins of the Republic," Sullivan said, "but don't forget that the uprising itself was financed largely by emigrant money. The Clann na Gael in the States have had a long history of supporting the Fenian movement." He paused. "Where does that word Fenian come from?"

"That brings me back to the present day. Fenian comes from the Fianna of Irish legend. Another example, if you like, of literature being assimilated into politics. The Fianna were a kind of cross between the old Knights of the Round Table and the Japanese samurai. We could do with a few of them around today."

Kelly remembered he had things to do and looked at his watch.

"It's 12.30," he said. "They'll be expecting you in the office in Lower Kevin Street. I've arranged for some of the lads to come round and take you off for the afternoon. Will you find your way back all right?"

Kelly pointed Sullivan in the right direction and said goodbye. Five minutes later he was sitting in the back room of Flannery's, a favourite haunt. He had planned to have about half an hour to think things over, but O'Flaherty's broad silhouette appeared in the doorway almost as soon as he settled to his beer.

When the waiter had brought a pint of Guinness and a plateful of freshly-cut sandwiches, which O'Flaherty promptly began to demolish, Kelly explained what he had in mind.

"Paddy, I've got a little job for you. Can you get away from the docks for a couple of days?"

"Nothing easier," O'Flaherty said eagerly. "It's all casual work, anyway. What do you want me to do?"

"I've had a message from Tom Magan. It's a bit worrying. You remember our talk about Jimmy Grogan? Magan says that Grogan's mother is sick in Kerry. He's taken off for a few days without so much as a by-your-leave. What with the ambush when we lost three men and Kevin O'Hara being lifted, I have a feeling something's not right. I'm not saying there's any connection, mind you . . . What I'd like you to do is to go down to Kerry. Act as if you're passing through on other business and tell Grogan that I'd like to see him in Dublin before he goes back."

Kelly leaned forward in his chair. "Now, listen carefully,

Paddy. If by any chance he's not there, don't let his people know that I'm looking for him. And don't mention my name to them. But try to find out if they know where he is. All right?"

"Sure. Shall I set off tonight? I've got a shift to do this afternoon, but I can go after that."

"No," replied Kelly. "I've told our people you're coming in to collect a car first thing tomorrow."

O'Flaherty ordered more drinks, Guinness for himself and a bottle of imported beer for Kelly. The two men sat talking for a while. When he got up to leave Kelly realised he hadn't touched his sandwich which still lay on the plate. He didn't seem to have much appetite these days, moving around so much.

"Finish that sandwich for me, Paddy," he said, punching the big man on the shoulder. "I don't like to see good food going to waste with you growing lads about." As he walked away he was thinking about his next appointment.

10

GROGAN WAITED IMPATIENTLY in the early morning light for Cathal Muldoon to get back from the garage. He was anxious to make an early start. The sitting room of the mews house was littered with the things they would need for their trip. Two fishing rods lay across the back of the old leather chesterfield. Below them were stacked piles of denim clothes, two pairs of heavy waders, and a bulging wickerwork picnic basket with leather straps. A collection of maps lay on the work-desk, a huge pair of wire-cutters acting as a temporary paperweight. Grogan moved his bag next to the two suitcases Cathal had put by the door. A large binocular-case stood beside them with a faded floppy jungle green hat on top of it.

It looked as though they were ready for a month's holiday rather than the two days Grogan was planning. He walked over to the desk and checked the route. From Kilburn, straight on to the M1, switch over to the M6 near West Bromwich and then up to Carlisle. He pulled out the large-scale Ordnance Survey map of the district in Roxburghshire in which he was particularly interested. He was so absorbed in studying it that he didn't hear the Big Six until there was a loud revving of the

engine just outside the window. Grogan looked out and saw
Cathal waving at him.

"Come and have a look," he shouted. Grogan went out into
the mews. "Isn't she beautiful?" Cathal demanded. "I like to
do some of the work on her myself, but there's a one-man
garage called the Normandie, specialising in Citroëns in South
Kensington. He's very good and can usually get spares. She's
just had an overhaul. What do you think?"

Grogan looked admiringly at the big car. Must be about
sixteen feet long, he thought. You could get a double bed in the
back. The paintwork glistened, a deeply polished black offset
by primrose-yellow wheels.

"Fantastic," he said. "What year?"

"Nineteen-fifty-three. Best-looking twenty-year-old banger
on the road. She's what the French call the Quinze-Six. They
started building them in 1933 and stopped in 1957. In all that
time the only modification was a change in the design of the
boot. Wait till you try driving her—she's as solid as a brick
shit-house."

"Come on," Grogan said. "Let's put the stuff in the car and
get going before you have an orgasm."

They loaded up quickly, some of their gear going into the
back of the car, the rest in the boot. Grogan carried out the last
few things while Muldoon slipped upstairs to say goodbye to
his wife, who was still in bed.

As they drove north through the suburbs of London the first
traffic of the day was moving in the opposite direction into the
city, bearing its wage slaves. The two men were sufficiently
attuned to know they were thinking the same thing. They
looked at each other and laughed. Today, at least, they were
free.

Once on the M1, Muldoon pushed the car up to a steady,
throbbing ninety miles an hour. Grogan saw that he had the
rare ability of the natural driver to be a part of the car, the big
machine becoming an extension of the man controlling it,
totally responsive to his will. Grogan had developed a similar
skill in the army. With him it had been weapons.

They started talking, filling in the gaps of the years and re-
viving old memories. As always, they found themselves back in
Kerry.

"Jimmy, do you remember that time the whole gang was nearly caught in the orchard down by the river? That old bastard of a farmer fired his shotgun and we were all scared out of our wits. Except that you suddenly wanted to jump him, to get hold of his gun and blast him to kingdom come."

Grogan remembered all right. He'd amazed them all. They'd been thirteen or fourteen years old and for years had pillaged all the fruit orchards in the area. One of the farmers was a notoriously cantankerous old man. On this occasion he'd nearly caught them and fired a shot well over their heads. Not that they were to know it. Cathal had usually been the organiser and leader of these sorties, but this time he'd been as cowed as the rest. Grogan remembered very clearly how his own fright had turned to anger, as he realised the old man was using a real gun against them. He had gone cold, his mind very clear. By the time the gang had persuaded him to clear out with them, the mood had passed. But it had marked a change in his relationship with the others. After that, they looked on him as having an indefinable quality which set him apart.

Muldoon turned the car in to one of the large, ugly motorway cafés as two ambulances roared past, bells ringing. The two men stopped briefly to fill up with petrol and walked across the bridge to eat a quick breakfast. In less than a quarter of an hour they were heading north again, this time with Grogan trying his hand at the wheel. The gears slotting into the dashboard were unusual, but he soon picked up the heavy rhythm of the car. It was comfortable to drive, but he kept the speed lower than Muldoon would have done. It occurred to him, not for the first time, that the car was conspicuous for the job they had in mind. But it was big and fast, and they should be in and out of the area so quickly that there should be no danger of connecting the car with the raid. Muldoon leaned over to switch on the car radio and sat back, knees against the dashboard, tapping with his fingers to the time of the music. Grogan could see that for him this was a holiday, a break from routine, with a little adventure thrown in. They slowed down at some temporary warning lights. There had been an accident. The ambulances which had passed them earlier and a police car had pulled in to the edge of the motorway beside an upturned lorry and the wreckage of a car. As they passed, ambulance men were gently lifting a man on to a stretcher. A blanket had been put around him, leaving his face exposed. It was covered in blood. They drove on for a few minutes in silence.

"You know, Jimmy," said Muldoon quietly, "I never talked to you about your old man's death. I don't think I even said how sorry I was . . . it just seemed to me you'd know how I felt and words would be useless. I knew that you'd taken it badly. Even blamed yourself in a crazy way, which is nonsense. Do you mind me talking about it now?"

"No, it's a long time ago," Grogan paused for a moment before going on. "It hurt a lot of people. Most of all Mother. We all took it hard, but she was the one who was really hit. Do you know, I don't think she's said more than a dozen words at a time since. Yet she used to be so full of life . . . I was beginning to find out a bit more about my father in the North."

It had been a crisp, cool morning with a bright early sun when they left London. Now it was getting warmer, with a foretaste of summer in the spring air. The country stretched away on both sides of the motorway, green and inviting and Grogan began to feel hungry. They changed places for the run into Carlisle, Muldoon settling masterfully at the wheel and Grogan looking carefully over the maps.

They left the motorway at Carlisle and for the next hour he navigated through a network of minor roads in the rolling Border countryside. They reached a spot Grogan had selected, and parked under a tree. They carried some of their gear down to the bank of the river. Only seven hours from London, it was like a different world. Muldoon was already wearing waders and his floppy hat, splashing near the riverbank as he tried out his rods. Fishing was one of the few country sports that Grogan had never much cared for and he busied himself preparing their lunch. He opened the picnic basket and took out some bottles of beer. Looping a length of string around the necks of the bottles, he lowered them into the moving current and fastened the end of the line to a peg which he hammered into the ground. He made a neat fire inside a wall of stones and when it was going nicely added charcoal from the bag beside him. Then he skewered meat, tomatoes and mushrooms to roast over it. He opened cans of beans, ready to warm in the ashes. Half an hour later they ate off tin plates, drinking cold beer from the river.

Afterwards Muldoon went back to his fishing while Grogan lay in the grass, looking up at the blue sky, content to let time pass slowly . . . He fell gently asleep.

When he woke an hour or so later, Muldoon was tidying up their small camp-site. The fire was out, the rubbish buried.

"No luck with the fishing?" he called out. Muldoon shrugged comically. Grogan splashed cold water from the river on to his face, then they carried their things back to the car. They moved what remained in the boot to the back of the car, leaving the boot empty. It was just before four thirty. They had about ten miles to go to the area where Grogan had pinpointed the quarries. He'd studied the locations on the map, and planned their moves very carefully. By six o'clock they had left the car off the road again, walked across the fenceless countryside to find a good observation point near the top of a hill.

Lying in the heather, Grogan looked through the binoculars and studied the small complex of quarry-workings below. Only a couple of the quarry-faces appeared to be currently in use, but the workmen had already left to go home. Grogan had been prepared to spend the next day, if necessary, reconnoitring sites. But it looked as if they had struck lucky at the first try. He refocused the glasses on a crofter's cottage. Then he moved them to the spot about a hundred yards behind it where there was a small concrete bunker, surrounded by newly erected wire and a mesh gate. Security precautions had been increased recently, but it still looked a walk-over. Smoke was rising from the chimney of the cottage. As Grogan studied the layout an old truck appeared over the top of a hill and lurched to a halt in front of the cottage. An elderly man got out, a dog at his heels, and fussed around a small outhouse before disappearing into the cottage.

"Bugger!" Grogan looked at Muldoon. "He's got an Alsatian. Otherwise it's perfect."

It was getting cold. Muldoon shivered in his loose sweater. "Will the dog bother us?" he asked.

"We'll make sure we don't wake it up. It's probably not trained, not like a police dog anyway. I've seen good dogs in action. A man doesn't have a chance unless he can kill a dog outright. They leave the ground about twenty feet away and go straight for the throat, all sixty or seventy pounds of them. Let's move, I've seen all I need."

They walked back to the car and drove away. By the time they stopped in the small town Grogan had chosen from a tourist guidebook, they were almost forty miles from the quarry and Grogan had explained in detail what they were to do later. They parked in a side street and walked to the hotel marked in the guide. After a drink in the bar they ordered dinner in the small restaurant and took their time over the simple, delicious country meal served by the landlord's wife. Smoked trout was followed by a beef stew. They drank beer from pewter tankards. After stewed rhubarb and fresh cream they sat back in their chairs over coffee. Muldoon patted his stomach.

"This beats the city life every time," he said. "Why don't we delay everything and take a week or more over the job?"

"After a week of this, Margaret wouldn't recognise you. I'm sorry, Cathal, the holiday's over. We'll do it another time."

Grogan paid the bill. An hour later they parked the car off a country lane. It was just after ten o'clock, a cold evening with the wind rising. A cluster of clouds obscured the moon and it became dark. Grogan got into the back seat and reaching into his bag, took out the Colt. When he had checked the magazine he slipped the gun into his coat pocket and lay back. Then they slept for three hours.

Grogan woke first and nudged Muldoon. Now it was very cold but the wind had dropped and the moon gave a clear light. Too clear, Grogan thought. He took a bottle of Scotch from his bag and passed it forward. Muldoon took a hefty swallow, wiped the top, and handed it back. Grogan tried some. His throat was parched. He felt the good, harsh, tingling as he swished the liquid round his teeth and swallowed it. He picked up the wire-cutters, moved into the front of the car and Muldoon started off. It was a quarter past one.

By half-past they were at the top of the hill, at the point where they had seen the old man's truck arrive the previous afternoon. Muldoon cut the engine and they rolled noiselessly down. Not far from the cottage the road branched into two tracks. Muldoon turned into the one leading directly to the bunker and braked just beside the mesh gate. Grogan passed him the heavy wire-cutters and Muldoon got out first. When Grogan reached his side the hasp-padlock on the gate had already given with a short, sharp clink as it fell open. Grogan pulled the chain away and pushed the gate. There was no latch. It gave immediately, and they went in. He moved the gate behind them so that it appeared closed.

The door to the bunker was only six feet inside the gate. It was sealed by an iron cross-bar and a more impressive padlock. Muldoon tried the wire-cutters but made little impression on it. Grogan slipped back to the car and returned with a steel file. He tried to keep down the noise of the file by limiting the length of its sweeps as it bit into the hasp. When he was almost through, he took the cutters and with a last effort the lock snapped. This time there was a loud crack.

A deep-throated barking came from inside the house. They froze. A light in the cottage went on. After a long moment they heard the door of the cottage open and then nothing . . . Moments passed and suddenly the gate crashed open and the dog was on them. Muldoon took a flying kick but went down and rolled over, trying to protect his head in his hands, with the dog snarling and snapping at his body. He shouted with pain. Grogan moved forward, the Colt in one hand and the cutters in the other. The dog sensed his movement, but as it turned Grogan put a bullet into its head and it dropped. A second later Grogan was outside the gate, running swiftly to one side of the cottage.

He crouched low. From this angle he could see the old man in the light of the doorway, standing behind two unused water tanks outside the cottage. He was in shirtsleeves and held a shotgun pointing towards the bunker. As Grogan watched, he loosed off one barrel, watched for a moment, then broke the gun to slip in another cartridge. Grogan moved silently in, picked up a rock and threw it to one side. As the man turned towards the noise, Grogan came in behind him, gun in his left hand. He hit him with the bunched knuckles of his right hand, a sharp blow to the kidney. The old man stiffened, dropping the shotgun. Grogan hit him with the side of the same hand, a blow to the base of the neck. He went down hard. Grogan dragged him into the cottage and trussed him, hands behind his back, with a length of rope from the kitchen. He reached into the old man's pocket, found a dirty handkerchief and stuffed it into its owner's mouth. Then he tore a strip from a kitchen tablecloth and tied it tight across the old man's mouth and knotted it behind his head to hold the handkerchief in. He went into the small living room next door and pulled the telephone wire out of its socket. That should hold him for a while, Grogan thought grimly. He turned out the lights when he left.

Muldoon hobbled towards him as he walked back to the bunker.

"Don't worry, I'm all right. Just a couple of pieces out of my leg. Let's get the stuff into the car. That's what we came for."

They swung open the heavy door and switched on the electric light. It was all there, everything they needed. The gelignite sticks were packed into twenty-pound containers. They took fifteen, stacked them in the boot of the car and locked it. Grogan collected the detonators, primers, time pencils, and safety fuse he would need. He put them in the back of the car, wrapped carefully inside a pile of clothes. He covered the pile with a blanket. Before leaving the bunker he insisted on having a look at Muldoon's leg, in spite of the other's protests. He made him sit on a table and rolled up the trouser leg. The wounds were bad, but not too bad. Grogan told Muldoon to sit tight and walked back to the cottage. Without turning on the light, he checked that the old man was all right. Conscious and breathing, he was still facing the wall where Gogan had left him.

"Just lie still where you are and wait till they come to find you in the morning. You'll be all right," Grogan said to him.

In the bedroom he picked a clean shirt out of a drawer. He walked back to the kitchen and poured water into a jug. Then he took the jug and the shirt with him. He stopped at the car for a moment before returning to Muldoon.

"Will I live, Doc?" Muldoon asked as Grogan tore the shirt into strips and washed the wounds. "As the sergeant said, staked out on the ant-heap, it only hurts when I laugh."

Grogan brought out the whisky from his coat pocket. They each had a swallow, then Grogan poured alcohol from the bottle over the leg.

"Fucking hell!" Muldoon shouted, jumping almost off the table.

"Here, you can finish it," Grogan said, passing him the bottle, which was still about a third full. "That'll keep you happy for a bit."

Grogan stuffed the bloodstained rags into the jug and took it with them.

"We'll drop this in the first river we cross," he said.

Grogan got into the driving seat and they set off, his friend cheering up as he finished the whisky. In an hour they had passed through Carlisle and were on the motorway south. Grogan turned the radio on but could find nothing and settled back for a long drive. By now Muldoon was fast asleep beside him and woke only when, several hours later, Grogan pulled in at the same all-night motorway café they'd breakfasted in yesterday. It was already dawn. Muldoon stirred, half awake, and Grogan told him to stay in the car. He got the waitress to fill up his thermos with hot coffee while he drank a cup himself, and he picked up a couple of packets of sandwiches.

On his way back to the car he stopped at a telephone booth and got through to Mairin's Dublin number. Her sister answered, but quickly put Mairin on the line.

"Sorry to wake you up so early," Grogan said, "I know you're not very sweet-tempered in the morning . . . It's all set for our little holiday. Can you meet me in Cheltenham the day after tomorrow? . . . That's right, Cheltenham . . . yes, England . . . Tuesday. Meet me in the railway station buffet at 8 p.m. OK, love. Take care."

From now on it was a clear drive through to London. Muldoon was fully awake when he got back to the car. They drank the coffee, ate the sandwiches and talked. The Citroën was running effortlessly now. Muldoon dozed off again but by the time they were approaching the outskirts of the city he was awake and singing old Irish ballads to himself. Grogan smiled wryly. As always, the songs were of war and death.

I I

PADDY O'FLAHERTY SPED THROUGH the Irish countryside in
one of the Provos' 'office' cars, an ageing Ford Consul with a
cracked rear-window and a lop-sided look about it. He'd taken
Kelly's advice and left Dublin that morning. He looked at his
watch and took a squint at the road-map on the passenger seat.
Mallow, County Cork, was behind him and, if he remembered
correctly, the turn-off to Tureencahill where the Grogan
family lived could not be more than a couple of miles away. It
was good to be out of the docks and back on a job.

He swung right at the Rathmore turning and drove along a
very narrow and very straight road which sliced through the
rural landscape like a pewter-coloured arrow. O'Flaherty was
a Kerryman himself but came from further west, a small village
on the shores of Dingle Bay. He had known the Grogan children
during his schooldays but only caught fleeting glimpses of them
since. He had, however, once worked with Sean, old Batty
Grogan's eldest son, in a garage in Killarney. He had visited
him years ago, after he'd taken over his father's forge in
Tureencahill. O'Flaherty was passing through a succession of
smallholdings now, as the rich green fields gradually gave way

to isolated outcrops of black rock and peat bog. A fat and ungainly duck, followed by a troop of fluffy ducklings, marched with determination across the road in front of the car and O'Flaherty swerved skilfully to avoid them.

He tried to remember exactly when he had last visited Tureencahill. It must have been at least four years ago, he thought. He had only a fragmentary memory of James Grogan from their school-days and what he had heard of him in Belfast had merely strengthened his dislike of the man. An arrogant bastard. As he drew closer to the hamlet O'Flaherty felt a sudden twinge of apprehension. He hoped that Sean would be there. He wasn't looking forward to confronting Grogan alone. Whatever happened, he must not give the impression that Kelly was checking up. At the back of his mind he felt that if this job went well, Kelly would have other missions for him.

It was after five o'clock when the grey Ford pulled into the small yard in front of Batty Grogan's forge. The screech of a sheet-metal cutter drowned all other sounds and silver and blue sparks from a blow-lamp flew in every direction. O'Flaherty was almost breathing down Sean Grogan's neck before the young blacksmith noticed him and turned the oxyacetylene lamp aside, raising his protective visor.

"Do you remember me?" asked the IRA man. "O'Flaherty, Paddy O'Flaherty from Dingle."

Sean Grogan screwed up his eyes and wiped the sweat from his forehead with a grimy hand. He looked at the stocky gunman. "Sure," he said slowly. "Of course I do. It was some time ago, wasn't it? What brings you down this way?"

O'Flaherty walked towards the entrance of the forge. He didn't want to be overheard by the two young apprentices at the workshop bench. His caution was hardly necessary. The cutter started up again as they stepped out into the sunshine.

"I'm on the way down to see my folk in Dingle," O'Flaherty said. "Thought I'd drop in and see how you were getting on."

"Well, that's kind of you. Look, give me another fifteen minutes and I'll be through. Then we can go down to the pub and have a few jars. While you're waiting," he added, "why don't you go along to the house and say hullo to my father?"

O'Flaherty hesitated for a moment, then said quickly: "I might as well wait for you here if you're not going to be long—

I'd like to check the exhaust of my car, it's working loose. I'll pay my respects later."

"Just as you like," said the blacksmith, looking a little closer at the IRA man. "See you in a minute." He turned and disappeared into the gloom of the forge. O'Flaherty went back to his car, opened the boot, took out some tools and swung himself under the tail-end. Lying on the ground he fiddled with the clamp that held the exhaust pipe on to the car's chassis. It *was* a bit loose but he had no intention of doing anything about it.

Half an hour later, Sean Grogan and O'Flaherty were at the pub at Ballydesmond. A long line of drinkers, stretched the length of the bar. Cloth caps pulled firmly down over their eyes, right arms extended, their fists were clasped around pint glasses. Behind the bar, facing them like squads of soldiers on the parade-ground, stood long rows of golden malts. At least half the men in the pub were completing the ritual of the rural Irish day. Mass in the morning, dole in the afternoon and the pub in the evening.

"My father will be along in a minute," Sean said, handing O'Flaherty a pint. "Will you be staying long?"

"No, I promised I'd get down to Dingle by supper time," the gunman replied. "How's your aunt, by the way?"

"Fine, just fine," said Sean, sipping his beer, "a bit old now, you know, but as tough as old boots and twice as healthy." He chuckled and wiped his mouth with the back of his hand. "And how's Jimmy getting on?"

"Well," replied O'Flaherty slowly, "it's an odd thing but I haven't come across him yet."

"He seemed withdrawn . . . a bit fed up you might say, when he was down here a couple of weeks ago. But he was always the quiet one. Nice girl from Dublin with him — good-looking too." He winked and laughed. He ordered two more pints and turned back to O'Flaherty.

"Jimmy will be sorry to have missed you, but you'll see him up North no doubt."

"Afraid not. Not after this," he pointed at the triangular scar on his right hand. Sean peered at it and looked impressed. "After escaping from Crumlin Road gaol and all that, they've told me to stay put in Dublin."

"Yes, I read all about it in the papers," said Sean. "You've had a terrible time of it. Now that's a pity though."

"What's a pity?" O'Flaherty asked sharply.

"Well, since Jimmy's been up there he's wanted to find out more about his father's death."

"But what more is there to know?" asked O'Flaherty, a small worm of doubt turning in him. "Surely you heard all about it at the time?"

He looked closely at the blacksmith. Sean Grogan had always struck O'Flaherty as a straightforward man, devoid of guile. He didn't seem particularly interested in what happened outside the narrow confines of his home, job and district.

"Ach sure, the cold details, you know," replied Sean. "He was shot and killed in an ambush crossing and you boys dragged him back. It's sad but it's history now, isn't it? After all, that was more than ten years ago. Times have changed. I don't think that sort of thing pays in the long run . . . Not that you lads aren't doing a grand job up there," he added quickly.

O'Flaherty relaxed and took a long draught of beer. It was all right. He smiled at Sean and was turning back to the bar when the pub door opened and an old man entered.

"Good night to you," said Batty. Jesus suffering Christ, thought O'Flaherty, he's growing more like his brother every time I see him. Batty's voice, as usual, was as high-pitched as if he were talking into a Force 8 Atlantic gale. He put out a massive hand which made O'Flaherty's look almost frail and greeted the gunman warmly.

"It's good to see you. That was a grand piece of work, that escape of yours. I won't ask for details—you wouldn't tell me anyway, would you now?—but from all that I read about it in the newspaper, it reminded me of a similar episode in '21. Now, if I remember correctly, it happened with Tom Barry's group over in Cork . . ." The old man was away and O'Flaherty nodded his head from time to time. He ought to be moving, he thought. Kelly would be pleased. But there was one more thing he had to find out. The old boy was asking him now if he had had a look around the forge. Had he seen all the latest electrical equipment that he and Sean had installed? The old part of the forge, with its open grate and blackened timbers, was still used but they rarely shod a horse these days, Batty explained. Now O'Flaherty wanted to get away. He turned to Sean.

"I'd better be on my way now," he said. "Sorry it's been so short. Can I give you a lift up to the house? I'd like to say hullo to your folk?"

"Thanks," said Sean. "But I think I'll stay on here for a bit. You know your way, don't you?"

"Yes . . . there was one thing I wanted to ask you," said O'Flaherty clumsily. "You don't know Jimmy's girl-friend's telephone number in Dublin by any chance?"

Sean grinned and looked at him slyly.

"Now, you old ram, what are you up to?" He guffawed and punched O'Flaherty on the arm.

"No, no . . . it's nothing like that . . . don't get me wrong," said O'Flaherty quickly, embarrassed.

"All right, I'm only joking. I haven't got the number with me but they'll give it to you up at the house."

O'Flaherty stepped out into the cold night air with a feeling of immense relief. He decided that he wasn't cut out for this cat-and-mouse game of words after all; the sooner Kelly gave him a real man's job the better.

An hour and a half later, the gunman was in Killarney. He'd kept his visit to the Grogan womenfolk brief. He'd always found old Mrs. Grogan difficult to get on with anyway; perhaps she sensed he and Grogan did not hit it off or maybe the death of her husband had had a permanent effect on her. She never mentioned that subject and for that, at least, he was thankful to her. He had got the telephone number—Mairin, it appeared was the girl's name—and having parked the car in the centre of Killarney began to look for a telephone box.

He eventually went into an hotel, broke down a pound note into small change at the reception desk and settled himself comfortably in a telephone booth near the main lounge. After a few minutes' delay, the operator put him through to a Dublin number. A girl's voice answered.

"Is that Mairin?" O'Flaherty asked.

"No, who's speaking?"

"I'm a friend of Jimmy Grogan," he said quickly. "Is Mairin there?"

"No, she's gone away—to see him. I don't know when she'll be back."

"Oh, I see . . ." O'Flaherty paused, not knowing whether to press further.

"I'm her sister," the girl said. "If you'd like to leave a message . . . Who did you say you were?"

"No, I won't bother . . . it's not very important," said O'Flaherty hurriedly.

"Well, she should be back in ten days or so—and Jimmy too, I imagine. I know she can't take England for much longer than that." The girl laughed in a friendly way.

"England!" exclaimed O'Flaherty.

"Yes," said the girl, "Mairin said Jimmy had asked her over for a holiday . . . Hullo, are you still there?"

"Yes, I'm here. Thank you very much . . . I'll ring again when they get back . . . Thank you, good night."

O'Flaherty put the receiver down and pursed his lips in a silent whistle. By Christ, that would make Kelly fall off his chair. He grabbed the receiver again and asked for another Dublin number. He drummed his fingers on the coin-box and then heard the familiar soft voice at the other end.

"It's O'Flaherty," he said briefly. "I've got some very interesting news for you. It'll make you fall off your chair. So hold on tight."

"What is it?" Kelly's voice sounded weary.

"Grogan's not here—and hasn't been here since he came down a fortnight ago. And his mother is as right as rain. That story about her being ill was pure codology. But there's more to it than that . . ."

"Go on, man. Let's have it," Kelly said impatiently.

"He's in England," said O'Flaherty triumphantly.

"Where?"

"He's gone to England. I phoned up his girl-friend's sister in Dublin and she says they have both gone to England for a holiday. They'll be back in about ten days."

"Oh God, more trouble," said Kelly, his voice leaden. "As if we haven't got enough on our hands. Whereabouts in England and when did he leave? Did they go together?"

O'Flaherty's elation evaporated. He'd forgotten to ask these questions.

"She wouldn't say," he lied. "I didn't want to press her too hard, otherwise she might have got suspicious."

Kelly heard the dejection in his voice. "Well, never mind, I'll find out soon enough. You've done a good job, Paddy. Now," he said more briskly, "book into an hotel down there for tonight—or go home, if you wish. But let's have you back in Dublin tomorrow. We need the car in the afternoon. All right?"

"All right." O'Flaherty felt drained. Escaping from gaol, he reflected, was child's play compared with this game of nerves.

One of the first tasks of an intelligence officer in a new posting is to know his city inside out. He must be able to find his way around quickly on foot, by car, by public transport. But he often moves in a manner rather different to that of the average citizen. By now Humphrey James knew certain parts of Dublin extremely well. He had an hour before his meeting with Interface and he had already spent twenty minutes taking counter-surveillance measures.

James had no indication that he was under scrutiny this morning, nor that he had aroused any suspicion of his true activities since his arrival in Dublin. His movements were therefore routine, but disciplined. He walked down O'Connell Street and turned into Woolworth's. There were very few customers as he stopped at a counter to buy a packet of razor blades. He turned to face the assistant, gaining a complete view of the entrance to the shop. Two people had entered behind him, a middle-aged woman with a shopping basket and a man who was buying a packet of sweets; the woman was browsing in the section selling men's shirts.

James collected his change and walked deeper into the store. The design of Woolworth's shops usually incorporates a rear exit and James walked casually out of the back of the store into a narrow alley. He walked along this to take a side street. Turning, he had a view down the whole length of the alley; nobody had followed him out of the shop.

Now he entered a main street on a regular bus route. He walked along at a natural pace, stopping from time to time to look in a window and going into a tobacconist's to buy cigarettes. A bus appeared at the end of the street, coming towards him. James arrived at the next stop as the bus, which had collected some waiting passengers, was about to move off. He hopped on and sat downstairs. He was the last passenger to get off two stops later and soon afterwards he arrived on foot at the safe flat. This was on the third floor of an anonymous modern block, with a lift serving all six floors. but no porter. James let himself in with the spare set of keys in his coat pocket.

He had taken some trouble setting up the flat as a clandestine meeting place for this case. After establishing through a contact in real estate what flats were available throughout the city, he and his secretary between them had examined the outside approaches and exteriors, narrowing the list down. A young male clerk who had just entered the service was fixed up with a cover job in a Dublin-based British company and brought over from London. He visited the apartments on the short list and James had selected this one in the light of his report. There was a lease for a year and the clerk would stay in Dublin for the duration of the case. Harriet, James's secretary, acted as a link to the clerk, the two meeting occasionally outside the Embassy. Harriet had only to call to tell him when to keep clear of his temporary home. She always used an outside telephone box in case the Embassy line was tapped.

There was still a quarter of an hour before Interface would arrive. James walked into the bedroom and took out his keys. He unlocked the lower section of a heavy dressing-table and, reaching in, pressed a button. Technicians from London had installed microphones and tape-recorders—everything said in the living room would be recorded. James went back there and stood by the window which gave a view of the street below.

He went over in his mind the instructions he'd been given. The case had still not developed very far. But it was curious how the codename had already taken on something of the personality of the agent. Not that he liked it much. Some sort of Americanism. When he first joined the service codenames were allotted by an old lady in Records, but she had finally run out of words. Now they were computerised, and some weird hybrids had emerged. The earlier ones had been more memorable. He could still recall some from his first years in the East—WORKHOUSE, WISHBONE, ZESTFUL—come to think of it, the old woman must have been getting near the end of her list even then.

From his position at the window James saw the agent appear at the end of the street, walking with his distinctive military bearing towards the entrance to the apartment block. James watched until he disappeared below, but there was no sign of anyone following. As he turned to the door it occurred to him that Interface would certainly think he was a unique source on the IRA, in Dublin anyway. He would be surprised if he knew that James had access, even at second-hand, to some of the very IRA Councils he sat on. That had been one of those strokes of luck, something that had fallen into James's lap. Definitely life was becoming more interesting in Dublin.

The buzzer on the door sounded and he opened the door to greet his visitor, ushering him into the sitting room and taking his coat. After a short exchange of pleasantries, most of them from James, they got down to business. James made the first move.

"Now that we have an ideal place to meet, I wonder if you would agree to more regular meetings?" he said. "Something which wouldn't form too much of an observable pattern, say every eight or nine days. But it would give us the chance to discuss events as we each see them."

His visitor folded his arms.

"Mr. James," he said quietly, "I suppose that your head-quarters must be pressing you hard to produce something concrete out of our relationship. I can understand that. But I hope you will accept that I can't be pushed faster than I wish to go."

"We have had three meetings," James replied. "You expressed a willingness to help us act against the Provisionals in the North. Forgive me, but I am still not clear how you propose to do that when at the same time you give us neither the identities of the men involved nor details of their operational plans."

"I would like to make my position very clear," he said slowly. "I am a senior officer in the Irish Republican Army; I have belonged to it all my adult lift. I do not believe that the present split into two wings is serving the purpose I've fought for, and have always believed in most passionately, the reunification of Ireland. Nor do I believe that the present tactics of the Provisionals, who came into existence only because of our internal dissensions, are serving that purpose. Therefore I have established a link with your service—with the express purpose of using that link to control a situation I cannot control from within our own ranks."

He paused for a moment and smiled coldly at James.

"You may think it's a dangerous game to play. It is— but these are dangerous times and the rules are changing all the time. Surely you're not surprised that I won't give you a list of names? I am no traitor, Mr. James, not to my country nor to the army I serve. If you and your service will be patient, you will discover that there are some areas in which we can both find common ground. I hope that for the moment you take my word for that. In the meantime, I don't object to meeting you occasionally, under the arrangements we have already made."

"Will you at least give me a way of getting in touch with you if I have something urgent to discuss?" James said. "I received your note safely, and of course it doesn't have your own signature on it, but that's a slow system. You could give me your telephone number at home so that I could ring you calling myself, let's say, Harry and arrange a time to meet. The place wouldn't be mentioned, but it would be understood to be this flat. That would give us an emergency system of contact. You, in turn, could ring me at the number I've given you, calling yourself Thomas, the name you signed on the note."

The lines of fatigue in his visitor's face suddenly relaxed. He shook his head to refuse the cigarette James offered.

"Very well," he said. "If it will make you feel better. Here, I'll write down the number."

He reached into the inside pocket of his jacket and produced a small notebook, tore a leaf of paper from the back and scribbled on it with the pen James gave him. How much the office would like to have that notebook, James thought.

"There are one or two points," James said, "that perhaps I could bring up, now we have a little time. We've heard from a source in Belfast that a former member of the SAS called Grogan is involved in Provo operations. Since we have his name, can you tell me anything more about him?"

"Jimmy Grogan. His father was shot in 1961 on the border near Sligo. You must have a lot of information on him—he was in the British army for about twelve years. When he got out he drifted about a bit, couldn't settle. The Provos approached him to help train some of the young hot-heads."

"Where's Grogan now?" James asked.

"He's in the North, based in Belfast. He was in a couple of scrapes—involved in operations, strictly against instructions."

"Are there any other SAS men in Ulster?"

The visitor looked hard at James. The cold smile reappeared.

"Only yours," he said.

"We don't have any. The SAS are not being used in Ireland." James could see that his visitor was looking restless. "We've picked up some indications that your Council has discussed possible operations in England. Is there any truth in that?"

"There is—it's always been discussed as a possibility. But there's no question of it happening. You've got to admit it's a tempting idea . . . but it's not our policy, and that's the end of it." He paused. James said nothing and he continued. "Since you're asking so many questions, there's one I should put to you before I go. You know our position on talks between the various interested parties, I think. Your government will have to learn the hard way, I suppose, that negotiations without us being represented, if not actually at the table, are valueless. No hypothetical solution found that way will ever be workable. However, we understand that the British and Lynch have been having secret talks, and we've noticed the odd Minister or two slipping away to London. Would you care to comment on these secret talks, and what they're supposed to achieve?"

"All I can say is that if they're taking place nobody's told me about them," James replied. "There's a lot more I was hoping to talk to you about this time. Can you . . ."

"I'm sorry, I really have to go now." His visitor stood up, the meeting was clearly over. "I shall be in touch with you again, Mr. James, and I hope you won't use your emergency arrangement unless you have something particularly important to tell me. Not just in order to earn your salary, if you understand me."

James saw him out, helping him into his coat and passing him his hat. He shut the door and walked slowly back to the bedroom. Then he switched off the recorders and changed the first spool, picking it up and locking the drawer. He could have hoped for more, but it hadn't gone too badly and at least he'd got him talking a bit. Not that he'd got anything out of him that carried things much further. James waited for a quarter of an hour, to leave a space between their departures.

When he got back to his office Harriet was bustling around as usual, managing in that original way of hers to be totally occupied without ever getting anything done properly. They were still in temporary accommodation after the burning of the Embassy. The combination lock on their one safe was meant to be changed every three months and James had asked her to do it as he left for his meeting—a simple job that should take ten minutes. He could see the lock was out of position at the back: she had managed to get it jammed again. That would probably take him a good half hour to put right. God, he had to do everything in this office. All he needed was a neat, tidy, preferably young, but above all *efficient* secretary. She looked at him despairingly, strands of wispy hair falling over her red, perspiring face. What could he say?

"Harriet, would you bring me the Interface file, please. And I could do with a cup of coffee, if you have a moment."

Vowing that he would write to Personnel in the next diplomatic bag asking for a secretarial replacement, he went through to his own room. He pulled forward a scribbling pad and drafted a telegram to London, a copy to go to Belfast.

INTERFACE

A. MEETING TOOK PLACE AS ARRANGED TODAY 1030–1105 HOURS.

B. INTERFACE AGREED TO EMERGENCY CONTACTING ARRANGEMENTS AND IN PRINCIPLE TO MORE REGULAR MEETINGS.

C. HE CATEGORICALLY DENIED POSSIBILITY OF IRA CARRYING WAR TO ENGLAND BUT ADMITTED SOME DISCUSSION AT COUNCIL LEVEL.

D. INTERFACE IDENTIFIED GROGAN AS EX-SAS NOW WORKING WITH PROVOS IN TRAINING CAPACITY. INTERFACE STATES GROGAN CURRENTLY IN BELFAST AND INVOLVED IN OPERATIONS. HE CLAIMS NO REPEAT NO OTHER SAS WITH IRA.

E. FULL REPORT AND TAPE IN TODAY'S BAG.

James looked up as Harriet came in with the coffee. For once it was not slopped into the saucer. It even tasted all right. He spoke first.

"Don't worry, I'll have a look at the safe in a minute."

He held the sheet of paper out towards her.

"Would you encode this and get it off right away, please. Whatever happens, it must go before lunch. And make sure everything's ready for the bag by three thirty. We mustn't go through that business of holding up the Chancery bag while we re-type half our correspondence again."

She stood looking at him, a mixture of helplessness and despair.

"OK, fine, off you go," he said, gently. Christ Almighty, she was almost in tears again. It really wasn't his fault.

12

BIG BEN'S CHIMES, MEASURED AND ALOOF, rang out over the confused grumble of London's morning traffic as Detective Sergeant Jack Fitchett walked briskly over to the wall-map in the high-altitude office in New Scotland Yard. He took a blue marker pin out of a box and stuck it firmly into the middle of England's western leg. Another quarry raid had been reported in the early hours of the morning. Fitchett made a quick count. "Five of them in the last two months, sir," he said, turning towards his superior.

"Where was the last one?" Bill Franks asked, without looking up from the papers on his desk.

"Dorset–Devon border," Fitchett replied. "Doesn't seem to be any pattern . . . they're all over the shop."

Franks shrugged. "Something will click into place, sooner or later . . . it always does."

Fitchett looked back at the map. It didn't seem likely to him. So far they had the names of a man and a woman—and that was it. They had no idea which part of the country they were in, what they were planning to do—if anything—or even what they looked like. He walked back to his desk and glanced at the

Identikit frames. James Grogan seemed to be long and lean in the face, Mairin Duffy round and fuller. There was nothing remarkable in that. Fitchett remembered a randy art master at his co-educational grammar school who had referred to the basic shape of men's faces as 'flower-pots' and women's as 'full moons'. He had always found *incomplete* Identikit pictures more confusing than helpful. They tended to make the wanted person look like Mr. Everyman and rob him of his individuality.

But then Jack Fitchett was new to the Metropolitan Police, and even newer to Special Branch. Twenty-six years old, he had spent most of his police career in the Essex force. He had shown promise in the CID in Chelmsford and, with the strong encouragement of his young wife, had joined the 'Met' and moved to London.

"Have those personal reports on Grogan come in yet?" Franks asked.

"All the army ones are here, sir," replied Fitchett. "But nothing from the Security Service yet."

"And MI6?"

"MI what?"

Franks looked up from his desk at the young, fresh-faced detective. Didn't they teach them anything these days, he wondered. He couldn't blame him, though. The Essex marshes obviously were not the place to acquire an understanding of the Whitehall machine.

"Come here, my lad," he said, getting up. He took Fitchett to the window and the two men stood silently for a few moments in a pool of pale April sunlight, looking out over London. It was a breathtaking view. Franks had tried to describe the precise location of the new Metropolitan Police HQ recently to an old ex-police friend who had been abroad when the big move away from the Embankment had taken place in 1967. He had found it curiously difficult. Well, he had begun, the new New Scotland Yard is off Broadway . . . then stopped. It sounded, his friend had said, like the latest bit of New York fringe theatre. But the description was precise enough. The new building, a huge twenty-storey edifice of mock marble, aluminium and glass faced Broadway and backed on to Victoria Street. It had originally been designed as an ordinary office-block and now, as the new home of the Met, cost the taxpayer a million pounds a year in rent. The all-round panoramic view — one of the best in London — was singularly appropriate for the city's police HQ, Franks thought, and included a magnificent sweep of the river on one side and an aerial view of St. James's Park on the other. The office the two policemen were in was part of the Special Branch complex on the eighteenth floor and looked out over Westminster Abbey, the Methodist Central Hall and the Houses of Parliament. Franks pointed down the river towards the city.

"Over there," he said, "is Millennium House, the home of MI6, or in plain English, the Secret Intelligence Service. They are, for your private information" — Franks gave the younger man a stern look — "MI5's counterpart which operates outside the UK and colonies. Oddly enough, they used to be over here once, in Broadway."

Fitchett nodded. He liked Franks despite the gruff manner. A tough old bastard, he thought, looking at his leathery face and military-style moustache. Avuncular and a bit out of touch with some of the new things they were teaching at Hendon these days, but a good operator and the right sort of man to be with in a crunch. Mean too, he thought, if necessary. Fitchett wondered for the hundredth time since he had joined Special Branch when he would eventually get into the real action. And what his own reactions would be to that. But he wasn't so sure about Barnes. Very senior and all that, though a bit on the soft side, he had decided.

"How did the first break come in this case, sir?" he asked. "It's still a bit of a mystery to me."

"The Governor pulled that one off . . . By the way, have you got everything teed up, he'll be in soon?" asked Franks, looking at his watch. Fitchett nodded and Franks went on. "We were going round in circles up in Belfast after that RUC oaf beat the shit out of one of the IRA men the army had lifted." Fitchett's eyes gleamed.

"He got Grogan's name but couldn't do anything with it," Franks continued. "And he was still sticking like a limpet to a pet theory of his that the IRA were going to intensify their ops in the North. You've seen all that in the files?"

Fitchett nodded again. He had taken off his horn-rimmed glasses and was polishing them vigorously. Franks tried to remember when he had worked with a policeman with glasses like those, but couldn't.

"What happened next was a classic example of the value of good contacts. He remembered he had an old chum in the Irish Gardai—police to you—in Dublin. A chap he'd worked with in Kenya years ago. I knew him too, as a matter of fact, though not so well."

"Are we that hand-in-glove with Dublin?" Fitchett asked.

"No, we aren't," Franks replied. "There is the usual exchange on criminal and civil matters, extradition and Interpol. But politics are more dicey. Anyway, to cut a long story short, the governor's chum scouts around on his own account and comes up with the girl's name and the fact that she's a bit of a left-winger. Even better, he learns that she has just taken off for England with her boy-friend, James Grogan. 'On holiday' was the way they put it."

"But I thought Grogan was supposed to be operating in the North," Fitchett objected. "What's he doing on holiday?"

"That's mainly why the Chief and I are back here. All we know for certain is that there is a potentially highly dangerous IRA gunman on the loose over here. Right?"

"Yes . . . but . . ."

The door opened and as Barnes walked in the telephone on his desk started to ring. "OK," he said, "I'll take it." When he had finished he turned to Franks. "What's the state of play, Bill?" he asked.

"Grogan and Duffy are on the watchlist—ports, airfields, train-ferries. Descriptions, such as we have, have been circulated to all forces. The Irish Squad are cross-checking on the local lads in London. During the next few days we're going to spread the net a good deal wider than we've done before. First big swoop is scheduled for dawn tomorrow."

"That will cause a bit of a stink—as usual," said Barnes calmly. "But I gather everyone is getting used to it since the Aldershot bombing."

"We still need more men," Franks said gloomily. "The Commissioner is about as sympathetic as this concrete," he tapped the wall.

Fitchett, sitting quietly in the corner of the room near the window, had his eyes glued to a file of reports on potential Irish subversives in the Anti-Internment League. But the young detective's mind was elsewhere. Fitchett couldn't quite get over his luck in being accepted by the Special Branch and then becoming immediately involved in this Grogan case. It promised some fascinating detective work as well as a bit of action. He had heard, though found it hard to believe, that the thing which had tipped the scales in his favour for the Branch had been his modest command of French and German. But if this was so, he was honest enough with himself to ascribe it less to his brilliance than to the average copper's total ignorance of foreign languages.

"Right, let's go through those War Office reports on Grogan," Barnes was saying. He picked up a buff-coloured folder. "Joined the army in 1955. Basic training Sherwood Foresters. Transferred to the Parachute Regiment shortly afterwards. With them for five years and spent the last six years of his service in the SAS. Demobbed in 1967 with the rank of sergeant."

"Got around, too," said Franks checking his notes. "The Suez invasion, Cyprus, Aden and the Radfan."

Barnes flicked over the pages. "He went for a commission in 1962 — but was turned down. His commanding officer gave him a glowing recommendation for the War Office Selection Board — though it didn't seem to do him much good. 'Grogan,' he wrote, 'is a first-class soldier. He combines a mastery of the skills of his trade with an equable temperament and a keen intelligence. Although lacking a formal education — he left school at an early age — he has made good the shortfall on his own initiative with the help of the Education Corps. He has a good disciplinary record, easily accepts responsibility and gets on well with his comrades, although by nature he is of a solitary rather than gregarious disposition.' "

Barnes smiled. "The colonel has quite an elegant pen . . . Well, not much else there — let's have a look at the WOSB report, they sometimes make good reading . . . Listen to this. 'This man has distinct leadership qualities, if somewhat under-developed at present. But there is an arrogant and stubborn streak in him too. There is no doubt, in the view of the Board, that Corporal Grogan has the capacity to lead small groups. He would make an ideal platoon sergeant. But we feel he is not yet ready for the responsibilities that an officer must carry.

There is also another reason, of a more confidential nature, for not recommending him for a commission.' "

"What was that?" asked Franks sharply.

" 'This is the delicate question of loyalty'," Barnes read on. " 'Grogan's father, it appears, was a long-standing member of the IRA, killed crossing the Irish border last year. Of course this should not be held against his son, who has an exemplary record as a loyal British soldier. However, in view of the closeness of his father's death and the undoubted strain that this must have placed on Corporal Grogan, we feel he should be reconsidered at a later stage.' "

"Did he ever try again?" asked Franks.

"No . . . he returned to his SAS unit and was promoted the next year to Sergeant. So there you are . . . neither an officer nor, you can be sure, a gentleman. Anything else?"

"A couple of things," replied Franks. "During his time in the SAS he did an advanced explosives and demolition course on attachment to the Royal Engineers. And then a little later, during his stint in South Arabia, he came back for one of those cloak-and-dagger courses with our friends in Millennium House. But we've had no response since we asked for their file on Grogan."

"And we won't—ever," said Barnes. "They keep their cards really close to their chests. More secrecy than service sometimes, if you ask me. But I've had a chat with Mike Cockcroft at 'Five' and we'll get a general line from him. We're due over at Brecon House, Bill, at ten forty."

Franks nodded and started putting away his papers.

"Get on to FIRMCOR, Sergeant," Barnes said to Fitchett. "See if they have anything on Grogan. A couple of the Irish Squad's sources say he worked with them after he left the army."

Fitchett said Yes Sir as if he were in the army himself.

"By the way, how's the agent running going? Getting used to it?" Barnes asked.

"Fine," he said respectfully. "I think I've got my hand in now." He sensed that he was already part of the unit. Taken for granted a little, but useful.

Ten minutes later Barnes and Franks stepped out of the lift on the ground floor. They walked out through the main lobby into Broadway. To the casual observer the most surprising thing about the public face of New Scotland Yard is the conspicuous absence of policemen. Uniformed policemen, that is. There are usually plenty of beefy, rather florid-looking men around, but invariably in plain clothes. Lawyers in black jackets and pin-striped bags abound and a fair cross-section of the general public find their way in from time to time. As the two Special Branch men passed the reception desk an old lady with pale pink hair and a moleskin coat was complaining bitterly about the loss of her miniature poodle.

Barnes breathed a sigh of relief as they cleared the building and headed down towards St. James's Park, London's loveliest patch of urban green, and a favourite walking place for Whitehall's mandarins.

"What do you think Grogan is up to?" Franks asked.

"Difficult to say," Barnes replied. "Might be on a dirty weekend or even going to the Continent."

"Two of them together, if they stay that way, should make it easier for us," said Franks, thoughtfully. "He sounds a bastard to me. How can a man fight for us for twelve years and then flip right over to the other side just like that?"

"It's odd, all right. He doesn't sound like the average Irish nut. A cold fish—and therefore doubly dangerous." Barnes paused. "I've been thinking about those quarry raids," he continued. "Let's suppose for a moment that Grogan was involved. Only the west country and Roxburghshire jobs happened after he came over. Dorset was a clumsy job—doesn't sound like him. But the Scottish one was neatly handled."

"Well, if it *was* him," Franks said, "he's got three hundred pounds of gelignite stashed away somewhere."

They crossed the Mall and walked through Green Park up to Piccadilly. Ten minutes later they were at the entrance of Brecon House, an undistinguished modern building facing Hyde Park. Five minutes after that the two Special Branch men were deep in conversation with their opposite number in Britain's faceless and highly efficient Security Service.

At the top of the long flight of stairs Grogan paused to find the Yale key, then let himself into the attic flat. Muldoon had certainly done a good conversion job, and the place was almost ready. It must be worth the best part of thirty thousand pounds, Grogan thought. He wondered what Muldoon's cut would be.

Grogan dumped his packages in the sitting room and walked over to the window to admire the view. This was the top flat in what used to be an old warehouse. The Thames, directly below, had a cold, grey, uninviting look, although it was a sunny day. Grogan had spent hours watching the river traffic since he moved in. Barges, steamers, tiny little motor boats, pleasure-cruisers, they all had their own rhythms and patterns on the water. At night the place was a dreamland, the twinkling light on the river moving against the sombre chiaroscuro backcloth of the huge buildings of the opposite bank. Grogan felt drawn out to the river, fascinated by the living quality of its movement.

He went into the kitchen and made coffee. It was only ten thirty but he'd done a few things already this morning. He'd visited a theatrical outfitter's near the Charing Cross Road and picked up what he would need to change his appearance. Nothing too dramatic, just enough to make a subtle but effective difference. Another trick he'd picked up in the SAS. He'd gone to his bank just after it opened and drawn out what was left in his account—just over four hundred pounds. Then he'd caught a bus back to Southwark.

Grogan took his coffee into the sitting room and sank into the one armchair that Muldoon had brought over for him when he arrived, together with a mattress, sheets and blankets, and a few kitchen utensils. He went over events. His disappearance would have been noticed by the IRA. The simplest of checks in Kerry would show that his mother hadn't been sick and that he hadn't gone back. It wouldn't take Kelly long to add it all up. But what would he do? Grogan supposed that Kelly *might* just sit back and wash his hands of the whole business. Kelly had seemed to like him, for his father's sake and for his own professionalism. But Kelly was an old soldier, and a tough one. On balance, he would most likely think of Grogan's action as a breach of discipline which could not go unpunished. But they'd have to find him first.

Muldoon was the only person in London to know where he was. But Muldoon's connection with him was unknown and he had no links with the Kilburn IRA. His trip to Scotland had gone unnoticed, as far as they knew, and the wounds on his leg were pretty well healed. At Grogan's suggestion he'd gone for treatment as an out-patient at St. Mary's Hospital, Paddington, rather than to a local Kilburn doctor, so that should have aroused no attention. Muldoon *did* have the gelignite, stacked away safely in his workshop where no one would light on it. And that was probably the best place to leave it. No, Grogan thought, it would be difficult to get to him through Muldoon. He was pretty safe so far, provided he went carefully and made no mistakes.

Grogan went out to the kitchen and poured himself some more coffee. By elimination he had already pretty well decided on three possible targets. But he wasn't going to make a final choice until he'd had a good look at them all. He looked out of the kitchen window across the river towards the newly developed parts of the city. Here the whole face of the city was changing rapidly, new roads and office blocks rising from the old slums. In shoddy counterpoint to the modern office blocks, looming above its surroundings, rose Millennium House. Grogan had even been in there once when an SAS course had assembled for half a day. Afterwards, the course officers and NCOs were taken by train from Waterloo to the extraordinary premises on the South Coast used by 'the firm', as the Secret Service was known to initiates, for training purposes That had been quite a trip.

Millennium House was a good target. The British Secret Service was probably the most potent of all the IRA's enemies. The Irish, after all, had a reputation second to none for breeding informers. The Secret Service seemed to him better than a military objective. Grogan had heard a lot about the Palestine troubles in the army, and developed a great admiration for the techniques of Israeli guerrilla groups like the Irgun. They hadn't messed about, they'd gone straight for intelligence targets, buildings and individual agents, with an undeflectable ruthlessness and determination that wasn't to be shaken. Now he could copy their tactics. Grogan looked at his watch. Eleven thirty. He decided to go out and have a look at the place to refresh his memory.

In a quarter of an hour Grogan had crossed the river and was

close to the Portland stone façade of Millennium House. There
was some window-cleaning going on. He could see the cradles
the workmen were using to lower themselves from the flat roof.
Grogan walked around the building. The front gave on to a
busy thoroughfare and there was no question of any casual
observer being challenged. Through the front doors, Grogan
could see at the back of a huge entrance hall a row of security
guards—behind a counter. He cut down the side street which
led to the back of the building. There were children playing
football near a concreted area that served as a parking lot.
Grogan couldn't tell whether this was reserved for Millennium
staff or used by the residents of the few small, narrow streets
at the back which were all that remained of the original
slum.

The children kicked a tennis ball through makeshift goal-
posts—piles of jackets. It rolled towards Grogan. He bent
down to field it and held it in his hand as a cheeky-faced, fat
little boy ran up to him.

"Here you are, son," he said, holding out the ball but letting
the boy come up to take it out of his hand. "Tell me, what's
that large building up there?"

"That's MI5, mister, where the top-secret coppers work."
The boy giggled and turned to his mates. Grogan grinned.
The boy hadn't quite got it right. But the location of SIS
headquarters was obviously a fairly open secret to the local
residents.

Grogan walked past the children into the series of streets
directly behind Millennium. Here, too, there was no restriction
on movement by the public. More concreted parking areas, all
packed with cars, surrounded the block. Suddenly Grogan saw
what he had been looking for. A one-room glass and concrete
hut stood by the side of a ramp leading down below the building. Two uniformed guards sat at a counter inside the hut,
facing the ramp. One was speaking on a telephone, the other
staring at the racing pages of a newspaper with the dedicated
concentration of the small punter. As Grogan passed, a black
Humber with a chauffeur at the wheel came up the ramp,
paused at the top while the driver waved at the two guards,
and moved gently away. Grogan saw a notice at the top of the
ramp before he turned the next corner—LIMIT 5 MPH. It looked

all right to him. He'd learned that simple schemes worked best. The ramp led directly below the back of the building.

There was an important factor to be considered. If he decided on Millennium, should he choose a weekday, in which case a hell of a lot of people, including secretaries, cleaners, and God-knows-what-kind of auxiliaries stood to be killed or injured? They knew who and what they were working for, so in a sense they knew the risk they were taking. Or if they didn't, they should have thought of it. The British had often dealt out wild justice to all and sundry in the history of Irish rebellions. On the other hand he could go for the weekend, when security would be even slacker and there would be only a skeleton staff in the building, with perhaps a few duty officers.

As Grogan was thinking it over he came face to face, in a sudden shock of recognition, with someone from his past. It was Lawrence Ferne. The last time he'd seen him was in Aden. Ferne was an intelligence officer who had liaised with the SAS in a number of highly delicate operations in the Far East and, later, during the British withdrawal from South Arabia.

"Hello, old boy. It is Grogan, isn't it?" Ferne held out his hand, smiling. "What on earth are you doing around here?"

Grogan registered the fact that it was a purely rhetorical question. "Just visiting some old friends. How about you? What are you up to these days?"

"The old firm's given me the boot. I've just been in to sign off, as a matter of fact. Sad, isn't it? Still, maybe it's just as well. One has to keep moving, don't you think?"

Ferne hadn't changed much in five years. Grogan had only seen him in tropical kit. Now he was wearing a dark blue pinstriped suit which emphasized the dapper, minor public school persona. A certain soiled yet innocent, shopworn yet undefeated, quality remained. Behind the thinning white hair, lined forehead and watery blue eyes shone a boyish enthusiasm that no institution could ever satisfy.

"Look here," he said, "this is something of a red-letter day. Why don't you let me buy you lunch at a splendid place I know just round the corner?" He frowned as he saw Grogan hesitate. "Yes, do come along. You can eat quickly if you're in a hurry."

Ferne led the way, talking compulsively in his high-pitched nasal drawl, loud enough to draw the attention of the occasional bystanders. Grogan managed to interrupt the flood of words from time to time.

"What happened to make you leave the service?" he asked.

"Well, you may remember my tastes in certain things were always a little unconventional." Ferne laughed. "I was discovered in what used to be called highly compromising circumstances. Very boring story, actually, but the firm reacted rather over-dramatically. Used it as an excuse, in a way. I hadn't done much of note for a few years."

Ferne's face had become clouded for a moment. But his temperament didn't allow for despondency, and he smiled at Grogan.

"But they've been more than generous with the gratuity, and there's a handy little pension when that's gone. Look, here we are. The Tun and Sack. It's an old wine shop. Been going for at least a couple of hundred years and still in the same family. Good cold buffet in the back."

They walked through a long narrow bar to take a table in the spacious back room. Ferne ordered two large dry sherries, with a bottle of the house burgundy to follow. He was obviously a regular customer. The elderly waitress treated him as something of a character.

"And what will you have to eat today, Mr. Ferne? Shall I make you up a plate of cold meats and a nice mixed salad? And then there's a very good Brie."

"Marvellous, Lucy." He looked at Grogan. "Will that suit you?"

Over sherry they soon fell into chatting about some of the experiences they had shared. In some limited operations SIS did the overall planning and obtained political clearances, SAS carried out the plans.

"The old *konfrontasi* days in Borneo were really quite something," Ferne was saying, "I know we said it in Aden, too, but it was the end of a whole era, you know. The British Raj may have disappeared from India after the '39 war, but his cousins and nephews were still at their old games for a good twenty years more." He leaned forward and raised his glass to Grogan.

"We were there when it really all came to an end and, by God, I believe it's a good thing it did. I remember teasing old Joe Hind terribly about Little Britain and all that—he couldn't take it at all. Do you remember him? Didn't he direct a number of you chaps, once?"

"I remember him very well," Grogan replied. "I was out on a patrol once over the Indonesian border, at least ten miles further in than we were officially supposed to go. We were in radio contact with Joe back at HQ. He ran that side of things for several months. Anyway, we suddenly stumbled on an old peasant, terrified out of his wits. We tied him up and gagged him. There had been some movement of the Indonesian army in that area and we were on look and report, no contact, patrol. Joe came up suddenly on the radio to say that an Indonesian Company had been reported moving out of a frontier town in our direction. He told us to sit tight and wait for further instructions. Those were the days when the SAS were working with Dayak trackers, and bloody good they were too."

Grogan paused as the waitress arrived with the food and the bottle of Burgundy. Ferne promptly filled their glasses up to the brim.

"The old peasant just couldn't understand that he was supposed to lie still and keep quiet. Kept thrashing about, eyes goggling. So one of the Dayaks tapped him on the head from time to time. Finally Joe came up to say we should move out fast and we asked what to do with the old man. However hard we hit him, we couldn't put him out for more than a few minutes."

Grogan hadn't touched his wine, but Ferne had already drunk most of his first glass and refilled it. As he carefully poured the dark red liquid he looked across the table, a moment of pain in his eyes.

"I remember hearing something about this a little later. There was talk about a misunderstanding. It all got swept under the carpet, covered up. What happened then?"

"There was no misunderstanding," Grogan said. "He came through clear as a bell. Knock him off, he said. So one of the lads throttled him as he lay there. None of us liked it too much, but it was war. A special kind of war, if you like." Grogan drank some of his wine.

"Something I've never been clear about," Ferne said slowly, "is whether killing becomes just a habit. Does it mean anything at all when you get used to it?"

"That's very difficult to say," Grogan paused. "In the SAS depot at Hereford they have a training room, a kind of gymnasium, known as the Kill Room. There you learn to kill with your hands—you don't need anything else if you can get close enough. After that you move on, learning to use all the bits and pieces of daily living. String, pieces of clothing, glass, nails, knitting needles, almost everything. By the time you get back to where most soldiers start—knives and guns—you know you've reached the aristocracy of killing. All that distance and space. . . . But in the end no one kills without thinking. Taking life is something even a brute understands. The important thing is to know why you are doing it. Then it's simple and can be nothing much more than a reflex action which follows the decision."

Grogan leaned back in the comfortable chair. "But we're getting a long way from the old days of the British Raj."

"Perhaps not," said Ferne quickly. "The British soldiers made the British Empire much more than all those fat, prosperous nineteenth-century merchants who were behind them."

"Anyway, I must be on my way." Grogan stood up. "Good luck with whatever you do next and thanks for a very good lunch."

"Perhaps we'll meet again soon. Where are you staying?" Ferne asked.

"With a friend, but I'll be out of London for the next week or so. Let me give you a ring when I get back."

Grogan took the card that Ferne produced from his wallet, finely engraved and bearing an address in Belgravia.

"Yes, I shall probably have to change my address in due course," Ferne said, reading his thoughts. "But not for a while anyway."

The two men shook hands and Grogan walked out past the narrow bar. The sawdust sprinkled on the floor, the sombre lighting, the heavy, winey smell from the vats along the wall, and the glowing mahogany furniture, all gave the place its period quality, a feeling of antiquity even. On the wall there was a sign — T. CRISPIN, FREE VINTNER — *Foreign wines by the Hogshead, Pipe and Butt.* Somehow it all suited Lawrence Ferne perfectly. Grogan wondered how Ferne would react to the plan he was now evolving.

13

SUNDAY, THOUGH NOT EXACTLY a day of rest, represented for Kelly a weekly break in his usual routine. He always attended Mass with his family and afterwards usually spent the morning walking with his two small daughters, while his wife prepared lunch. This morning, on an unusually warm spring day, he was playing with them in the garden at the back of their suburban home.

They finished an exhausting session of their version of rounders. The girls, out of breath, flung themselves on the ground and built a castle from a set of bricks they'd had for years, interspersing into its walls fragments of twig and stone from the garden. The whole edifice was in danger of collapse as Kelly watched their flushed, excited faces. With long, red hair and freckled, pale skin, Tara, aged nine, and Melanie, a year younger, were unmistakably sisters. Kelly had married late, having led too active and dangerous a life in his earlier years to allow for any kind of settled domestic routine. But it had been worth waiting for, and he had surprised himself at the ease with which he had taken to family life. His wife Mary — younger by fifteen years — was a born home-maker. Their life was happy and contented, organised to fit around his tightly organised schedule. Lately Kelly had taken to holding more frequent business meetings at home. It was just as secure as most of the IRA premises and since they led a fairly social life anyway, neighbours and friends popping in and out, he could always lose a few business contacts in the middle of them. From time to time he was aware of some attention from the Gardai, but by and large they left him alone when he was at home.

The girls' castle had fallen for the third time when his wife called from the back door. Kelly sighed and went into the house. He winked at Mary as he passed her in the kitchen, hands covered in flour — they each knew what the other was thinking. The telephone was in the small entrance hall and Kelly took the call.

"Fine . . . and you? Yes." It was O'Flaherty, anxious to get his new instructions.

"Paddy, why don't you come by for a drink this evening around nine o'clock? The kids will be in bed and there will be some peace and quiet for an hour or so. . . Yes, do that. I'll be out myself until eight, eight thirty, so I'll see you then."

Kelly replaced the receiver and walked thoughtfully through to the front parlour. This Grogan business had been taking up a lot of his time just lately and he had been reluctant to make up his mind about it. Kelly sank into the deep leather sofa and, stretched his legs. From the moment Grogan had disappeared there had been danger. Grogan had apparently accepted his decision, perhaps not with good grace, but as a professional soldier would. But now he'd gone off to England with his girl-friend, leaving no trace. The more Kelly looked at it, the less he liked it. Grogan had jumped the gun. A stupid, impulsive action — it could ruin everything, Kelly thought bitterly.

Mary poked her head round the door.

"We'll be ready to eat in a quarter of an hour. Shall I bring you some beer?"

Kelly nodded gratefully and she disappeared, to return in a minute with a tray, which she placed on the table beside him. He sipped the beer and settled deeper into the corner of the sofa. There was another angle he had been thinking about. Supposing Grogan took things into his own hands and succeeded in blowing up some high-level military headquarters — with his training and expertise he might pull it off. Kelly remembered a reference Grogan made to the British royal family. Supposing Grogan even knocked off someone like Prince Charles. British security was not that tight, and he was a determined man. In circumstances like those, if Grogan were disavowed by the IRA, could they lose by it? The point would have been made that IRA splinter groups could get at specially selected targets. Could the British Government, wide open to such attacks, fail to take the point? The IRA could hold it to ransom. But how could he control Grogan now? For what he had in mind, he needed him on a tight rein. Grogan's defection now gave him even more problems in the power struggle within the movement. If there was a blowback his enemies might try to make him the scapegoat.

Kelly poured the last of the beer into his glass. It wouldn't really do, not quite. There was only one clear course of action; to stop Grogan. For that he would do well to get clearance from the Council meeting later this afternoon. He would give the job to O'Flaherty, a good, tough nut of the old school who already had a healthy dislike for Grogan. O'Flaherty was not what you'd call a sophisticated operator, though he'd led men well enough in the North. But for straightforward operational stuff, requiring guts and determination, he would do. Just to make sure, Kelly thought, he'd send someone with him. After all the trouble he'd had with the older Grogan, he should have known better than trust the young one!

As usual when he had a meeting with Kelly, O'Flaherty was in very good time. He was driving another office car, this time a new Cortina, and he enjoyed manoeuvring it quickly and lightly through the light Sunday evening traffic. He had a solid meal and a couple of pints of Guinness in his belly. He was sure that Kelly would have something for him, and he could make a good guess what it might be. He parked the car a few streets away from Kelly's house and walked around for fifteen minutes before arriving on the stroke of nine o'clock.

Kelly greeted him formally, shaking his hand and showing him into the parlour. A tall, thin young man was already sitting there, legs neatly crossed to show trim, bony ankles. "You know each other, don't you?" Kelly said, waving his hand towards the Shoeman. O'Flaherty nodded and they shook hands. The name had come from an incident in Belfast where he and another Provisional had been trapped in a shoe store and shot it out with a platoon of British soldiers. They had made a spirited defence and got away over the rooftops, leaving a sergeant and two privates dead behind them. At that early stage in the conflict it had been considered the first major battle-honour for the IRA and became part of the burgeoning legend of the war. Since then the Shoeman had proved himself more than adept with a gun: he had a detached, cool-headed quality. He had become a specialist in meting out the punishment order by the Provisional field courts, dealing death or that traditional IRA mutilation—the bullet through the kneecap— with impartiality. O'Flaherty had met him a few times in the North. He didn't like him much, but he was a good man to have on your side.

"I've brought you two boys over for a special reason," Kelly said, as he put a glass of whiskey into O'Flaherty's fist.

"You both know the background to Jimmy Grogan, what he's been doing for us in the North. He's been causing some problems up there, but now he's gone to England there's real trouble."

Kelly looked at O'Flaherty.

"I've put the Shoeman into the picture, Paddy, and outlined to him what I told you yesterday. I've had a session with the Council tonight. They've agreed to what I reluctantly had to recommend. We've got to stop Grogan, I want you two to work on it."

Kelly turned to the Shoeman.

"Paddy's the senior man and he'll be in charge, but I want you to stick together. I'll put you in touch with a good man in our battalion in Kilburn, who will keep me informed on a daily basis. He will pass on my instructions. Whatever plan you come up with must be cleared with me before you do it. Is that absolutely clear?"

The two men nodded. Kelly went on.

"Here's the situation. First of all, we have to locate Grogan. The Kilburn boys will help, and I'll be digging around for information in various places. We have a good contact in London in FIRMCOR, where Grogan worked for a time, who put us in touch with him in the first place. He may come up with something. We don't know how far the Duffy girl is involved. He may be using her as cover. When we find out where he is, I want you to keep close to him. Are there any questions?"

"What about the girl?" asked O'Flaherty. "What shall we do with her?"

Kelly thought for a moment before replying slowly. "I would prefer her to be left out of it. But we can't afford to leave any loose ends. You'll have to check with me all the time."

Kelly got up and refilled their glasses. He smiled suddenly at O'Flaherty.

"By the way, Paddy, you'd better think up another of your disguises for England."

The Shoeman laughed. O'Flaherty had a reputation in the Provos for being a master at changing his appearance, a talent which had its comical side. O'Flaherty's greatest coup had been after his escape from the Crumlin Road gaol in Belfast. With the entire British army on the alert, he'd crossed the frontier wearing a blond wig and heavy glasses. The thought of the man in that get-up, let alone fooling a British patrol with it, was just absurd. But it had happened—and O'Flaherty had witnesses in the car to prove it.

"Don't worry," he said, grinning. "I'll fix up something special."

"Well, boys, that's about it," Kelly said. "Come in to the place in River Street tomorrow morning and we'll fix up the final details. Money, tickets. I'll arrange for you to collect weapons when you need them in London."

They left the house separately, according to the usual drill. Kelly ushered O'Flaherty out first, saying there was something he still had to talk about with the Shoeman. O'Flaherty walked slowly back to his car. Life produces some curious twists, he mused. Now there was another Grogan out of step. Like father, like son.

The buzzer on the front door of Grogan's apartment rang. He looked through the peephole, saw it was Muldoon, and opened the door. He'd rung him earlier and asked him to come over.

"How's the leg?" Grogan asked.

"Fine, just fine. Don't worry about the gelignite, it's nicely stashed away. Margaret's being a bit tricky, but she's off to Dublin tonight for a few days to visit her family. There's a cousin getting married."

"Is she now?" Grogan considered for a moment. "She could deliver a message for me while she's over there. Do you think she'd mind?"

"Not at all," said Muldoon quickly, then hesitated. "You're not exactly top of the popularity polls with her since my little accident." He looked across at Grogan. "Don't worry, she's taken it all right, but she doesn't want it to happen again. You know how it is with women." He shrugged helplessly.

"She's right, Cathal. I want to keep you out of my problems."

Muldoon began to protest, but Grogan stopped him. "Look, you've been a great friend and I'm grateful for everything you've done, but you're out of the action from now on, and that's that."

Grogan looked at Muldoon who had slumped into the arm-chair. He could see that, for all his protests, Muldoon was relieved. Things were moving fast and he was getting out of his depth, Grogan thought.

"But there are a couple of things I'd like to ask your help on," he said. Muldoon's face brightened. "The first thing is the message. I'll give you a note for a girl I know in Dublin. There'll be no risk. All Margaret has to do is to go and see the girl, slip the note to her and leave."

It was stuffy in the room. Grogan got up and opened a window.

"The other thing may be more difficult," he continued. "I shall have to get out of the country for a while and I can't use my Irish passport, at least till I get somewhere like Sweden. There'll be a watch at the ports and airports for some time. If I can get to Scandinavia, they're fairly used to political refugees and sympathetic to movements like the IRA." He laughed sardonically. "Let's hope that's how they'll be, anyway. From there I'll probably go on to Canada or the States."

"Why don't you go back to Dublin or Kerry?" Muldoon asked.

"I'm not going to be popular there for a while either." He

paused. There was no point in going into more detail. "You mentioned once you'd come across someone in Kilburn who could arrange for people to leave the country quietly. Are you still in touch with him?"

"Sure I am. Julius Avakian, one of the arch fixers of all time. An Irish-Armenian, of all things. A friend of mine did him a big favour once. Avakian is a successful fence, with sidelines in all sorts of directions, including arranging the kind of thing you have in mind. Why don't I take you along to see him today?"

"No, I don't want you involved. Just get in touch with him, tell him you've got a friend who needs his help and arrange an appointment. Give him a phoney name, why not call me Seamus something? How about Seamus Pearse?"

"Right you are, Jimmy. I'll use the telephone here. When do you want to see him?"

"As soon as possible. No point in wasting any time."

In a few minutes it was fixed. Grogan had to go to an address in Kilburn which Muldoon wrote down. He would meet Avakian there at seven o'clock. Then Grogan wrote a short note to Mairin, putting it in an envelope bearing her name and address in Dublin. It was simply to confirm that the arrangements for Tuesday stood. Instead of signing it, he quickly drew a child's picture of a happy face. He put it in the envelope and sealed it. He held out the letter to Muldoon. "If by any chance the girl isn't there, Margaret can leave it with her sister or just push it through the door."

"I'll give it to Margaret right away and the girl should have it tomorrow night." Muldoon winked at Grogan. "Any verbal messages?"

"None that Margaret would like to deliver," Grogan replied, grinning.

A few minutes later Muldoon left with the promise that Grogan would telephone later to say how the meeting went.

At a few minutes past seven the same evening Grogan got out of a taxi in Kilburn High Street. He turned into a side street and came to the address he was looking for. An old four-storey house had been converted into offices and behind the dingy, open front-door stood a staircase leading upwards. On the third floor there was a brass plate—JULIUS AVAKIAN AND ASSOCIATES, LTD. Grogan rang the bell, and heard it tinkle thinly somewhere in the interior. He waited for a moment, then the door opened.

The man facing him looked much younger than he'd expected. About thirty, possibly thirty-five, of medium height with a swarthy, dark complexion. The most surprising thing about him was the thick black, fuzzy hair which framed his lean face.

"Julius Avakian?" Grogan asked.

The man nodded.

"My name is Pearse. Cathal Muldoon said you might be able to help me."

Avakian looked at him carefully for a moment, then held the door open. He led the way through a small empty reception room into the office behind. After the dinginess of the exterior of the building and the staircase, the sumptuousness of the large office was striking. The furniture was antique and highly polished. Ornate silver and brass objects were laid out on leather-topped tables. Bookcases lined the walls and beside one of them stood a small mahogany book-ladder of the kind found sometimes in libraries in order to reach the higher shelves. Dominating the room was a magnificent wide desk with two green lamps. There was remarkably little correspondence lying on it.

Avakian smiled at Grogan and beckoned him to sit down. It was a careful smile, which began slowly and ended by illuminating his face. A beautiful smile, one that was meant to be admired.

"Please tell me how I can help you, Mr. Pearse," he said. "I have reason to wish to help any friend of Cathal Muldoon." Avakian's voice was harsh and he spoke in totally accentless English, yet Grogan had a strong impression that it was a second language to him.

"I want to go to Sweden," he replied. "Quickly and quietly."

Avakian studied him. "But I imagine you have no papers and you are unable to take the conventional forms of transport?"

"That's exactly the problem," Grogan said briskly. "I understand you can fix such things."

"It can be done, Mr. Pearse. It requires a certain amount of manipulation, and that takes time. I can arrange, for example, a seaman's identity card. And I can see that you are allocated in the pool to a ship sailing for Scandinavia. You will then have to pass with the ship's crew as a perfectly normal seaman. It may, of course, be rather hard work . . ." Avakian looked enquiringly at Grogan.

"Don't worry about that," Grogan said. "I know something about boats."

Avakian nodded approvingly.

"Good," he said. "You'll simply jump ship in the first convenient port. The poor captain will be a man short for the rest of the trip. You'll have signed on for a round voyage, of course."

"That sounds fine," Grogan said. "How much will it cost?"

Avakian shook his head regretfully. "Because you come in the name of your friend you will pay only the price it costs me. That is two hundred and fifty pounds. Cash. I shall need some photographs and the personal particulars you wish to use on the trip. Date and place of birth, full name and so on. It may take a day or two."

Grogan nodded and stood up. He took a bundle of ten-pound notes from his pocket. He counted off twenty-five and placed them on the desk in front of Avakian.

"I'll bring the photographs tomorrow morning, if that's convenient," he said.

Avakian stood up to show him out. "Not before noon," he said, smiling. "I am not an early riser." He got up and showed Grogan to the door.

Grogan walked down the shabby staircase. Avakian was obviously a sharp operator. He could probably be trusted, as far as anyone could in this kind of business. Above all, Grogan thought that he would probably deliver the goods. He stepped out into the street and decided to walk for a while before taking a taxi back to Southwark. It was a fine night, quite warm, and Grogan was pleased with the way things were going. He had his plan of action pretty well worked out. The precise timing would depend on the length of time Avakian took to fix his papers.

Grogan walked past a noisy pub. It was the stage in the evening when the solid drinkers were beginning to warm up. He could hear the sound of a musical group somewhere in the back. On impulse Grogan turned back. He walked through the public bar to find a larger, squarish room behind it. A packed bar ran round two walls, with the traditional blowsy, dyed blonde barmaid and her two assistants busy behind it. On a raised platform at the far end of the room was the band, four men in green suits playing for all they were worth. In between about twenty tables were packed with customers, laughing, singing or shouting to make themselves heard. Two burly waiters were twisting their way through the crowd, packed trays held high above their shoulders. It was so much like one of the many Dublin singing pubs that Grogan laughed. He walked up to the bar and slowly elbowed his way through the throng. He saw a notice on the wall—MUSIC, WEDNESDAYS, FRIDAYS AND SATURDAYS ONLY.

As he stood there, sipping his beer and enjoying the atmosphere, there was a sudden commotion close by. A big Irish labourer, face flushed, was prodding a small man hard in the chest with his forefinger. The crowd of drinkers split apart expectantly. It was difficult to tell what the argument was about, but it was clear that the Irishman was going to give him no chance to apologise. Grogan could see that the drinkers were enjoying the distraction and weren't going to make way for the waiters to intervene. With another prod that was almost a blow, the Irishman forced the man to his knees. The crowd laughed as he made him kiss his dirty boots.

It was the kind of bullying that Grogan loathed, a big man mindlessly humiliating a weaker and unequal opponent. He felt himself about to move. His hands clenched and he felt the joy of rightful combat rising inside him. He checked himself. He had been taught to think, then move. Instinctively he knew it would be wrong to draw attention to himself simply to correct what was after all a minor wrong. He had a much bigger project on his hands. The big Irishman lost interest in his game and turned back to the bar. The crowd jostled back into place. The incident was over.

As Grogan picked up his glass, two men walked in from the public bar. They stood in the door, looking over the crowd. One was a solid, chunky figure with a shaved head and a thick red beard. Beside him was a young, white-faced man. He stood there, an elegant figure in a dark suit, his cold eyes impassively checking through the room. It was the Shoeman. Grogan calculated quickly and decided not to move. He knew very well what the Shoeman's role was—official executioner for the Provos.

The two men, apparently satisfied, moved into the room. They sat down at a table against the far wall. A waiter came up and while he leaned over to take their order, Grogan quietly walked out. A few minutes later he found a taxi. He hadn't been recognised but now he certainly had something else to think about.

14

WITH A SUDDEN SQUALL, the steady rhythm of the rain changed and it became violent and penetrating. Chief Superintendent Charles Christie pulled the upturned collar of his raincoat tightly about his neck. As he did so, he felt a flush of water run down his back.

Jesus Christ, he thought bitterly, this is all I need. He'd been sitting in his office at RUC Headquarters only an hour before, working all through his lunch hour, as usual. At least he was warm and dry. The Deputy Commissioner had walked in to say there might have to be an official court of enquiry into the Kevin O'Hara incident. The British Army medical officer, that interfering colonel, had refused to take responsibility for O'Hara's condition and raised hell. The DC was making it clear that this was one complaint too many, though Christie remembered the hypocritical bastard hadn't complained when they'd got all that information out of Long Kesh not so long ago.

Just as the DC was letting him have it, the telephone rang. It was McQuaid, whom he hadn't seen for some time, using the false name they had arranged. He said he wanted to see Christie urgently. Christie's first thought, with the DC standing there in front of him, was to try to make the whole thing sound smooth and well-organised. Unfortunately the only meeting place they'd used recently was out of doors over by the Linfield Football Club. Since there was a cuptie replay this afternoon McQuaid would already be there, so Christie, with one eye on the DC, barked into the telephone that he'd be over in half an hour at the usual spot. At least, Christie thought, the DC had looked reasonably impressed when he hastened to explain that it had been his top agent and added that it must be something important, implying that it would be something good. By Christ, he needed it.

Now he had arrived punctually, walked up and down the railway embankment, but there was no sign of McQuaid. Christie was getting soaked, he could feel his trousers hanging wetly and heavily around his legs. He leaned down to shake off the rain and jumped at the soft voice behind his shoulder.

"I'm very sorry to be late, Superintendent," McQuaid said. "You don't look too comfortable. Shall we go off and have a glass of something to warm you up?"

Conflicting thoughts raced through Christie's head. First, he'd look an idiot if he insisted they stayed out in this rain. And the thought of a large whiskey warming his stomach in a few minutes was almost irresistible. But he'd made a great point in the past of explaining to McQuaid how concerned he was that they shouldn't be seen together, in the interests of the other man's safety. For that reason he'd said they should continue their meetings out of doors.

"Good idea," he said at last, gruffly. "There's a pub just the other side of the railway bridge. Let's try that."

Fortunately the pub was almost empty. It was coming near to closing time and most of the regulars had gone off to join the football crowd. They found a cubicle empty, took off their coats and shook out the rain. Then they ordered two large Powers. Christie took a huge gulp and felt a little better.

"Well, Joseph," he said, "I hope you've got something for me this time. What's it all about?"

McQuaid's blue eyes gleamed. "I've got something you'll find interesting, and something you may not like."

Christie looked at the old man carefully. McQuaid was a picture of health, with clear eyes and pink cheeks.

"I'll tell you the good part first." McQuaid was enjoying himself. "Last time we met, you asked me to find out everything I could about this man Grogan you had a lead on. Well, I did. It seems he's a loner. He's gone to England against orders. The talk is he's going to try something big. Something like assassinating one of the royal family."

"Jesus suffering Christ!" Christie exploded. "Are they going to let him get away with it?"

"That's the thing." McQuaid picked up his glass, finishing his drink slowly. "They've sent a squad after him from Dublin. Two of the hard boys, I don't know their names."

"What are they going to do, kill him?"

"Possibly. Or perhaps bring him back to Dublin for court martial. Anyway, they're going to take care of him."

"And what if they don't manage it?" Christie realised he was shouting and lowered his voice. "The stupid bastards can't even control their own people, it's just bloody typical."

The pub was about to close and Christie called for two more drinks.

"They'll manage it all right," McQuaid said evenly. "There's been a lot of trouble between the Provos and Officials about this, but one thing that's certain is that they'll all go after him if need be. The word's out, Superintendent, and they'll get Grogan, whatever they have to do. I wouldn't like to be standing in his shoes right now."

"Does he know they're after him?" Christie asked.

"It would be an intelligent guess, I'd have thought. Depends whether he's got anyone tipping him off from the inside."

"It just goes to show I was right all along," Christie said. "I always said the IRA would step up the campaign here, not in England. There's too much against it. But just try to convince those bloody English coppers—impossible to get through to them!"

He had a sudden thought.

"Look here, Joseph. This is all interesting information. How did you get hold of it?"

"Friends of friends, Superintendent." McQuaid looked at him calmly. "You know I have my contacts. I can guarantee it's all sound."

"The point is although I believe it, I have to convince my

commissioner. But he wants to have a good idea where it comes from. Otherwise, how can it be evaluated? Who told you now?"

"All I'm going to say is it came from the top. Someone close to Cathal Goulding."

Christie flushed angrily and stared into McQuaid's face which lost none of its composure.

"You will remember, Superintendent," McQuaid said calmly, "that it was always part of our arrangement that I wouldn't be pressed to answer questions if I felt I was particularly vulnerable. I would remind you that I'm taking considerable risks already, seeing you. I have a family as well as myself to consider."

"For God's sake." Christie was shouting again. "We're all taking bloody risks. I've got a family too, you know."

"But, if you don't mind me pointing it out, you are paid to take risks. It's your job, but it's not mine."

"You mean you want to be paid?" There was a long pause between them, and Christie realised that he was going badly wrong. He tried to backtrack, speaking in a more reasonable tone.

"Look here, Joseph, you've been helping us out in a difficult situation and we're extremely grateful. We're all working together, aren't we, to save Ulster from being totally destroyed? Look what the IRA have done to our commerce, with their bombings and murderings."

Christie looked at the older man, trying to will him into agreement. He went on, speaking quietly now, but passionately.

"Now Bill Craig and the Vanguard movement are saying, from the opposite side, that if necessary they are prepared to see Ulster destroyed rather than the IRA win. I'm not saying they're right or wrong, though you can see their point of view. The fact is unless we, the responsible, mature people, get together to stop it there is going to be a holocaust here, a civil war that will move south and rip the whole country apart. You don't want that any more than I do, and we both have families to keep out of it."

Christie stopped talking and there was total silence. It was as if a machine had wound down. He felt tired and drained of emotion.

At last McQuaid spoke. "I appreciate everything you've

said, don't think otherwise. But I told you earlier that I had something to say that you might not like. Well, here it is. Quite simply, I do not wish to continue the arrangement between us. Over the years it may have proved of some use, certainly I hope so. But in present circumstances, I've had enough. When it started, the terms of the relationship were, it's true, rather vague. But I've been feeling increasingly uncomfortable with it. Where I had hoped to be some kind of buffer between the two parties, even between the two communities, if you like, I find that I am being manœuvred into the position of a common informer. It's a word that in Ireland, as you are well aware, Superintendent, one shrinks from. But it's a fair description of the way the pressures are going."

Christie started to interrupt, but McQuaid, with a sudden authority, waved him down.

"Please let me finish—I've heard you out. Times have changed. Perhaps I'm being carried away, as many people have been misled on this island, but I believe that the course of history is at last changing here. You know of my early years ... I won't say I would ever go back to an active role, I'm too old for all that, but I've been stirred. I find that my position is suddenly untenable. At my age, all I can do is sit back and watch. To do that, in all conscience, I must discontinue our arrangement. I hope you will understand and accept my statement, because I'm a stubborn old man and my mind is made up."

Christie sensed defeat, with him an animal instinct that usually made him fight that much harder. But this time fists were useless and he could think of no powerful arguments.

"I can see you've thought hard about this and made up your mind. I'm sorry. All the more so because I think you're wrong. The few responsible Catholics like yourself who've helped us are working against terror and violence, in the best interests of both the communities. If you all back out, how is any understanding going to be achieved?"

Christie paused. Perhaps he could salvage, if not the wreck, at least a few pots and pans. "I'm very sorry indeed, Joseph, but I accept your decision. Unwillingly, but I accept it. However, there's one thing that I would ask you to agree to. If you don't want to continue our regular meetings, very well. But at least meet me from time to time if some specific issues come up that you may be able to help on. Will you leave the door open at least that much?"

By now the pub was completely empty and they realised that they were holding up the landlord who was standing impatiently behind his bar. They put on their coats and went out into the rain. Just outside the door McQuaid turned to face Christie.

"Let me think about it, Superintendent. Give me a few days and I'll get in touch."

To Christie's surprise, McQuaid put out a hand for him to shake, then walked away. Christie watched him, a stocky figure disappearing down the wet, cobbled street in the direction of the football ground. As Christie began to go over in his mind what McQuaid had said he had a sudden moment of panic. As near as he could place it, he felt marooned. It was a strange kind of feeling to have standing in a side street, in his native Belfast.

For Wally Figgis it was turning out to be a good day. He made his living off the city, doing the best he could, in a number of unorthodox ways. Two or three clubs in Soho paid him a retainer and expenses for his activities on their behalf. If he were ever asked what these were, he liked to describe himself as an entrepreneur, an all-embracing term he had picked up early in life from a rather bigger fish in the same line . . . A small-scale entrepreneur, perhaps, but that was how he liked to see himself. Some of his victims, the punters, in the jargon of the clubs, might use words like touting, pimping, even blackmail. But Figgis had a more delicate, elliptical view of his professional skills, which he used in a truly vocational sense, working outwards from a solid base of contacts and a wide knowledge of human failings. Although he owed his loyalty to the clubs that retained him, he was not above operating on a freelance basis from time to time. This led to disputes once in a while, and Figgis was the kind of person who could never have survived without the patronage of powerful backers who could be brought into play in an emergency. These backers might be from inside or outside the Establishment. It didn't make much difference to him, and he paid his dues in full, as expected of him.

One of these backers, dating from a time long past when there had been a nasty incident involving drugs and manslaughter, was the Special Branch. What had resulted from the encounter was a natural market phenomenon — the meeting at a certain point of supply and demand: in this case the supply of and demand for information relating to a rather specialised section of the criminal underworld. For Figgis was a born observer, fascinated by people and, above all, by their weaknesses, and he saw things of interest almost everywhere he went. Because he was half Irish and still lived in the small house his mother left him in Kilburn, he had drifted into the net of the Special Branch Irish Squad when they began to concentrate their activities.

Today Figgis had met his new contact in Special Branch, Sergeant Fitchett. Although he had been reluctant to be passed on to such a young, evidently inexperienced officer, he had to admit that Fitchett was taking an enlightened interest in his job. In return for a few titbits on Kilburn-Irish personalities and one little gem about the location of a couple of Thompson machine-guns, Fitchett had congratulated him and slipped him twenty-five quid, which by Special Branch standards was a very decent sum. Fitchett also told him that the heat was on for an IRA gunman called James Grogan, who was thought to be somewhere in England, possibly London. He'd made it very clear that there would be money and kudos in it if Figgis could help locate Grogan. Afterwards Figgis had spent the afternoon at his local bookie's and had come up with two good doubles. By late afternoon he had the best part of a hundred and fifty pounds to show for his day's work.

Figgis felt on top of the world. A celebration would be in order, he decided. He went back home to set out, bathed, shaved and changed, at seven thirty in the evening. He left his car behind for the time being, thinking he might have a drink or two and come back for it, before going on to the West End. He walked down towards Kilburn High Street, a small, wiry man of indeterminate age, smelling of Palmolive soap and cheap aftershave. As he passed Julius Avakian's office, he looked up automatically and saw that a light was on. He knew quite a lot about Julie and rather admired him for the class of the operations he ran and for his obvious success. If Julie had a weakness, it was an inordinate and expensive taste for young girls, little girls even, and Figgis had once or twice done a little business catering for it. He knew it was unusual for Julie to be working in his office this late. Even more unusual since on this particular evening he knew that some special entertainment to suit Julie's tastes had been arranged at one of the big private houses in Mayfair. Figgis decided, out of sheer curiosity, to hang around for a while. It was getting dark and he melted into a doorway which gave him a clear view of the lighted window opposite. From there he would see any visitor leaving Julie's office. It crossed his mind only while waiting that Julie's many activities included spiriting away men on the run.

He didn't have to wait long. The street door opened and a tall, dark-haired man appeared. Figgis couldn't believe his eyes. The man fitted the description Fitchett had given him perfectly. His luck was really in today. The man he was looking at had to be Grogan.

He looked up at the office window. The light was still on and a moving shadow showed that Julie was still there. Figgis moved off after the tall man, following at a discreet distance. They turned into Kilburn High Street and walked along. Figgis saw the man hesitate outside the Golbourne Arms, turn back and go in. Figgis went after him. At the long bar in the back Figgis saw the man order a drink. A rough hand slapped him suddenly, a little too hard, on his thin back.

"What are you up to, Wally, you little rat? This isn't one of your regular haunts, is it?"

He looked up, an eyelid twitching in a nervous tic he'd had for years. It was Jack Garritty, a bookmaker he'd had one or two run-ins with when he'd accumulated some bad debts. In the end he'd managed to pay them off and smoothed things out, but Garritty had banned him from any of his places and there was still bad feeling. Figgis muttered something inaudible and weaved away through the crowd to order himself a whiskey. By the time he had it in his hand and moved into a good position for watching his man, a group had gathered at the other end of the bar around a big Irishman picking a fight.

Figgis always shrank from physical violence and he concentrated on studying Grogan. Figgis saw him suddenly become tense and wondered for a moment if he was going to go after the Irish navvy. Then, quite suddenly, Grogan drained his glass and walked out of the bar. Figgis went after him. He wished there had been time to get to a telephone.

In the street outside, Grogan, walking more quickly than before, went almost the whole length of Kilburn High Street before stopping to hail a taxi. Figgis hadn't expected this, but fortunately there was another taxi behind it. He waved it down and jumped in.

The leading taxi headed southwards. It turned down the Edgware Road towards Marble Arch. Figgis settled back in the corner of the back seat as the two taxis followed the same route down Park Lane, past Buckingham Palace, along Birdcage Walk and across Westminster Bridge. He looked at his watch. It was eight forty-five.

Not far from Borough High Street in Southwark, an area Figgis hardly knew, the front taxi drew in to the kerb. Fortunately he had a friendly, elderly taxi-driver who didn't mind playing games—all he cared about was getting paid. Figgis told him to drive past and stop further down the street. He paid quickly and nervously, glancing up the street, and saw Grogan about fifty yards away walking in the opposite direction. The taxi-driver was still fumbling with change. He didn't have time to wait; he shouldn't risk losing his man now. He told the driver to keep it and walked briskly up the road. When Grogan turned off the well-lighted High Street, Figgis ran after him to close the distance, falling back into a walk before reaching the corner. He looked round it cautiously to see Grogan turning off into a smaller street, waited until he disappeared and started off again. The trouble with these side streets and alleys was that you could lose someone so quickly. They should have cleared them away years ago, Figgis thought angrily. They were the last damp relics of the old borough, built in the Middle Ages over the riverside bogs and marshes. He moved fast down the street and again peered carefully round the corner. He couldn't see Grogan and cursed under his breath. He was slightly out of breath and he could feel his heart pounding. He must have been crazy to come so far. He should have let the man go and simply telephoned Fitchett to say Grogan had been sighted. After all, it might be the wrong man.

He walked quickly and almost silently up what was not much more than a back alley. There was a street lamp at the far corner but its light didn't extend far and the alley was mostly in darkness. As he walked along he remembered he still hadn't eaten. His stomach was beginning to feel queazy. He'd slip into a pub in a minute and get a sandwich to hold him until he went up to the West End. Then he'd . . . Something that felt like an iron bar closed on his neck and throat. Even as he gasped the noise cut off. There was a fraction of a moment of nausea before total blackness. Inside his head, long thin streamers of white light flashed to a myriad of tiny dots like pinheads.

Wally Figgis lay across the doorstep in a Southwark alley, like a seagull abandoned on a rocky shelf, his neck broken. It had not, after all, turned out to be a very good day.

PART III

The Deception

"The business of the Final Hour shall be accomplished in the twinkling of an eye, even less."

The Koran

15

CHELTENHAM STATION WAS VIRTUALLY DESERTED when Mairin walked into the buffet a few minutes after seven thirty. She had come down from London that afternoon and killed time by wandering around the town which she instinctively disliked. The Georgian terraces reminded her of Dublin but here they seemed to be on show, museum pieces rather than living houses. There was also a smug coyness about the place which brought out all her strongest anti-British feelings. She sat down at a table in the corner of the tea-room and looked at the tired waitress behind the counter. The girl stared back with a blankness that was more offensive than outright hostility. She seemed bolted to the floor and eventually Mairin got her cup of tea by shouting across the empty room. She looked at her watch. The next train, another one from London, was due at eight ten. That must be the one Jimmy will be on, she thought. Why meet in Cheltenham, of all places? She shifted in her chair so that she could see the door from the buffet. The station was beginning to come to life now and a few people were being served by the reluctant waitress. For the hundredth time, Mairin tried to puzzle out what her boy-friend was up to. She had become used to his uncommunicative manner which had originally annoyed her but which she now accepted as part of his character. But those telephone calls and even the note had been cryptic in the extreme. None of all this seemed like a holiday to her.

She was just finishing her second cup of tea when she heard the train. The platform was crowded now and porters had begun to spread out along the platform, like well-drilled markers on a military parade. Mairin left exactly the amount on the bill and got up. She was easing her way through the crowd at the entrance of the buffet when she felt a strong hand grasp her arm. She looked up. "Jimmy!" she cried, startled He smiled down at her and guided her out onto the platform. "But I thought you were coming here by train," she said, as they walked towards the exit.

"I did," he replied, "but earlier this morning, on the one before yours."

"You are a mysterious old sod, aren't you!" she said, laughing. She leant over impulsively and kissed him hard on his right ear as they almost collided with a couple of old ladies in twin-sets and pearls trying to steer three uncontrollable dachshunds through the crowd.

"What in the name of Mary, Holy Mother of God and her sanctimonious son is this all about?"

They gave up their platform tickets at the barrier and walked out into the street. The eight-ten from London had stopped with a clank and a shudder behind them and no one, not even the observant young police constable who was reprimanding a group of rowdy schoolchildren, noticed them leave the station.

"I'll tell you all about it," Grogan said, taking her hand, "when we get to the hotel."

"The full story?"

"The full story."

"Where are we staying?" Mairin asked.

"At an inn called the Old King's Head, central, snug and good food, they say," he replied. "I've booked us in. Ever heard of Mrs. Langton?"

"No."

"That's you, and I'm your dutiful husband."

"James Bond again?" Mairin looked up at him mockingly.

"Not really, but we have to take a few elementary precautions, you'll see why later. Now," he said, stepping out more briskly, "tell me how you've been."

They arrived at the hotel about half an hour later having picked up Mairin's bags from the central bus station where she had left them. Grogan dealt with an obsequious assistant manager at the reception desk as if he had lived in hotels all his life. Mairin, who had only once before been outside Ireland with him, again caught herself thinking how chameleon-like he was: over here he blended perfectly into the cool, bland landscape of the English personality. He looked the part tonight, she thought. His dark hair was long at the back but carefully groomed, the navy-blue brushed-denim suit making him look slight and slimmer than he really was and the soft natural-tan Italian shoes rounding off a very self-possessed and disturbingly good-looking man.

The assistant manager, flashing gold at wrist and mouth, treated Grogan with respect but couldn't resist a smirk when he looked in Mairin's direction. She tossed her red hair and scowled at him, turning away. "I'll have the porter take your bags to your room right away, sir," the assistant manager said to Grogan. "Paddy," he called out. "Paddy, Paddy . . . Where on earth is he?" he said, turning to Grogan with an air of apology. "These Irish—they seem to spend half their lives asleep or daydreaming . . . If you'd like to go up, I'll send up your things as soon as I can find the porter."

Grogan took the key but Mairin had already gone ahead. He had heard her snort of disgust and knew she was seething with rage. Bloody women, he thought, they're completely dominated by their emotions. He would have loved to have kicked the man in the crutch, but where would we all be if people didn't have some sense of order and restraint? He suddenly remembered what he was here for and grinned to himself.

He caught up with Mairin in the corridor and they walked in silence to their room at the end. It was large and comfortable with an old-fashioned double bed, feather-mattressed, high and stately. Mairin dropped her handbag on the floor and rounded on Grogan, her face a picture of fury.

"That bloody man, I could have killed him. Jimmy, why didn't you do something?" she cried.

"Kill him?" He raised his eyebrows.

"Don't be an idiot," she said angrily, "you know what I mean. But you did nothing, nothing. You just stood there taking all that crap . . . all that smarmy, greasy, sycophantic, racial crap without saying a word . . . you looked like God knows what . . ." She was groping for words now. "A waxwork dummy or some inbred Englishman . . ."

Grogan said nothing but stood looking at her, smiling.

"Stop grinning at me, you stuffed gombeen . . . God, you make me mad sometimes, what are you made of, James Grogan, what are you made of?"

She leant forward and pinched him viciously in the loose fold of flesh just below his ribs. He sucked in his breath with pain but leant back, quickly side-stepping in the same movement. Mairin tumbled forward, lost her balance and found herself spinning head over heels as Grogan pulled her deftly across his hip. She landed with a thud on the floor with the wind knocked out of her and Grogan sitting firmly on top, pinioning her arms to the carpet.

"Let me up," she cried as she recovered her breath, "let me up, you bastard." She twisted her head from side to side, tears of rage in her eyes. "Just you wait, you brute . . ."

Grogan leant down gently and kissed her forehead. She tried to tear herself away from him, bucking her legs and bottom and twisting her hips. She managed to catch him a glancing blow on the side of the head with a wild left-footed kick but he simply spreadeagled her more firmly, pinning her to the carpet like an exotic butterfly. He moved his face down to hers. "Now, now," he said soothingly, "this is no way to begin a holiday."

She was still spluttering with rage when he kissed her on the mouth and ground his groin into hers with a deliberate movement. She responded in the way he knew she would though he sensed she hated herself for it. He was careful not to relax the pressure on her but he could feel her changing mood in the way that a child's emotions, from tears to laughter, can sometimes be felt through contact with its body. He felt a great wave of tenderness for her, for her youth, her passion, for the harmony between her body and her spirit. She had closed her eyes and let herself go limp. He whispered in her ear: "Are you all right!"

She opened her eyes and smiled at him. "You're still a

bastard and a brute, but I'm used to you that way and I don't really suppose I want you to change, though you're so soft-centred sometimes, in spite of all the superman stuff."

"Any complaints here?" he asked as he pressed his pelvis against hers.

"None," she said laughing and fumbling with her clothes. He helped her and then she undressed him, with a slow, loving care. He moved towards the bed but when he turned back to look at her she was lying on the floor in the exact position he had pinned her a few moments ago. "Here," she said simply, "here."

Grogan refused to tell her anything until they had taken the edge off their ravenous appetites an hour or so later in one of the town's best restaurants. They shared a liking for good food and drink which was part of the physical harmony that had grown up between them. When Mairin had disposed of a large slice of home-made paté and Grogan had worked his way through the smoked salmon, he felt he was ready to talk. She topped up his wine glass and kicked him gently under the table. "Come on, Jimmy," she said, "you're not working for the *Guide Michelin*. I want to know what's going on."

"All right, it's simple enough," he replied. "You know I had a row with the big men over in Dublin?"

She nodded, slowly sipping the pale gold wine.

"Well," he continued, "I had a plan which I offered them, they turned it town—out of hand, really—and told me to go back to the North."

"But you went back, didn't you?"

"Don't jump the gun," he said, frowning. "Yes, I went back but not to work for them again, just to sort myself out and prepare. That's when I phoned you from Belfast. By that time I had decided to go it alone."

"What is that supposed to mean?" she said quickly, a look of alarm crossing her strong-boned face. "What are you going to do?"

"Exactly what I say," he replied, "I've been fed up with the way things are going in the North. What you don't know is that I've seen why everything has been such a balls-up from the inside."

"But, Jimmy, wait a minute . . ." Her voice was now brittle

with tension. "What you're saying is you've disobeyed Kelly and the others in Dublin, cut yourself off from the movement and now you're about to do something over here—*all by yourself?*"

"That's about it."

"You'll get yourself killed," she burst out.

"What about in the North? I wasn't going to finish up with a medal on my chest or nomination for mayor. A bullet in the back, more likely."

"Yes, of course . . . but there you had a reasonable chance of surviving, while here . . ." She looked at him and lifted her hands off the table in an expression of disbelief. "It's crazy." She continued staring at him and was about to say something when the waiter appeared at her side. It was even more crazy, it occurred to her, to be eating like this in sedate Cheltenham and talking with the man whom she loved—though from time to time completely failed to understand —about challenging the might of England.

"What are you going to do, madman?" she asked after the waiter had left them, her voice dropping to a whisper.

"Select an important military target somewhere in this country, attack and destroy it," said Grogan.

Mairin saw a gleam in the eye and recognised the stubborn set of his mouth. She had once seen a photograph of his father in Kerry, taken about the age James was now, with the same expression.

"But, Jimmy, is this the right way?" Her earlier disbelief and panic were giving way to a more rational approach. "Can you take all that on? And, even if you succeed what good will it do? Besides . . ." She paused.

"Besides what?"

"It doesn't seem to me," she said slowly, "that it's correct politically if you accept—as I know you do—that we are all part of the Republican movement. We are bound to follow within reason what our leaders lay down for us. What would happen if everyone took it into their heads to rush off and strike an independent blow for the cause. Chaos, sheer bloody chaos."

Grogan sipped his wine. "Listen carefully, because I mean every word I say. The aim of the IRA is to reunite Ireland

by militarily defeating Britain or forcing her into such a position
that she will negotiate with us directly and give us what we
want over the table instead of across the battlefield. Right?"

Mairin remained silent.

"Now," he continued, "if you look back, but not very far,
you'll see the political mentality and tactics of the British as
clearly as you see the wine in your glass. If the threat is great
enough, the British always negotiate—no matter what they've
said in the past. Kenyatta, convicted of involvement with the
Mau Mau, was described by a British governor in Kenya,
when the country was actually on the way to independence, as
the 'leader to darkness and death'. He duly became president
of Kenya."

Grogan shrugged. "The Stormont Government was saying a
little while ago 'no negotiations with the murdering IRA'. But
we already have direct rule. And why? Because violence pays
and because the British are not fanatics. Unlike the OAS in
Algeria or the Portuguese in Africa, the Brits do not believe in
the ultimate logic of violence which is self-destruction. They
always call a halt and talk." Grogan stopped and smiled at
Mairin. "I've become quite political, haven't I?" he said.

"In a cock-eyed way," she replied. "You realise everyone
will be against you, don't you? And, Jimmy," she said despairingly, "how can you, singlehanded bring the British to the
negotiating table? David killed Goliath but that was a long,
long time ago."

"Look, Mairin," he said earnestly, leaning across the table.
"The IRA campaign has been a mess in the North. I was
involved in a couple of major operations, including the shooting
of the Minister and both were balls-ups."

Mairin's eyes had opened wide and she was staring at Grogan
with a peculiar intensity.

"Even then," he went on, "the campaign has paid off politically. The trouble is now it could go on for ages, brave but mis-
guided, vicious yet inefficient, becoming bloodier all the time
and dragging in more and more innocent people, both Catholics
and Protestants. As long as it stays over there, in Ireland, the
British people don't care a damn. And therefore they don't force
their leaders to take the drastic steps we want."

Mairin had never heard him so articulate before. But she

felt instinctively that the motive for what he was doing was less political than personal.

"Now," he continued, "doesn't it make sense that if Britain was hit hard where it hurts—here at home—they'd give way?"

"So what are you planning?" she asked simply. She knew now his mind was made up. Nothing she or anyone else could do would change it. They were alone in the restaurant now and it was very quiet, very peaceful. She would remember this moment.

"I've spent most of the day having a look at the Government Communications Centre near Bath," he replied. "But it's a non-starter—too many buildings, and too many civilians. It's a pity though, because this is where all the monitoring and cypher work is done. I heard all about it when I was on a special job in the SAS . . . It would have made the right sort of impact politically," he added reflectively.

"And now?" Mairin asked, suddenly feeling tired and flat.

"Tomorrow morning, I have to see an old friend who works in the Concorde Flight Test Centre just down the road from here. He's a good Irishman, Padraig Kenny—I don't think you've met him."

She shook her head and he went on. "You'd better stay here, if you can take another day in Cheltenham." He saw her grimace. "I won't be long. We'll spend one more night here then move on. We can stay together quite a bit. It looks more natural. But we'll have to keep our heads down from now on. All right?"

"Jimmy," she said a little wearily, "why did you ask me over here? Was it just because it 'looks more natural'?"

"Don't be silly, Mairin," he said, reaching out and taking her hand. "I want you with me and you can help more than most people. You know that . . . You will help me, won't you?"

She nodded and raised his hand slowly to her lips.

In the basement of an old house not far behind Trinity College, Dublin, there was the usual Wednesday evening commotion going on. Jade and Tula McGurran had rented the damp, empty apartment and converted it into a combination of community centre for university drop-outs, publishing head-quarters for their political broadsheet and sparsely furnished home.

The broadsheet's basic platform concentrated on the role to be played by youth in Europe and the USA in the transformation of the world's socio-political structures. The transformation was, of course, to be a very gradual process and its exact nature was still largely undetermined. Jade and Tula were both twenty-three. They married a year ago when they left Trinity College.

The search for a name for the broadsheet, which was now being produced as a fortnightly basis, had caused much soul-searching. Tula, who had a more literary bent than her husband, had come up with a quotation from Dante, later used also by the Alexandrian poet Cavafy. *Il Gran Rifiuto — The Great Refusal*. Jade finally agreed when he'd visualised the full political implications. *Refusal*, as they now referred to it in conversation, soon became an integral part of their lives. Printing took place early on Thursday mornings, so Wednesday night always tended to be frenetic. People rushed in and out, contributions were chased up and the scene generally was one of friendly confusion.

On this particular Wednesday evening, Jade was waiting to receive an article which was to be featured prominently in the following day's edition. He'd asked a young IRA Provo officer from the North to write up a kind of war notebook from inside the barricades of Free Derry. The officer had been given permission to do so by the Provos and was due to deliver his copy at any moment. Jade cleared the room which acted as the editorial office. He told Tula to keep everyone out for half an hour when his visitor arrived.

A few minutes later Tula showed the visitor in. He had an older man with him, whom he introduced as a colleague from the IRA, Sean O'Kane. He passed across a neatly typed manu-script in a cardboard folder, with the legend *Free Derry — 3,000 words* written on the cover. Probably all worked out for him by their publicity people, Jade thought a little sourly. He'd wanted something personalised that would get through to his student readers by its immediacy and vitality. He hoped he wasn't getting the Provo spokesman's views instead of the field officer's.

O'Kane offered cigarettes around, lighted them and leaned forward in his chair to speak. He was a big man, probably about thirty, with a lot of booze fat on him but very solid underneath it.

"I wanted to come and meet you, McGurran, because I've been following up a matter that interests us. I understand you're a good friend of Mairin Duffy?"

It sounded like an accusation.

"That's right," he replied defensively. "Mairin was at Trinity with us. She helps us out around publication time. What's the problem?"

"The problem is that she's been going around with a man called Grogan. And we want to find out where he is." O'Kane moved in his chair and Jade could see the heavy stomach protruding over his belt. There was no doubt about the threat suddenly implicit in his voice. "I am assuming you can keep your mouth shut about this conversation."

"Why don't you ask Mairin about it?" Jade asked.

"If she knows, then I reckon you know too. Or can find out." O'Kane smiled unpleasantly, showing a row of bad teeth. "Girls who get involved with the wrong types tend to get the wind up easily. Or flustered. Right?"

Jade tried to think fast. He could deny knowing anything, in which case O'Kane might get nasty. It was clear to him that O'Kane was not a man to mess around. And after all, he knew damned little. But if he spoke, he would be letting Mairin down.

Jade jumped as O'Kane, moving very quickly, brought his fist down on the table with a hard crack.

"You're taking a long time to answer, young man," O'Kane said. "I'm telling you that I'm here on serious business." He nodded towards the young Provo officer. "My colleague here can vouch for that. I can't believe that you would want to hold us up on something important . . . Well?"

Jade felt his stomach turn. He ought to resist this bullying. But then, why should he? The information he had couldn't be very important and he *was* a supporter of the IRA. He was about to publish their article, wasn't he?

"Look, all I know is that my wife and I were round at

Mairin's place last week when a woman came in with a note. She only stayed a few minutes and she'd obviously never met Mairin before. She said she was visiting Dublin with her kids and she'd been asked to leave the letter, that's all. Mairin just said it was from her boy-friend."

"Didn't she ask the woman anything else?" O'Kane demanded.

"The woman said she couldn't say anything more. Then she insisted on leaving, almost immediately."

O'Kane looked at him, as if unsure whether he was telling the whole story.

"Look, I was there—we both were—the whole time," Jade said. "That was all that happened, nothing more."

"Did you see the letter?"

"Of course not. It was private."

"Didn't the woman give a name?" O'Kane asked brusquely.

Jade hesitated. He decided he'd better tell what he knew.

"Yes," he said. "She said she was a Mrs. Muldoon. She said her husband ran a workshop in Kilburn. In London. He's an old friend of Grogan's apparently."

"Apparently," O'Kane repeated thoughtfully, drumming his fingers on the table.

There was a knock on the door. Tula's head appeared.

"I'm sorry to be holding you up, Mrs. McGurran," O'Kane said, standing up. "We'll be getting off now." He turned to Jade. "I hope that article is what you want. And I'll be grateful if you'll keep our conversation to yourself. Good night to you both."

When the visitors had left, Tula looked enquiringly at Jade.

"Whatever was all that about?" she asked.

"They were asking about Mairin's boy-friend. They're looking for him and must have found out she spends a lot of time with us."

"You didn't say anything, did you?"

"No . . . No, I didn't." Jade grimaced. "They can be very unpleasant though. I just said we knew he'd disappeared and that was all. What do you think we should say to Mairin when she gets back?"

Tula looked at her husband, surprised. "Why, we should tell her what happened, of course. What else could we say?"

Jade nodded and smiled, suddenly relaxed. "Yes, of course," he said. "They just threw me a bit."

That evening Kelly was working even later than usual. He was still in his office when O'Kane came in to report, and he sat on after the other man had gone. He had almost worked out a plan of campaign. It was a little complicated and he didn't like the fact that one or two elements were outside his direct control.

Kelly stood up and put on the old coat he kept in his office for late nights like this when it suddenly became chilly. He said good night to the guard who always stayed on the premises. He walked down the staircase and out into the bracing Dublin air. A wind was blowing in from the sea and ruffled his dark hair as he walked along. He went past his car and walked, a small, upright figure, to the end of the street where there was a public telephone booth. He didn't like using the phone for this kind of thing. But time was important now. In less than a minute he was through to the Kilburn number in London.

"Is that you, Frank?" he asked in his soft voice. "How are my two boys doing?"

"They're fine. As a matter of fact Paddy's here with me now having a drink. Just a moment. I'll put him on the line."

O'Flaherty's loud, harsh voice suddenly rasped.

"We're having a spot of trouble finding our man," he said. "We're trying everything. Frank's put a few fellers on to it, too, but no luck so far."

"Don't worry, Paddy, I've got a lead for you," Kelly said. "Now listen carefully. Your man has a friend called Muldoon, who runs a workshop of some sort in Kilburn. Muldoon's wife and kids are over here. I'll have someone looking out for them tomorrow, but in the meantime you chase him up there. I think he knows where your man is—his wife brought a message over for the girl-friend, the one you got on to. All right?"

"I've got that," O'Flaherty said.

"Good. Now this is very important. Find out from Muldoon where his friend is and get hold of him, however you can. Then I want you to hold him, and wait for my instructions. But just hold him, you understand? Nothing else without word from me. Have you got that?"

"I've got that," O'Flaherty said again.

"Good. Well, go and do it. Then get in touch through Frank."

Kelly gently put down the receiver. As he walked back to his car he hoped O'Flaherty and the Shoeman would pull it off. They'd have the element of surprise. But Grogan was still an unknown quantity.

16

GROGAN SMILED AT THE GIRL behind the Merlin Car Hire
counter and said he wanted a small car for a few days. She
smiled back at the tall man, her first customer of the day, and
pulled a brochure out of a drawer. The girl, in her early
twenties with a trim figure and upturned nose, looked at him
a little more closely as he glanced down the list of cars under
two litres. She decided she liked what she saw.

"How about the new Fiat 128?" he asked.

She said they had a couple available, the tourist season
hadn't really got off the ground yet, and he could have it right
away. Would he be going far? No, just around the Cotswold
villages and maybe down to Somerset to see friends but no
Monte Carlo stuff. She smiled again, an open smile, full of
creamy teeth, with the suggestion of an invitation in it. Grogan
put down a cash deposit, took full insurance and signed the
papers.

The girl looked at the form he had filled up and said: "Could
I see your driving licence, Mr. Lawrence?"

Grogan reached into his jacket pocket and a look of dismay
crossed his face. "Damn it," he said, "I'm terribly sorry, but

I've left it in the hotel. Would you mind very much if I brought it along later?"

"No, of course not," the girl said casually, "but could you tell me the county of issue and the date of expiry."

"Roxburghshire County Council, expiring the end of this year. And the number is 4939 — an easy one to remember." He grinned engagingly, enjoying the control of a human situation with its delicate sexual overtones. It was a game, he thought, that most people played to a greater or lesser extent every day of their lives.

"By the way," he said as he turned to go, "it's just possible I may have to cut short my holiday and return to London. Do you have an office there where I could check the car in?"

"Yes, we do," she said, a trace of disappointment in her voice, "in the Strand. But I hope you don't have to leave this part of the world too soon."

Grogan thanked her politely and walked out onto the street aware of her eyes on his back. He looked at his watch. It was only nine thirty. Mairin, whom he had left at the hotel, would still be in bed and it was too early to set off for Fairford. He decided to take another quick look at the Government Communications Centre and then reconnoitre the countryside around the Concorde Flight Test Centre at Fairford itself.

Three hours later Grogan pulled into the New Inn in the small Gloucestershire town that had been put on the map by one of the most controversial aeroplanes ever built. The Communications Centre near Bath was definitely out. He had driven around the main buildings just as its employees were arriving. The work done there had a direct bearing on the British Government's military capacity. The establishment had grown out of the famous codebreaking team that had cracked the German Secret Service's cyphers during the Second World War. It couldn't really be described as a 'military target'. If he could blow up the costly and complicated equipment at the Centre, then it might make some sense. But he had no way of finding out where that was or of taking reasonable precautions so that dozens of people working in minor jobs didn't go up with it. Concorde was a much better proposition. A project that had indirectly already added to Britain's military potential and was so spectacular that it made his heart pound just to think of it.

Mairin had talked of David and Goliath. Well, this could be the sling-shot that might bring the giant crashing to the ground.

Grogan parked the car around the corner and walked back to the pub. In Fairford Concorde was king. On his way in he had passed the Concorde Launderette, the Concorde Café and noticed postcards of the supersonic plane on sale outside every newsagent. The New Inn, the best pub in town, he'd been told, was packed with lunchtime drinkers. He saw Padraig Kenny almost immediately, sitting in a corner talking with two other men. Kenny caught sight of him and Grogan waved him over. The two men hadn't seen each other for years, but the skinny little technician hadn't changed. They'd originally met in Cyprus during the Eoka campaign. Grogan had been in the paras and Kenny was a sergeant mechanic in REME, working on Saracen and Saladin armoured cars. A bright, vivacious man, Grogan had always remembered him as a good companion. It was an unusual relationship, especially since the paras rarely mixed with men from other units as a matter of principle, but they had been drawn together by their Irish background.

"Welcome to Concorde," Kenny said with a cheerful smile. "A drink, then I'll fill you in."

Grogan liked his style, as crisp and economical as his appearance. While Kenny fought his way back to the bar, Grogan looked around the place. It could have been a Royal Air Force local anywhere in the country at the time of the Battle of Britain. British fliers have a distinctive plumage, more than just the handlebar moustaches, though Grogan could see quite a few of those around. The Concorde pilots had already become Fairford's folk heroes . . . It was the way they dressed, the way they held themselves, the way they talked. He looked at a group of them at the bar. Their fraternity, he thought, was as secure and confident as that of a Masonic Lodge with none of the hole-in-the-corner secrecy. They advertised themselves with the flair of a good public relations organisation.

Kenny returned with the drinks and they spent a few minutes catching up on their lives since they had left the British army.

"I've been working down here for the last couple of years now," Kenny said. "It's a bloody good job—interesting, well-paid, and all that. Though we never know from one day to the next whether the Government is going to cancel the whole shooting match."

"How do you feel about Concorde?" Grogan asked, wondering how much of the Celtic nationalism that Kenny had been famous for in the old days had survived.

"I love all the machines I work with," he replied without hesitation. "But I know there are more important things, age-old things of the blood." Grogan had the answer he wanted. Kenny was at heart a romantic of that peculiarly Celtic breed who talk incessantly of the 'old country' from afar but rarely became politically involved and often never return. It would be wrong—and cruel—to call his bluff and ask him to *act* instead of *talk* after all these years of friendship. But there was no harm in asking him to come half-way and lend a hand without compromising himself.

"You can guess why I'm here?" Grogan said.

"They sent you from Dublin, I suppose," Kenny replied.

Grogan nodded. "I'm to have a good look round. No panic, no rush. They don't want any more mistakes. Just good information from the inside."

"Got you," said Kenny.

Grogan stood up. "Let's go somewhere else, this place is terrible."

Kenny looked at his watch and said: "Perfect timing. Come with me and you'll see our bird fly . . . there's a test flight due at two o'clock. Princess Margaret and some of the royal brood are going up in her."

"Great," said Grogan and led the way out to his car. On the way to the airfield, Kenny explained that it had been a V-bomber base before the Concorde project and that it still belonged to the RAF. They walked into the public viewing enclosure packed with sightseers. It was a blustery day with a cold edge to it, but there was a holiday mood among the crowd. Grogan wondered how many times they had seen the Concorde fly already and yet made a special outing today because royalty would be aboard.

Kenny was busy pointing out the main features of the Test Centre in his vivid way. The factory where the prototype and production models were manufactured was fifty miles away, at Filton, near Bristol. But Fairford had expanded as the project advanced. A large servicing and maintenance organisation had formed around Fairford and the airfield, growing like coral, a living organism. Kenny pointed a boney forefinger down to the massive hangars and workshops where he spent his day.

"Several hundred of us work down there." He swung his arm in the opposite direction. "But most of the structural and engine tests are done over there."

"What's security like?" Grogan asked, carefully studying the layout of the area, slotting the component parts into place in his memory like a mental jigsaw puzzle.

Kenny was about to reply when there was a gigantic roar from the far end of the airfield followed by a banshee wail. Heads swung in unison, as if pulled by a string. Grogan saw the Concorde roll slowly out of a feeder runway on to the main strip. The watery sun shone on its silver back and the air quivered behind the four huge engines encased in elongated coffin-like boxes beneath its belly. As it turned slowly on its cluster of wheels Grogan saw the predator's head, dropping in the position of rest, in profile. He sucked in his breath. It was a marvellous-looking aircraft, with the proportions and suppressed power of a natural athlete. The noise of the engines died away for a moment, then returned with a shattering intensity. Children on the viewing platform covered their ears with their hands. A final shriek and the plane began to roll gently forward. The swept-back wings trembled as it gathered speed, then it was level with the spectators, moving effortlessly down the runway at over a hundred miles an hour. Grogan returned to his study of the airfield. When he looked at the Concorde again it was high up in the sky, its nose still hooked but more impressive than ever as the full delta shape of the body came into view. Four greasy plumes of smoke trailed from its engines as it finally disappeared into the clouds.

The two men walked away from the airfield deep in conversation. Security, Kenny explained, was not as tight as people might expect, though precautions against sabotage and tampering were taken. But industrial espionage also worried the Corporation and anything vital like draughtsmen's sketches, performance figures and flight tests were treated as top secret and protected with as much care as embassies give to their diplomatic mail.

"That's all right," said Grogan. "I'm not interested in that side of it. But tell me more about the security around the planes themselves."

Kenny looked at him closely, frowning.

"During the daytime it's difficult, virtually impossible for someone who doesn't work there. We all have passes with photographs on them." He pulled out a small identity card in a plastic holder. "But at night," he continued, "it might be possible to get in, though anybody who tried it would need someone on the inside . . . Look, Jimmy, I don't want to stick my nose into your affairs but if . . ."

"Don't worry," Grogan cut in, "I'm not going to involve you in this and the less you know the better." He paused. Kenny was looking a little unhappy.

"One way of getting close to the plane during the day," Kenny said, as if a thought had just struck him, "might be with the press groups that are going round all the time A free-lance photographer friend of mine told me once that they don't check up much. A normal press card and a few cameras slung round your neck might do the trick."

"That's an idea," replied Grogan. "But what about getting something on to the aircraft?"

This time Kenny looked thoroughly alarmed.

"Christ, you're not planning to blow it up, are you?" he said, stopping and turning to look at Grogan. "They rarely fly these days without at least half a dozen passengers as well as the crew on board. It would be murder."

"Now, now," said Grogan, gently putting his hand on Kenny's arm. "No one's going to get hurt. If we do anything at all, it'll be when the thing's on the ground and everyone's safely asleep. But these are early days; I'm only here to have a preliminary look round, you know." Grogan grinned and guided the other man back towards his car.

"No," he continued, "this has to be played very cool. You've helped us, Padraig, and I'll mention that when I get back to Dublin. The thing now is just to forget everything we've said. All right?"

Kenny looked relieved and nodded his head. "Don't worry, Jimmy . . . silent as the grave. I'd better be off now. Good hunting."

Grogan got into his car and started the engine. As he drove off he stuck his hand out of the window: "Keep the faith," he said.

Humphrey James was in his office earlier than usual, preparing a report for the Ambassador's mid-week briefing session, when the telephone call came through. The quiet, precise voice identified the speaker as much as the false name they had arranged. He said he would like to see James as soon as possible and suggested nine thirty the same morning. James agreed. There must be something moving. The agent had never used the emergency contacting arrangement before.

As he left the office, Harriet looked up anxiously. She was struggling with a large parcel that had arrived in the last diplomatic bag and had contained spare reels of tape. The parcel had split open and they lay in a confused heap over her desk. James noticed with irritation that the top two buttons on her blouse had come undone and somehow an old line from his army days ran through his head . . . she couldn't fight her way out of a paper bag.

"I've had a call from Interface," he said. "I shall have to take counter-surveillance measures, so I'm off now. You'd better call the Ambassador's PA and explain that I won't be at the morning meeting. I don't know exactly when I'll be back, but certainly before lunch. I'll have to get a telegram off right away, so wait for me anyway. OK?"

Harriet nodded, over-emphatically.

"You have an appointment to see the Head of Chancery at eleven o'clock," she said. "To discuss the locally employed staff — especially that new driver. And Miss Good wanted to talk to you about one of the girls in the typing pool." Harriet blushed. "Apparently she's been having an affair with the archivist in the Saudi Consulate. I told her you might be free about twelve."

"Oh, God . . ." James groaned. "Cancel them both. Say something important came up. Apologise nicely, and say I'll give them both a ring the first chance I get."

James pointed to his chest in farewell. "And better get your-

self buttoned up." As he went out, he wondered why he
bothered. Harriet must be the joke of the Embassy by now.
Forty minutes later he was in the safe flat, having arrived with
a few minutes to spare.

As usual, his visitor arrived punctually at almost the precise
moment arranged. As they sat down, James noticed that he
looked more relaxed than usual. The lines of strain and over-
work had eased.

"I have a formal proposition to make to your Government,
Mr. James," he began at once. "I believe that your service is
the most secure channel for it. Perhaps I could now explain to
you the reasons why I was unable to speak before . . . certain
preparations were necessary. Now they are complete."

He looked directly at James. "I assume our conversations are
being recorded? Otherwise, you may wish to take notes."

James nodded, without replying, and took from his inside
pocket a small leather notebook and a slim gold pencil.

"Good . . . I'll begin by referring to previous conversations
when we have spoken, at your initiative, about the possibility of
the IRA carrying the war to England and about a former
British Army sergeant, James Grogan. I can tell you that we
are now in position and prepared to hit certain selected targets
in England. I can also tell you that Grogan, whom you have
been searching for without success, is under my control."

Interface smiled briefly at James, who was taking notes.

"Before I go on, I think you are entitled to a little explana-
tion of our strategy. When I say 'our', I mean the Irish Republican Army, regardless of splits into separate wings. I am talking about the hard-core cadre, the IRA that will continue to
exist as a surety that the settlement we shall determine will not
be betrayed by future generations either in London or Ulster."
He paused for a moment to allow James to catch up with his
notes. "I told you before that it was not our policy to attack
England. You know the arguments already. They are valid
enough. But now we believe that we are faced with the possibility of a cheap sell-out solution in which a token trend towards reunification in ten or twenty years will be exchanged for
peace. We will not tolerate it, Mr. James."

He looked across the table and James studied him carefully
before speaking.

"I would have thought such a conclusion, supposing it were possible, to be rather more than most people consider the IRA deserve. And with Protestant feelings running as high as they are, you'd be damned lucky if you could pull it off."

Interface shrugged.

"I can see you are a sound tactician," he said. "But I don't accept your premise. Not at all. We are not to be foisted off with a partial solution that can be diluted over the years into something even less than it sounds. If a united Ireland is ever to emerge, and pray God it will, it must be this time."

He leaned forward in his chair, his voice hardening. "No, Mr. James, this time we are playing to win. I'll explain our plan to you. We've deliberately allowed Grogan to expose himself, in order to give your Government a glimpse of the destruction we can wreak. Let me put it to you that we have twenty Grogans, all in England, and all ready to move against a variety of targets. Supposing we made one attack a week for a month or two, beginning with someone like Prince Charles and moving on to your Foreign or Home Office, for instance. Or striking at Cabinet Ministers. How long would it take Mr. Heath to agree to negotiations? Of course, public opinion would be against us. But how often in British history has it been against nationalist movements? And how often has that stopped the movements succeeding?"

James looked at his visitor coldly.

"You could be bluffing," he said, measuring his words. "Aldershot wasn't much of an operation, and come to that, neither are most of the things you're doing in the North. Who do you think is going to believe your blackmail threats?"

"I understand your anger," Interface replied, "I might even consider it justified if I didn't know only too well the history of British military and civil oppression throughout the world. And in Ireland in particular. Because times have changed and now both your political parties subscribe to a loose, progressive system of socialist democracy, you may not be allowed to forget the recent past. In Ireland that past still conditions the shape of the present."

Interface relaxed into his armchair, one arm raised as if in supplication towards James.

"No . . . please do not let us argue that particular toss," he continued. "If you want proof, I can supply it. But I sincerely hope that more bloodshed and destruction can be avoided. To begin on that course in England, in any case, can only lead to the same conclusion. The one I am offering now."

James took a cigarette from his case and lighted it carefully. "What exactly is your proposition?" he asked.

"It's very simple. We want secret negotiations with the British Government. They should begin within a week. The main item on the agenda will be the reunification of Ireland. And I mean reunification now, with all the necessary safeguards . . . In return we will stop all operations in the North and cancel the operational plan to attack England."

Interface paused and smiled. "I will also pull out that particular thorn in your flesh — the former British army sergeant."

James began to speak, but his visitor held up his hand.

"I'll make two last points, then I have finished. As a token of goodwill I have chosen to talk first rather than act . . . I could have done it the other way round. Historically, that would have been more usual. Secondly, time is an important factor. I am asking you for a quick response. Without it, there may be unfortunate consequences."

There was a long moment of silence before James spoke. "Naturally, all I can do is report your proposition . . . I shall do so immediately, of course. Supposing it's agreed, I take it you will be part of the IRA negotiating team? Who else would be there?"

"That is still to be decided, but I would certainly expect to be present, if not to lead our side. You know a little about my background, Mr. James. Enough, I think, to realise that I would be one of the few figures acceptable to both the Official and Provisional wings. I have never accepted that arbitrary division in the movement. This is the moment, I believe, to pull them back together. There are a number of powerful figures in the movement who believe as I do. I have taken great care to hold them together. What I am proposing to you today is on behalf of a reunited, strengthened IRA. Any dissident voices will be quickly silenced."

James scribbled down a last note and closed the leather notebook with a snap. "Very well," he said. "I will pass on your proposals just as you have put them to me." He looked across the small table. "When you ask for a quick response, what kind of time period have you in mind?"

His visitor stood up, picking up his coat from the side of the armchair. "Let's simply say the quicker the reply the less chance there will be of any accidents. I don't want to set a deadline. But it would clearly be in the interests of both sides to produce an agreement to talk within two or three days . . . I, too, have problems of co-ordination that will depend upon your reply."

James accompanied his visitor to the door. He reminded him of the arrangement they had made for James to telephone his house, giving the name of Harry, to fix their next meeting. He promised to be in touch as soon as possible. As he watched him walking down the corridor towards the lift, James, in spite of himself, felt a touch of respect. The old fox had certainly laid it on the line. He wondered what the reaction from London would be.

17

THE DEATH OF WALLY FIGGIS spurred Special Branch into new efforts to find Grogan. It wasn't that Figgis himself mattered very much—he was a useful but minor nark—but now the Branch felt that it had come under direct attack. There was little doubt in Barnes's mind as he sat in his office staring gloomily out over Westminster Abbey that there was a link between the murder of Figgis and the Grogan affair. He knew he had to avoid becoming paranoic about Grogan and solid evidence remained as elusive as ever. But the man had such a distinctive style about him, the way he operated, the way he killed, that Barnes felt he could recognise it with his eyes shut. He tugged at his right ear, annoyed with himself. His whole nature and background resisted a personal vendetta, yet unless he settled his account with Grogan—and quickly—he felt this was the way things were moving. He turned back from the window and asked Fitchett to get them all some coffee.

"Southwark, why Southwark?" Franks seemed to be talking to himself. "Well off the beaten track for Paddies like Figgis, I would have thought," he added raising his voice.

"I don't like it . . ." said Barnes. "Too close to our cloak-and-dagger friends in the City. Anything new on the Figgis investigation, Sergeant?"

"Nothing, I'm afraid, sir," said Fitchett. "Still a case of the three wise monkeys."

"The what?" Barnes said sharply.

"Hear no evil, see no evil, speak no evil," said Fitchett nervously, feeling that he had overstepped the mark.

"Ah . . . yes," murmured Barnes burying his head in the papers piled on his desk.

Frank's telephone rang. He picked it up, listened for a few moments grunting occasionally, then said: "Right, I'll deal with it."

"Southwark?" Barnes asked.

"No. The Irish squad. They've spotted a Belfast IRA man in the Kilburn area. Known as the 'Shoeman'. A big fist, they say." Franks paused. "No direct connection with Grogan, but they could have come over at roughly the same time. The Shoeman has been around for a week or more, but lying low. They think it's worth following up."

"You bet . . ." said Barnes, a glint in his eye. "It might be a long shot but he could be part of Grogan's unit."

Fitchett was already on his feet, thumbing through the card index — KNOWN IRA OPERATIVES AND SUSPECTS — in a mud-green filing cabinet over by the far wall.

"Here he is, sir," he said quickly. "Looks more like a hatch . . . more like a strong-arm man employed to keep discipline within the IRA than on ops outside it," he said, correcting himself. He liked a colourful turn of phrase but realised that, with Chief Superintendent Barnes, there was a time and place for everything.

"Surveillance?" said Franks, looking at Barnes.

"Yes . . . good idea."

"How about. . . ?" Franks nodded over to Fitchett who was still poring over the cards.

"All right by me," replied Barnes. "Put Jenkins and Nelson with him." He paused, rubbing his chin thoughtfully. "I doubt if we can raise another team to make it round the clock. They'll never wear it up there . . ." He raised his eyes in mock reverence to the ceiling. "But a good long look at our friend the Shoeman during daylight is better than nothing at all."

"You're drafted," said Franks to Fitchett, not unkindly. "Get onto Jenkins and Nelson straight away. You'll need two-way radios. Then call into the Irish Squad and they'll give you all the rest of the gen—description, whereabouts, usual movements, street plans. OK?"

"Great," said Fitchett, trying valiantly to hide his enthusiasm and make it appear that trailing IRA gunmen around the streets of London was something he did every day of the week. "I'll keep in close touch."

"Got your gun?" Franks asked, the shadow of a smile at the corners of his mouth.

"Yep . . ." said Fitchett, pulling aside his jacket and giving Franks a glimpse of his shoulder holster.

"One word of advice," said Franks.

"Yes?"

"Have a good piss before you start."

Fitchett laughed, an infectious boyish guffaw.

"Don't worry . . ." he lowered his voice, "I can always tie a knot in it."

Franks grinned and slapped him on the back. "On your way then, and take it easy . . . they're rough bastards."

At three forty-five in the afternoon, especially on a sultry afternoon, the upper end of the Edgware Road is at the nadir of its day. The pubs have spilled out their late lunchtime drinkers, the cafés are flyblown and empty. Most shops, except the bookies, cope offhandedly with a desultory trade. The great artery of traffic on the road continues to pump back and forth but the tramp of feet on the pavements has diminished almost to the point where individual footsteps acquire an identity of their own.

That was what was worrying Detective Sergeant Jack Fitchett. He and the other two Special Branch men had picked up the Shoeman's trail at a pub just off the Edgware Road at lunchtime. They had followed him and a burly man with a shaven head for the next hour around a maze of smaller streets. The pair made a number of what seemed to be personal calls. Now they were out in the open walking slowly along the Edgware Road, on the right-hand side, in the direction of Marble Arch. Fitchett wished like hell the pavements were more crowded. He was currently the lead man, with Jenkins almost level on the other side of the street and Nelson, also on that side, fifty yards behind him in the classic L-shape surveillance pattern.

Fitchett had given Franks a quick thumb-nail report on his radio via the local police station. It didn't amount to very much but Franks had sent back a word of encouragement and told them to carry on until nightfall. The fact that the Shoeman and Shaven-Head never seemed to part company was of some interest and Fitchett kept wondering idly who the second man was. Fitchett suddenly slowed his pace. They had stopped. The Shoeman was cupping his hands to light a cigarette. He lit one for Shaven-Head and they strolled on. Fitchett stopped and pretended to stare into a milliner's window. A middle-aged woman at his side suddenly turned to him and said tartly: "Are you really *that* interested in lady's underwear, young man?" Fitchett mumbled something and moved on. Stupid cow, he thought bitterly. Why couldn't the great British public mind its own business just once in a while?

He looked up the street. Shaven-Head had vanished. But the Shoeman was still there gazing into a dingy-looking shop window. Articulated container-trucks roared past, obscuring Fitchett's view of his team. When they were past he gave a quick hand-signal to Nelson, the rear man, and began to cross. Jenkins slowed his pace and dropped back towards Nelson who, after pausing for a gap in the traffic, crossed over and took Fitchett's vacant place. Fitchett stopped to light a cigarette and had a quick glance at the Shoeman who hadn't moved. He was gazing in a cool, detached way at the display of contraceptives, trusses, anti-haemorrhoid pills, books on sex technique, and other 'surgical goods'. Just as Fitchett was about to continue walking, Shaven-Head came out of the dark interior of the shop putting a small packet wrapped in brown paper into his pocket. Who's the lucky girl, thought Fitchett?

For the next three hours, Fitchett and his team slogged on. Neither the Shoeman nor Shaven-Head seemed to be engaged in anything urgent. They visited a bookie, had several cups of tea and an unanimated conversation in a café. While the members of the team managed to grab a cup of tea and something to eat, Fitchett had sent a couple more reports back to Franks. Later it looked as if they were going into a cinema. Fitchett watched Shaven-Head hesitate for several minutes beside a billboard advertising I WAS A SEMI VIRGIN and SEX IN THE SUBURBS. But the Shoeman had looked at his watch, said something to him and they had moved on. Now they were off the Edgware Road once more, on the Kilburn side. The pavements were full again as the lemmings of the city, intent on their distant destinations, streamed homewards.

As the light began to fail, they had a break. The IRA men went into a pub just as Fitchett was thinking of calling it off for the night. They reappeared out of a side entrance which Nelson was covering from a transport café on the opposite side of the street. Fitchett, nodding towards Jenkins who had been sitting on a bench reading a newspaper, set off in pursuit. The Shoeman and Shaven-Head had been joined by a third man, short, bow-legged with thin sandy hair. They turned a corner and walked fast down a curving road that followed the railway track. It was almost dark. Fitchett looked behind him and saw that Nelson was with them. There were few pedestrians around now, so the Special Branch men dropped back. The trio ahead crossed the road once, turned left, right and left again. Fitchett reached the last corner in time to see them disappear into a tall Victorian house with a steep row of chipped stone steps. He noted the number and the street name and waited for Jenkins to come up. It was ten minutes past eight, very dark. A chill wind was rising, a sudden reversal of the earlier promise of summer.

Fitchett had a quick council of war with his colleagues. The house, they told him, was already on the suspect list for use by one of the top IRA men in the area. Fitchett realised that the Shoeman and Shaven-Head might be in there for hours, even all night. He had no right to keep Jenkins and Nelson hanging around any longer. He told them to sign off. They would pick up the trail the next day. He told Jenkins to make a detailed report to Franks and say that he would telephone him later. He had a couple of urgent calls to make on foot, he explained, which would hang him up a bit. He said good night and walked off. When he was sure they had gone he walked back round the

14

block and stood for a moment staring at the big house. He was damned if he would give up now. It was against the rules and all that and he was bloody tired, but he had a feeling the IRA pair would reappear and didn't want to miss them. He looked, at his watch. He would give them until midnight. If nothing happened by then he would quit.

Three hours later, stiff and cold, with his spirits at a low ebb, Fitchett was beginning to think that he might advance his deadline. But lights in two of the front windows kept him doggedly at his post. As he looked at his watch for the hundredth time both lights went out. Two minutes after that the door opened and the same three men appeared. They stood together on the threshold talking, then they walked down the steps into the street. They moved off on the opposite side of the street and disappeared around the corner. He hurried after them. They were walking briskly with a purposeful air. Fitchett realised that there was more chance of being spotted alone, but he was determined not to lose them now. It had just gone half past eleven and the streets were deserted. The wind had continued to rise and Fitchett could smell the dust of the street in his nostrils. They were back on the long curving road that ran parallel with the railway line. Fitchett increased his pace. The two Irishmen suddenly swung left and disappeared. At first Fitchett couldn't see where they had gone, then, as he drew nearer, he saw a small turning on the opposite side of the road to the embankment. It was a narrow cobbled road leading down to what looked like a mews. Fitchett slowed and walked past the opening. No one. He doubled back and began to walk as silently as he could over the cobbles. Twenty paces brought him to a right-angled bend. He pulled into the side of the street by a house with an orange door and peered cautiously round the corner. Again no one. He waited for a few moments then continued down the mews keeping close to the wall. As he passed another doorway a brawny arm shot out and clamped itself around his neck. Fitchett gasped but instinctively let his body go limp in an attempt to drop down out of the hold. Then he felt a gun barrel in his kidney. He still couldn't see the man but smelled the beer on his breath. From the bulk of him, he guessed it was Shaven-Head. "Walk backwards," the man hissed, easing the pressure around Fitchett's throat but keeping the crook of his arm hard up against his Adam's apple. The two men did a strange shuffling movement backwards into a dark narrow alley running up the side of two of the houses. After a few yards they stopped. The arm on the throat tightened again and Fitchett felt the gun move up his back. Fear engulfed him and he began to struggle desperately. He now knew the gun had a silencer on it. The barrel bored into his back between the shoulder blades. There was a sharp PLOP. Fitchett's body shuddered as if electrified, the air rasping in his throat, and then sagged. The big man allowed the corpse to slide slowly to the ground. The moon, suddenly bright through the racing clouds, glinted on the shaven head as it swung in a graceful arc over the fallen man, the finale of a macabre ballet.

If anyone had been walking along the road beside the railway a few minutes later that night, they would have seen two men—one large, the other slim—carrying a third. The pair took their burden, crumpled and inert, quickly across the road up to the fence that separates it from the railway. With a quick heave, they rolled the body over and let it tumble down the embankment. It finally came to rest in the long grass and nettles a few feet above the track. There were no witnesses, however. The street remained deserted and Detective Sergeant Jack Fitchett's lifeless body lay unseen in the damp spring grass.

18

ON THE SECOND FLOOR of the Old King's Head Hotel in Cheltenham there are four rooms set apart from the others, overlooking a cobbled yard. This is the oldest wing of the building, dating back to the early thirteenth century. The rooms are in a cul-de-sac at the end of a long corridor and are probably the most comfortable and certainly the quietest in the entire hotel. At a little after nine this April morning, a soberly-dressed man of medium height and middle age walked along the corridor towards this wing. The normal sounds of the hotel were muted, the bustle of breakfast past and the cacophony of the morning cleaning operation yet to come. All that could be heard here was the soft tread of the man's shoes on the carpeted floor and the occasional creak of leather or ancient floorboard. He reached the end of the corridor, looked at the numbers on the bedroom doors and knocked firmly on the one at the far end on the left.

There was no reply so he knocked again.

A sleepy, feminine voice said: "Come in."

The man turned the doorknob gently and stepped into the room.

"Good morning," he said pleasantly, "I'm Chief Superintendent Barnes of the Special Branch, and you, if I'm not mistaken, are *not* the young lady mentioned in the hotel register."

Mairin, her long hair tousled, struggled to sit up, pulling the bedclothes around her.

"What the . . . ? Who are you . . . ? Oh no . . ." Her voice tailed off as she rubbed the sleep out of her eyes.

Barnes looked around the room. It was in a mess. A tray of dirty supper dishes lay on the bedside table. Clothes and books were scattered all over the place. A flimsy undergarment lay twisted on the floor, entwined in its death throes, it seemed, with a pair of tights. A cork shoe, with a high, built-up sole, looked as if it had been kicked across the room against the wall. There was a faint trace of cigarette or perhaps pipe smoke in the air.

"Mind if I open the window?" said Barnes, walking over to the big bay window and opening it.

Mairin was still half asleep but the cold blast of spring air snapped her to her senses. What had gone wrong? Jimmy had given her no warning that anything like this could happen. Thank God he'd gone, though she could still smell his body in the sheets. How had they got onto her so quickly? She had only been in the bloody country two days. And why? The worst thing, she suddenly realised, was being curled up in this wretched bed, her hair all over the place, clutching the bedclothes like a frightened virgin in front of this calm, moonfaced Englishman.

"I'd like to get up," she said brusquely.

Barnes bent down and picked up a dressing gown that had fallen on the floor.

"I'm not stopping you," he said, sitting down on a chair with his back to the window. "Go ahead."

Mairin felt embarrassed and hated herself for it. She sensed that he was aware of her feelings and that made it worse.

"Look," she said determinedly, "I'm not getting out of this bed—or talking to you, until I get dressed."

"I'll look the other way, Miss Duffy," Barnes murmured, turning to gaze out of the window.

Damn him, she thought. But she got out of the bed, shivering in the draught, picked up her nightdress and slipped it over her head. She ran a brush over her hair, looked at herself fleetingly in the mirror and abruptly turned away. Then she pulled on her dressing-gown and threw herself down in the armchair on the other side of the bed.

"Now will you please tell me what all this is about?" she asked, beginning to feel more collected, even a little confident. "I am an Irish subject here on holiday and know my rights."

Barnes turned back towards her slowly, almost as if his mind were on something else.

"Where is James Grogan?" he asked mildly.

"I haven't the faintest idea what you are talking about."

"Now, Miss Duffy, you are an intelligent young woman. You and Grogan checked into this hotel two days ago under the names of Mr. and Mrs. Charles Langton. The names you wrote in the register are false."

"Is there a law against that?" Mairin asked aggressively.

"No, there isn't," said Barnes soothingly. "But there are several against blowing innocent women and children to bits."

"What is that supposed to mean?" the girl said, sitting bolt upright in her chair.

"What I'm trying to say is that your boy-friend is a dangerous man. I must have a talk with him." For the first time Mairin was aware of a note of urgency in his voice. It made her more wary than ever, and, in a curious way, more sure of herself too.

"He's a good Republican and there's no crime in that, Inspector," she said.

Barnes ignored the jibe. These bloody university-educated women, he thought.

"Do you smoke?" he asked suddenly, reaching inside his jacket pocket.

"No thank you, I . . ."

"He was here this morning, wasn't he?" he said sharply. "When did he leave?"

"So what. You're wasting your time, you know."

"Probably not more than an hour or so ago," said Barnes, more to himself than to her and looking at his watch.

"Look, I don't think you quite realise the situation. While your friend is on the loose he represents a threat to society, and to a number of innocent people in particular. It's my duty to see that he doesn't do anything rash."

"And what about *his* duty," the girl said with spirit. "You British always try to give the impression that you're seeing problems from both sides. But that's just a trick to conceal your own interests. You talk of the innocent, what about the Irish innocents? What about Derry? Over there it's your soldiers that threaten *our* society."

Barnes frowned and stared hard at her. "There's nothing in the world we'd like more than to get out of Ulster," he said slowly. "You know as well as I do there'd be a bloodbath if we did. We simply have to stay for the time being until the two communities have learned to live together in peace. But England's different. We're already at peace here and no one..." He paused momentarily and repeated the words with, Mairin thought, a touch of menace. "No one has the moral right to disrupt it."

Mairin pulled her dressing-gown more tightly around her. For the first time since she had arrived in England she felt afraid.

"I think this is a fuss about nothing," she said, as calmly as she could manage. "Jimmy and I are here on holiday. We used that name because you know how stuffy hotels, especially English hotels, can be about unmarried couples . . . 'cohabiting', I think the word is. Now would you be kind enough to leave me so that I can get dressed?"

"I must talk to Grogan," said Barnes bluntly, ignoring her question. "Why has he suddenly taken off?"

"I haven't the faintest idea," the girl replied. "He often does that. And I do the same. Why not? We're free agents, aren't we?" She stopped. She wished she hadn't used the word though it was innocently meant. "We're not in the habit of clocking in and out with each other, you know." She stopped again. There was no point in overdoing it.

Barnes sat silently watching her. Grogan was on the loose all right and, he felt instinctively, up to something big.

"Have you ever seen the effect of a bomb exploding in a crowded place, Miss Duffy?" he said, eventually.

"No, I haven't," she said warily, "but what . . ."

"Let me try and paint the picture for you," Barnes went on

in the tones of a strict but kindly schoolmaster. "First there is the sheer impact of the explosion. It pulls and sucks at the flesh ripping it apart and peeling it off the bone in the way that the meat falls off the leg of an overcooked chicken. The structure of the body simply collapses. Muscular containers, like the stomach, burst open and their contents fall out. Limbs are literally torn off. Eyes can be sucked out of their sockets." He paused.

Mairin was sitting immobile, her face pale and her lips drawn together in a straight line.

"And then," Barnes continued remorselessly, "there's the havoc wreaked by the objects which the blast picks up and hurls at its victims. Glass, stones, bits of metal, fragments of concrete fly at terrifying speeds, scything through people's bodies like a hot knife through butter. The overall effect is totally indiscriminate and usually far more devastating than gunshot wounds." He paused again. "Lastly, there are the psychological aspects, people who shake for the rest of their lives . . ."

"All right, all right," said Mairin quietly, "you've made your point." She fell silent.

"Look, Miss Duffy," Barnes said, leaning forward in his chair, his plump, well-kept hands on his knees. "I can also understand your loyalty to your boy-friend. You're in love with him, anyone can see that. So it's natural . . ."

"Stop being so bloody patronising," she burst out, "and for God's sake go and leave me alone."

She leapt out of her chair, tossing her head so that her hair fell in a red-gold cloud around her face. "If you don't get out of my room immediately I'll call the manager. Or make a scene. You English hate scenes, don't you," she said, moving towards him. She caught the look in his eye and stopped. She unclenched her fists and laughed out loud. There wasn't the slightest chance of the manager, or anyone, coming to her aid but she felt she had won a moral victory after being very close to defeat.

Barnes watched her like an ornithologist studying a rare species. Then he put his hand inside the breast pocket of his jacket and pulled out an envelope. He took the letter out slowly and handed it to Mairin. She stared at it suspiciously then recoiled, the colour draining from her face.

"You recognise this, don't you, Miss Duffy?" Barnes said gently. "It's from an Irish friend of Grogan's who works at Fairford. It was sent to Dublin three weeks ago and it's signed Padraig."

"Where did you get it?" Mairin said, her voice almost a whisper.

"We looked through your room half an hour ago while you were asleep. We must have missed Grogan by minutes. But one thing struck me as odd."

"What?"

"Are you in the habit of keeping your boy-friend's private mail in your handbag?" Barnes paused. "I think he would be very upset if he knew."

"I found it lying around in the flat and I was going to give it back to him . . . Oh, God!" Mairin sat down heavily in her chair, the fight gone out of her. "What are you going to do?" she asked dully.

"Pursue our enquiries, as we say," Barnes replied standing up. "That will be all for the moment, Miss Duffy. Thank you," he added politely.

"Just a minute," said Mairin, getting to her feet.

"Yes. . . ?" said Barnes, turning back from the door.

"How did you find us here?"

"Aha," he smiled. "People often underrate country police forces. Some of them are really rather good."

Barnes paused for a second as he turned to go.

"Have a nice holiday," he said.

19

BARNES HURRIED ALONG THE CORRIDOR. It was all very well playing little games with hot-tempered Irish girls but he had urgent business to transact. The pace was quickening. There had always been a temptation, he'd found, to linger over minor victories in the chase. He had trained himself to avoid indulgence of that kind. That way the scent often went cold. But so far there hadn't been much of a breathing space. He had been woken up at 3 a.m. that morning by an excited Franks who was already at the Yard with the news that a girl answering Mairin's description had been seen the afternoon before in Cheltenham. The local police, though sound and painstaking, didn't have the same concept of urgency as people like Barnes and Franks. It had taken some time for the information to filter through to the operations rooms in New Scotland Yard. Franks had driven straight into the office and contacted Barnes. Within half an hour the two Special Branch men had been in an official and very powerful car on the M4, heading westwards.

When Barnes came down the stairs Franks and a senior

officer of the Gloucestershire Constabulary were waiting for him in the lobby of the hotel. They were chatting with the manager, a florid-looking man in a canary-coloured waistcoat. "How did it go?" asked Franks, detaching himself from the others.

"Not bad," said Barnes, smiling. "She's a tough one all right." He gave Franks a quick run-down of what had happened. "Now, I'd better get going," he said. "Is the car ready?"

"Standing by."

"Fine. Give the girl a few minutes to get dressed, then pull her in," Barnes said briskly.

"What are we going to do with her?" asked Franks.

"Hold her for a few hours. Let's see what comes out of Fairford. She may be very useful yet."

Franks nodded. "Good luck in Fairford," he said. "It sounds a bit like the proverbial needle in the haystack to me."

Barnes shrugged. He went over to have a quick word with the Gloucestershire police officer and the manager. Five minutes later he was being driven out to the Concorde Flight Test Centre on the road Grogan had taken twenty-four hours before.

The chief security officer, a sallow-faced man in his late forties who had spent twenty years in the Military Police, was waiting for him at the entrance of the main office block of the Test Centre with two local CID men. Barnes shook hands and was led into a comfortable office in the corner of the building. It looked out over the airfield and the main hangars.

"Your message was passed on to me at home, Chief Superintendent," said the security officer. "I've been working on it since I came into the office, but I'm afraid it doesn't make much sense to me. We've never had any trouble here before, you know," he said sceptically. "Are you sure this is not some sort of elaborate hoax?"

"Dead sure," said Barnes coldly. He handed the other man the letter they had found in Mairin's handbag. The security Officer took it gingerly as if it had been brushed by the plague. He placed it carefully on the desk in front of him and read it slowly, his hands propping up his head. "I see it gives the Centre as an address, but that doesn't mean a thing."

"Do you know anyone with this name?" Barnes pointed to the signature.

"No. I can't even pronounce it," the security officer said gloomily.

"It's Padraig," said Barnes, looking towards the two CID men who shifted uncomfortably in their chairs.

"Sounds Irish to me," said one of them cautiously.

Barnes took a deep, silent breath.

"How many employees do you have here?" he asked, turning back to the security officer.

"Eight hundred and fifty-six men and two hundred and thirty women."

"You have personal files on all of them?"

"Yes . . . and a card index system too," replied the security officer. "Everyone is carefully vetted before being taken on. We don't employ any riff-raff here, you know."

Barnes groaned inwardly. Why were these sort of people always so bloody defensive? It would save everyone so much time and sweat if they could simply accept that occasionally a bad apple could slip into the barrel. And that the only logical thing to do was to root it out.

"I'd like to have a look at those cards," he said shortly.

The security officer, moving at the slow, deliberate pace of a man on his second career and comfortably cushioned by the pension derived from his first, led him up the stairs to the next floor and through a door marked: PERSONNEL OFFICE — AUTHORISED STAFF ON OFFICIAL BUSINESS ONLY. A mousy woman in her fifties with a crisp manner guided Barnes over to a phalanx of filing cabinets in the corner of the room. Barnes smiled at her pleasantly and sensed he had an ally.

"Could we run through the cards quickly and pull out any with the name 'Padraig'? Also any Irish-sounding names, no matter how remote?"

The archivist nodded briskly and started flicking through the index. Soon there was a pile of thirty or so on the table. Barnes thumbed through them. There were no 'Padraigs' either as a surname or a Christian name.

"Would you mind having another look?" Barnes asked.

The archivist, with good grace, started at the beginning again. Only one card, a Kennedy, joined the stack on the table.

Barnes stared at the cards. "Just a minute," he said sharply.

"Padraig is Gaelic for Patrick—let's sort out the Patricks among this lot."

Five Patricks—all first names—became a separate pile.

"Good," he said. "Now let's have the personal files to match these names."

The archivist went off to another filing cabinet and returned carrying five dark-green folders. Barnes took them from her. He divided them amongst the two CID men and the security officer, keeping a couple for himself.

"I want you to take a careful look through. Tell me if any of these men had any connection at all in the past with the British army," he said.

Nothing could be heard for the next five minutes except a rustling of papers and the chirping of birds on a large elm tree outside the window.

"There's an ex-army chap here," the security officer suddenly said. "Patrick O'Sullivan, joined the Irish Guards, September 1939, promoted corporal January 1942, Normandy campaign. Awarded the Military Medal for bravery in the field."

"When was he demobbed?" Barnes asked sharply, looking up.

"October 1946."

"No good I'm afraid."

The security officer grunted and pushed the file aside.

"Here's another," said one of the CID men.

"Let's have it," said Barnes.

"Patrick Kenny, born in Ireland 1932; joined the Royal Electrical and Mechanical Engineers in 1955, having become a qualified motor mechanic after leaving school; did his basic training in . . ."

"Where did he serve?" Barnes cut in.

"Let me see . . . yes, here it is. British Army of the Rhine, 1956 to 1958, a year back in England attached to Western Command, then Cyprus . . ."

"That's our man," said Barnes jumping to his feet. "Where is he now?"

"Working in No. 2 Maintenance Bay, I should imagine," said the security officer, peering at Kenny's file. "Bloody hell, I never thought he was an Irishman."

"Get him up to your office, at the double," said Barnes, the authority now unmistakable in his voice. He thanked the archivist and hurried out. The two CID men exchanged looks and followed him downstairs.

Kenny had been up to his elbows in an intricate part of the Concorde's Rolls-Royce-Snecma engines when the summons, delivered in person by the chief security officer, came. For a moment, his mind went completely blank. Then he knew. His head spun and his legs felt weak. As he preceded the security officer along the passage-way connecting the workshops with the administrative buildings, he pulled himself together. He had done nothing, after all. He hadn't committed any crime. What was wrong in having a chat with an old mate? They had no evidence. His talk with Jimmy couldn't have been overheard, could it?

Barnes was sitting beside the security officer's desk, his legs crossed, when Kenny entered the room. The two CID men were standing by the window, talking quietly.

"When did you last see James Grogan, Kenny?" Barnes said, sizing up the little Irishman in the greasy overalls.

"Years ago, back in the army I think it was," Kenny replied carefully. "And who might you be, if I may ask?"

"This gentleman is a police officer—from Scotland Yard, Mr Kenny," the security officer said hurriedly. The thought that all this upheaval might lead to trouble with the unions had just struck him.

"Don't bullshit me, my friend," said Barnes, getting slowly to his feet and going across to the technician. "We know all about you—and Grogan."

He paused. "You saw him here yesterday, didn't you? What did you tell him?"

"Nothing . . . I mean I didn't see him . . . I haven't seen him for years." Kenny smiled nervously and looked at the others, as if for corroboration. His usual brisk chirpiness seemed to have deserted him.

"Then what the hell is all this about?" said Barnes in a hectoring tone, waving the letter in front of Kenny's nose. "Would you deny this is your handwriting? It looks remarkably like the spider's shit scrawl on this application form of yours here." Barnes picked up Kenny's green personal file from the table.

The Irishman stood silent, his thin arms hanging at his side.

"How many kids do you have, Kenny?" Barnes asked.

"Three . . . and a fourth on the way," Kenny said miserably.

"You value your job, don't you?"

The technician nodded. The silence hung heavily in the room. For a moment no one moved or said anything, a frozen tableau of four men breaking the will of their defenceless victim.

"And you want to keep it, don't you?" Barnes continued remorselessly.

Kenny nodded again. His voice had abandoned him, like everything else it seemed.

"Right," said Barnes, breaking the spell. "Let's talk business. You tell me all you know about Grogan and I'll see what I can do for you. You've got yourself far deeper in the shit than you'll ever know. Now sit down and be careful not to miss a thing."

Kenny slumped onto a chair but, remembering how dirty he was, he kept his arms on his lap. The posture was awkward and emphasised his vulnerability. In a quiet voice he told Barnes of his exchange of letters with Grogan, finishing with a description of their meeting in Fairford and their visit to the airfield. One of the CID men made notes. Afterwards Kenny read them through and signed them, Barnes told him he could go back to his work but not to leave the area for the next ten days. As he turned to leave, Kenny looked back at the Special Branch man.

"Grogan wasn't going to hurt anybody," he said. "It would have happened at night, if it had happened at all."

Barnes looked at him thoughtfully. "So you fell for that," he said. "Use your head, man, it just doesn't make sense. Grogan isn't the sort of man for sneaky bangs in the night. He's in the first division. With him it would be an explosion in the air, with as many people on board as possible."

As the door closed, Barnes swung round on the security officer.

"Two things—fast," he said abruptly. "First I want a thorough search of the aircraft, the workshops, the maintenance sheds and these offices. Second, the tightest possible clampdown. Double security checks and guards. And this story must stay inside these walls."

The security officer was looking worried but nodded. Barnes told him to get BAC's managing director or his personal assistant on the phone and to put in a call to the director of the Test Centre. As he was talking the telephone rang. The security officer passed the receiver to him. It was Franks, his voice taut.

"Can you get over right away? I've just had a flash from London. Jack Fitchett was shot dead in Kilburn last night."

Barnes motioned to the CID man. The security officer spoke as they were going through the door.

"What shall we do about Kenny?" he asked anxiously.

"Sack him, of course," Barnes said.

"Of course."

The last few days had been busy and full of suspense for Humphrey James. A flurry of telegrams had passed between London, Dublin and Belfast. It appeared from this distance that Interface's proposition was being taken very seriously It was also being restricted to Secret Service channels. Finally, three days after his meeting with Interface, a telegram arrived from London saying that John Calvert-Jones, the Controller responsible for Ireland, was flying over the next day. James was to arrange the earliest possible meeting with Interface. James was lucky and got through to his home that night. He would be at the safe flat at eleven thirty the next morning, which meant James could meet Calvert-Jones at the airport and take him straight there.

The following morning in the car, legs elegantly crossed in the front passenger seat, Calvert-Jones brought James up-to-date.

"As you can imagine, we've had the most awful chaos. Chaps running to and from the Cabinet Office, FCO, Home Office and us, like balls on a pin-table. The Chief and Frank Robinson have had to see the PM twice. In the end we've got a pretty open-ended brief, as you'll see."

James looked at his Controller. Calvert-Jones was wearing an immaculate grey flannel suit with a red pin-stripe, a cream silk shirt and a maroon tie. James couldn't help glancing down at his own suit, which looked like something from a shop in Shaftesbury Avenue in comparison.

"Are they taking his threats seriously?" he asked.

"They're bound to, Humphrey." A flicker of irritation crossed Calvert-Jones's smooth face. "You know what security in the UK is like. Wide open. Another of the prices of running a democracy, if you like. If the IRA really have a number of men like Grogan ready to strike, we're in trouble. We don't know who they are. Nor where they'll strike. It's a politician's nightmare, of course."

Calvert-Jones uncrossed his legs and smoothed the knees of his trousers.

"The point is," he continued, "the IRA are asking for secret talks. That we can deliver. And I might say I'm glad to see our service being used in its proper role for a change. Now whether the IRA are bluffing—though I am inclined to doubt it—and whether our friend can pull together the Official and Provisional wings, that remains to be seen. All I can tell you is that the problem is being handled in a number of different ways, if you understand me. What *I* am authorised to do is to talk. At this point in time, my job is to hold off any IRA action in England."

"Do you want to brief the Ambassador later in the day?" James asked.

"No. For the time being this is between SIS and the Cabinet Office. I'll probably be staying in Dublin for a few days, possibly a week, and things may change in that time. We'll see."

James parked the car a few streets away from the safe flat and they walked there. Once inside, James went into the kitchen to make coffee, bringing a tray into the sitting room, as the front-door buzzer sounded.

"Shall I introduce you by your own name?" James asked.

Calvert-Jones grimaced.

"Might as well play this one by the book. Call me John Holland."

A moment later, James showed the visitor into the sitting room. He seemed not at all surprised to see another person in the room. James took his coat.

"Mr. Kelly," James said, "may I introduce a senior colleague from London, John Holland?"

15

Calvert-Jones stood up and the two men shook hands. They sat on opposite sides of the table while James served them coffee.

Calvert-Jones spoke first.

"The Cabinet Office has authorised me to be its representative. You may take it that I shall report back directly. This, in effect, means that our conversation will go to the Prime Minister himself." He paused for a moment. "We have examined your proposition very carefully, Mr. Kelly. I think you will understand what I mean when I say that, in giving you a first reaction, we are aware that we are taking a number of your statements on trust. However, you have declared that as a token of goodwill you wished to talk first rather than act—a statement that, in the context of present difficulties, we appreciate. In return I am authorised to tell you that the British Government is prepared to discuss, informally, without any prior commitments and through the channel of my service, possible solutions to the present problems. I would suggest that in the first place you and I between us can go quite a long way towards establishing our respective positions, without calling on any other persons from either side to be present. Is that satisfactory to you?"

"It's a step forward, Mr. Holland," Kelly said without much enthusiasm. "But there's a limit to the time I can spend acting as a kind of Lone Ranger. We have now formed a special IRA Council, from both wings. People with power and influence in the movement, who wish to see a speedy end to the present divisions. I can act as their spokesman in a preliminary meeting. But I thought I had made it clear to Mr. James here that what we want are secret negotiations, not a series of informal talks, tête-à-tête, between me and the British Secret Service."

The two men studied each other carefully before Calvert-Jones broke the silence.

"I accept your standpoint about negotiations," he said, "I hope that in return you will accept me, initially at least, as the negotiator on our side. If you wish to bring some of your colleagues to our next meeting, I would also agree to that. But there is one proviso I am instructed to make before we can take things any further . . . It appears that your gunmen are con-

ducting some kind of private war in London." Calvert-Jones
was speaking now in a tightly-controlled voice. "We believe
this man Grogan is somewhere in the middle of it. We've just
heard that a Special Branch officer has been murdered in
London. We want this war to stop. And we want Grogan."

"I've already told Mr. James that I can control Grogan,'
Kelly said evenly. "But let's be quite clear about this. I am not
going to hand you Grogan on a plate. What I will do is stop
him."

"Then do so," Calvert-Jones said tersely. "When you've done
that, we can discuss an agenda."

Kelly stood up. "I understand," he said softly, looking at
Calvert-Jones. "I'll deal with Grogan immediately. I will contact Mr. James when it's done. Then, perhaps, we can begin
talks in earnest."

Calvert-Jones stood up. This time the two men didn't shake
hands. James felt the tension between them lying heavily in the
room. At the door Kelly nodded, without his normal courtesy,
by way of farewell. James turned back and before rejoining
Calvert-Jones he breathed in, once, very deeply. He felt a sense
of disappointment. The meeting had been something of an
anti-climax, yet he knew that there were developments still to
come. Somehow, he felt that a lot of movement had taken
place, almost too fast, and that what was left from now on
would be just hard slogging, monotonous work. It occurred to
him suddenly that he must choose the right psychological
moment to ask Calvert-Jones for a change of secretary.

As Kelly walked out of the building, he sifted over his im-
pressions of the man he'd just met. Pretty much what he might
have expected. Trust the British to appear to agree to something and at the very same moment pull back so as to give the
minimum ground possible. And that only in exchange for
something they wanted badly.

But on the whole, Kelly decided he was satisfied. He was on
the verge of success. He'd been lucky so far that Grogan hadn't
made his move. Of course, if he had, Kelly could have blamed
it on the slowness of the British Government's response. He had
been walking a tightrope but he'd managed to keep his balance.
What he had to do now was settle the issue. Since he couldn't
see Grogan listening to reason from O'Flaherty or the Shoeman,

there was only one way of doing it. Kelly turned into a post office and went into a telephone booth. There was a delay in getting through. But soon he was speaking to Frank in Kilburn. He'd briefed him the night before to stay by the phone.

"Any news?" he asked.

"Not a thing. Nothing since last night's spot of trouble."

"Well, listen carefully. The boys have got to get Grogan right away. We can't afford any more delays—or mistakes. When they find Grogan they've to finish him. A nice clean job. Then they're to get back here as fast as they can. Got that?"

"I'll be in touch with them right away."

"Good. Give them all the help you can, Frank."

Kelly replaced the receiver carefully and stared at it before shaking his head slowly. It ought to work. If it didn't, well, he still had room to manœuvre. A series of alternatives presented themselves to him as he walked out into the street. He smiled wryly to himself. Politics was a demanding occupation.

20

THE NEXT FEW HOURS in Chief Superintendent Barnes' eventful life were among the most frantic he could remember. Fitchett's murder gave the crisis a vicious twist. But he knew he had to put it to one side for the moment. He was bound to see things through here first. Half his problem was that he had an imagination. Yet even if he fell back on cold logic, the scenario remained unnerving. James Grogan was a professional killer and a demolitions expert. He was in England and had just carried out a reconnaissance of the Concorde testing gound. Gelignite had been stolen in various parts of the country and one of the robberies—the biggest, as it happened —carried the hallmark of a man of Grogan's calibre. There were almost a million Irishmen living freely in England. From the Republic they shuttled back and forth to England every day of the week without passports, exempt from immigration controls. The Irish in England, Barnes reflected, represented a potentially terrifying fifth column. Kenny had helped Grogan when he clearly wasn't a member of the IRA and had everything to lose—and nothing to gain—by sticking his neck out. And yet he had done it without, apparently, a second thought. How many other Kennys were there around? It was as bad as the bloody Mafia. There was another depressing thought. Had Grogan come over with other IRA men? The Duffy girl was obviously mixed up in it and the IRA usually operated in small commando units. It would be highly unlikely that he was working alone.

The telephone on the security officer's desk rang. Barnes, who had taken over the office temporarily while its owner was busy with the search operation, picked up the receiver. It was the secretary of the British Aircraft Corporation's managing director. Her boss, she said, could see Barnes in half an hour but, she added tartly, he was a very busy man. Barnes swore under his breath but said a polite thank you and rang off. He wondered what the Corporation's reaction would be when they heard the news. The Concorde, its development costs now hovering near the thousand million pound mark, had been savaged in the press recently. *The Observer*, he recalled, had launched a broadside over the plane's controversial operating costs. And though the British Government had given the green light to the aircraft, it was still far from certain whether the major airlines would take up their increasingly expensive options. An explosion in mid-flight, sabotage on the ground, even a mysterious 'scare' could well scupper the whole project — or at least set it back with disastrous effects on its sales. And then what about the Frogs — they owned half the thing, didn't they? Barnes groaned and made a mental note to contact Dufournet in Paris as soon as he had a moment.

There was a knock on the door and one of the Gloucestershire CID men came in to report that police reinforcements were on their way from Bristol and Cheltenham. The search was going on, discreet screening of Irish members of the staff had begun and the Corporation's security force had been given a special briefing on extra precautions they were to take. Barnes thanked him and put a call through to New Scotland Yard. He'd better put things straight with his boss before the local police started complaining about Special Branch poaching on their domain. They'd done it before, admittedly with good reason, Barnes thought grinning, but the salvoes were still echoing. In any case, the new tough Commissioner, Robert Mark, would want to know exactly what was happening.

Christ, it could develop into a national emergency! That was
the trouble, he thought, you get so involved in the details of a
case that you often lose sight of its wider implications.

But it wasn't all gloom. There was no indication, he reflected,
that Grogan had been in Fairford earlier than yesterday.
Kenny had appeared to be telling the truth when he swore that
it had been the first time he'd seen Grogan for years. According
to the hotel manager the IRA man and the girl had only
checked in the day before. Though they could have been in the
area for some time, perhaps under another name.

If no other trace of IRA activity in the Fairford district was
found then it seemed likely that Grogan's mission was a recce,
nothing more. Barnes rubbed his chin reflectively. But you
could never be sure. And then if Grogan was thwarted there
where would he strike next? Barnes wrenched his thoughts back
to the present. He picked up the telephone and asked for
Cheltenham police headquarters. He must talk to Franks. An
idea, a strategy of attack, was slowly forming in his mind.

The phone rang again just as he put the receiver down. It
was London.

"What's going on down there?" the familiar fruity voice of
his boss boomed, as if he were in the room. "We've already had
a query from Bristol CID. Fill me in."

Barnes winced. Modern communications could work against
you sometimes, damn it. He gave a succinct summary of what
had happened and outlined the measures he proposed to take.

"That's fine," said the other man, "but don't take the law
into your own hands. Clear all the major moves with the BAC
people. I'll back you up to the hilt at this end, though if the
thing escalates, you realise it will go over our heads." The traditional buck-passing operation grinding into motion, Barnes
thought sourly. When police officers reach the age and seniority
of his superior, their primary consideration seems to be to keep
their lily-white records clean so that nothing happens to their
pensions.

"Will you inform the Commissioner?" Barnes asked.

"Yes, and the Security Service. But," he added, "let's hold
this one for the Branch as long as we can—at least on the
operational level. Right?"

Barnes said: "Fine." Now the crafty bugger wanted the

glory too. He sighed, cut the connection and joggled the receiver rest until the Fairford operator answered. This time he got straight through to Franks. It was a relief to hear his businesslike voice.

"How's the girl?" he asked.

"Shouting for a lawyer and refusing to eat." He laughed. "You'd *need* to be a gunman to keep her in line."

"We must hang on to her for as long as we can," said Barnes tersely. "She's all we've got—and don't let anyone get near her." He knew he was edging out towards the brink but it had to be done.

"Don't worry," said Franks calmly, "I'll see to it. What next?"

Barnes spoke rapidly for the next five minutes. Franks interrupted him one or twice and seemed to be taking notes. When Barnes had finished he said: "What about Concorde?"

"I think I can handle most of it from here," Barnes replied. "I've set up a kind of ops room in the Test Centre and the Chief's in the picture."

"Do you need any help from London?" Franks asked.

"I could do with one of the bomb boys—preferably someone who knows a bit about aeroplanes, hijacking and sabotage techniques . . . that sort of thing."

"Right," said Franks. "By the way, a piece of news from London. You remember asking for a follow-up on the quarry raid in Scotland? Well, apparently two men were seen in the area in a foreign car. An old Citroën, black with yellow wheels."

"Thanks," Barnes said.

Franks said he would keep in close touch and rang off.

Barnes looked quickly at his watch. It seemed incredible that it was only mid-morning. He must try to keep his mind on his first responsibility—Concorde. But there was, he realised ruefully, an unrelenting temptation to veer away and pursue Grogan while the scent was still fresh. There was a knock on the door and one of the CID men came in and agreed to hold the fort for the next hour or so. Barnes stood up, stretched like a big cat, picked up his notes and left the room. He had decided that, tactically, it would be better to have a talk with the director of the Centre before bearding the Corporation's top man. As he turned into the corridor he heard a noise which at first was meaningless and then, suddenly understanding, made his blood run cold. Christ Almighty! He sprinted along the passage, swung left at the end, almost colliding with a cleaning woman and her bucket, and tore over to the open window. Below him, in a perfect bird's-eye-view was the Concorde, glistening silver in the sun, slowly rolling out of its hangar onto the tarmac apron. Barnes opened his mouth involuntarily to shout a warning then closed it with a snap. A lot of good that would do. A blast of noise rolled up from the hangar's walls as the aircraft pivoted slowly beneath him.

Barnes swung round and ran back down the corridor. The director's office, he had been told, was on the floor above at the opposite end of the building. He reached the stairs and leapt up them, two at a time. For such a solidly built man he moved with surprising speed. A couple of chattering mini-skirted secretaries stared at him in astonishment as he raced past them down the corridor. His eye flickered over the polished brass name plates as he ran. There it was: DIRECTOR OF OPERATIONS. He burst through the door, past a severe-looking middle-aged secretary who half rose in her chair, bristling like a Staffordshire bull-terrier, and then he was through the second door into the inner officer.

"STOP THAT PLANE," Barnes yelled, face flushed, fighting to regain his breath.

A grey-haired man with a strong square face and clipped moustache stared at him as if he were insane.

"Who the hell are you?" he said angrily, rising to his feet. "What the devil do you mean by breaking into my office like this?"

Barnes raised a hand, as if he were blessing the multitude, and said more calmly: "I'm Barnes, from Special Branch . . . We spoke on the phone half an hour ago. I've been investigating an IRA case here with your security officer. I'll give you the details later but first you *must stop that Concorde*." He could see incredulity in the other man's eyes. "You've got to believe me," he went on hurriedly, "one of your employees has been giving restricted information to an IRA sabotage squad . . ." Soup it up, he thought, as long as the message gets across . . . "They may not have moved yet, but we can't afford to take the risk."

The director had sat down again and was listening intently. Bewilderment was supplanting disbelief on his face. "But it's a special test flight we've had scheduled for ages. It's also a pre-paration for tomorrow. We've got PAN-AM and several other very important customers coming down for the demonstration flight. It could be crucial for sales."

"What I'm trying to say," said Barnes, his voice rising again, "is there may be a bloody bomb on board your precious air-craft!" He said it slowly, like a patient teacher dealing with a retarded child.

This time it worked. The director's ruddy face paled a little and he began to look alarmed.

"All right," he said. "I'll do it but I warn you that there will have to be a post-mortem into this at the highest level. We simply can't hold up work every time there's a minor security scare . . . we're already far behind schedule." He picked up the green telephone on his desk.

"Control Room," he said, a new decisiveness in his voice. "Hullo, Norman, something important's come up. We've got to cancel Flight 127 . . . Yes, that's what I said, cancel it imme-diately . . . I know, I know . . . I'll tell you later, but get that plane back into its hangar as fast as you can . . . OK? Oh, and Norman . . . I want this kept as quiet as possible . . . tell them that there has been a re-scheduling of flights due to more customers coming down . . . yes, anything that sounds con-vincing. And for Christ's sake don't let anyone talk to the press until we've had time to think something out."

Barnes let his body go limp in the chair. It was done. All he had to do was pick up the pieces. The director was talking again, on another phone, to the Centre's public information officer. Barnes waited until he had finished, then briefed him in detail, again playing up the dangers a little more than the facts warranted. The man took it more calmly than he had expected and showed a refreshingly practical turn of mind now that the initial shock had receded. He lost no time in putting his finger on the central dilemma.

"All right, so we carry out the security clamp-down you say is necessary," he said bluntly. "But how on earth do we stop word getting out? The press, especially those anti-Concorde bastards, will have a field-day. It's not even a question of plugging leaks. If Concorde stops flying—that's news, no matter how we dress it up."

"I think I can arrange for a D Notice to go out," said Barnes quickly, plunging into deep water. He hoped like hell his boss was still with him.

"That's all very well as far as the *reason* for the cancellation is concerned; but it won't prevent the local press and the agencies simply reporting the fact that the Concorde has stopped flying. *That* doesn't endanger national security, does it? And then," he added, sounding harassed again, "what about our customers? PAN-AM, absolutely vital for American orders, what about them?" He stopped suddenly. "Oh, Christ . . ."

"What's wrong?"

"Princess Alexandra . . . she's due to fly next week . . ." He consulted a well-thumbed desk diary, "Wednesday afternoon."

"Don't worry about that," Barnes said soothingly, "we'll have everything tied up by then. One of our best explosives experts will be down here later today and with luck we may have everything sewn up tomorrow."

The director looked dubious but nodded his head. Barnes told him of his appointment with the managing director. He should have been there twenty minutes ago. The director suggested that they should go together. He told his secretary, who scowled at Barnes as the two men walked through the outer office, to let him know that they were on their way.

About the time Barnes was closeted with the managing director of the British Aircraft Corporation, James Grogan entered a telephone booth in Waterloo Station. He asked the operator to put him through to the Old King's Head hotel in Cheltenham. A girl's voice came over the line.

"Can I help you?" she said.

"I'd like to speak to Mrs. Langton, room 216, please," Grogan replied.

"I'm awfully sorry, sir, but she's not here . . . who's speaking?"

"This is her husband," said Grogan shortly. "Do you know when she'll be back?"

"I . . ." The girl seemed to be talking to someone else in the room. "Here is the manager, sir," she said abruptly.

"Mr. Langton," the voice was deep and meaty, "I am afraid I have some very bad news for you. Your wife left the hotel this morning at about ten o'clock. To do a little sightseeing, I presume," he added unctuously. "As she was crossing the road she was knocked down by a car which had swerved to avoid a dog."

Grogan was stunned. It couldn't be right.

"Is she all right? Where is she now?" A moment of panic struck him. Mairin, so healthy, so alive . . . to be maimed or killed in a road accident to save a bloody dog, it just couldn't be.

"She was rushed by ambulance to Cheltenham General Hospital," the manager said. "I couldn't really say what her chances are, Mr. Langton, but when I phoned half an hour ago they said she had sustained severe head injuries and was being operated on."

"Do you have the hospital number there?"

"Yes . . . Cheltenham 24718," the manager said. "I'm sorry I can't do more. You have my deepest sympathies, Mr. Langton." The PR touch even to the grave, Grogan thought sourly. "Should I hold your room for you? I imagine you will be down right away—there's a train in forty minutes' time from Paddington."

"Yes . . . do that. And thanks." He rang off then dialled the operator again. His call to Cheltenham General Hospital was taken by an efficient young woman who confirmed that a Mrs. Charles Langton had indeed been admitted earlier that morning suffering from head injuries received in a traffic accident in the middle of the town. Mrs. Langton was still undergoing surgery and they could not give a considered estimate of her condition until the operation was over.

"What are the chances?" Grogan persisted.

"I'll put you through to a senior house surgeon," the hospital receptionist said.

The surgeon, a gruff-voiced man, refused at first to meet Grogan's question head on, but finally put them at about 'fifty-fifty'.

Grogan put the receiver down and cursed under his breath. He had thirty-five minutes to get across London and catch that train. But he needed time to think. His mind was spinning. He walked out of the station, hailed the taxi at the top of the rank and settled back to think as the driver swore his way through London's congested streets.

Grogan decided to take the Cheltenham train, then re-jected the idea. He wavered again. He would have to make a decision by the time he reached Paddington. After the immediate blow had fallen, his first thoughts were about the effect Mairin's accident would have on his operational plans. She might have her Irish passport with her or other papers identifying her as 'Mairin Duffy'. But so what? She had used a false name at the hotel. That wasn't a crime, was it? And there was no reason why the police should be on to her . . . or himself, for that matter. So, on the surface, there was a mini-mum of risk to be run by going down to see her. It could be a little embarrassing with the hospital over the 'husband and wife' gambit which was blown, but he could ride that easily enough. And then, of course, he *should* go down, for Mairin's sake. He knew the psychological effect of seeing someone close can sometimes make the difference between life and death. He'd seen soldiers die not because they lacked adequate medical attention but because their mates were not around them at the crucial moment. If Mairin died without him having made the effort to be with her and comfort her, would he ever forgive himself? He thought again of his father, who had died alone. There seemed to be a malignant spirit guiding his destiny whenever his affections were involved.

The taxi swung round Marble Arch with a screech of tyres. The driver was one of that London breed who always goes fast whether you tell him or not — and probably had an ulcer to prove it. But the swaying movement broke Grogan's train of thought. He sat upright. What if the police *were* on to him? Wouldn't they look around for a way to trap him? And what better way than to use his girl? He had no evidence. Only a feeling that some-thing wasn't quite right. As the taxi turned into Paddington station, Grogan's mind was made up. He paid the man and headed for the nearest phone box. As he dialled a number he was almost deafened by an announcement booming out of a loudspeaker above his head. The Cheltenham train, a sepul-chral voice said, was subject to a delay of fifteen minutes.

Grogan looked at his watch. He had almost twenty-five minutes in hand. With luck, he thought, that should be enough.

Muldoon was at home.

"Cathal," Grogan said urgently, "I may be in a bit of trouble. There's something I've got to check up on quickly . . . Do you know anyone reliable who has good contacts in the nursing profession. There must be thousands of Irish nurses working in hospitals all over this country?"

"There are . . . Margaret was a ward sister herself for several years, in Bart's," Muldoon replied. "But she's been out of touch for some time . . . let me see . . . I could take you along to see a cousin of mine tomorrow . . ."

"Tomorrow's too late," said Grogan tersely. "I must find out something from Cheltenham General Hospital now, right now."

"Cheltenham, Cheltenham," Muldoon pondered for a moment. "Look, Jimmy, I'll get on to an old friend of Margaret's who knows someone working in one of the big Bristol hospitals. Give me your number and I'll ring you back as soon as I can."

Grogan stood in the box, idly flicking over the pages of a telephone directory, trying to keep calm. It was a long shot, but he had to try it. If only he knew more about hospitals, he might be able to edge in under the protective shield the police had thrown round their bait. Assuming that it was a trap of course. There was a knock on the glass door of the booth. A red-faced man in a brown trilby and a British Warm was tapping on the glass with his signet ring. "Have you finished?" he mouthed. "I must say you've been a devil of a time in there. You don't seem to be using the phone."

Grogan swung round and saw a line of people waiting. Sod him. He stared at the red-faced man, mouthed a piece of soundless gibberish back and returned to the directory. The next minute the phone rang.

Muldoon, triumph in his voice, had traced the woman in Bristol and had just finished speaking to her.

"But there's more to come, Jimmy," he went on excitedly. "She worked in Cheltenham herself until a couple of months ago and has friends there. What do you want to know?"

"Can she find out, discreetly and without going through the main channels, whether a young woman called Mrs. Charles

Langton was admitted and operated on this morning after a bad road accident?"

"She can have a bloody good try," said Muldoon cheerily. "Stay with it, kid. . . . I'll ring you back."

Grogan ducked his head and looked out at the station clock. The red-faced man had half-turned away. He was gesticulating angrily to the next man in the queue. Fourteen minutes to go. the man in the next booth finished his call and left. Grogan now had 'Red-Face' on his flank. He gave him a cold stare and turned his back. What can you do in a public telephone box when you're waiting for an urgent call? Grogan pulled more loose change out of his pocket, put it on the coin box and stared into the mirror. He looked haggard; the vertical lines on his face were deeply drawn. He sensed that Red-Face on his left was scowling at him again. He checked his watch. Five minutes left. Then the phone rang. A marvellous sound.

"Jimmy . . ." Cathal's voice seemed strained.

"Yes?"

"She talked to an Irish girl who works in the theatre at Cheltenham hospital."

"What did she say?"

"Never heard of your lady. All they had this morning was one burst appendix, a cartilage and a five-year-old kid who swallowed a sparking plug."

"Is she absolutely certain?"

"As sure as pigs don't fly," Muldoon said. "She checked yesterday's operations too . . . nothing there either. Who is she?"

"I'll tell you later. Cathal, I always said you're a great man, now you're canonised. The heat's on. So don't try and get in touch with me—whatever happens. Can I keep the attic for the time being?"

"As long as you like," Muldoon paused. "Ring me when you can. See you soon." He rang off.

Grogan put the receiver down slowly. His mind was racing. The bastards, the clever bastards. They'd got Mairin, God knows how, and set the whole thing up . . . The manager, the hospital receptionist, the 'house surgeon', probably half a dozen others too. A good operation. But The Irish 'underground' had punched a hole in it. They couldn't hold Mairin indefinitely. Nor could they pin any charges on her. She'd do the sensible thing, he was sure, and make her way back to Dublin as soon as they let her out. But he wasn't going to stop now. It would have to be Millennium.

Grogan stepped out of the telephone booth at precisely the same moment as the red-faced man. The station was swarming with people now, the early build-up to the rush hour. The red-faced man was still determined, it seemed, to have the last word. He turned towards the tall Irishman and opened his mouth. The two men, jostled by the crowd, appeared to be locked together for a fleeting second. There was a sharp crack that sounded like hard leather on bone, a deep groan and then nothing as the pale, taut faces swirled by. It was only when a commuter almost tripped and fell over an inert body that the forward movement of people past the telephone boxes was checked. A small circle gathered round. Looking down they saw a middle-aged man dressed in a British Warm overcoat lying on the ground. He had a red face and underneath his arm was a crushed brown trilby.

21

O'FLAHERTY AND THE SHOEMAN turned into the cobbled street and walked up it for a hundred yards. They swung right at the end and found themselves in a cul-de-sac. On the left was the double mews house with its workshop and garage underneath, and the ornate sign above: CATHAL MULDOON & SONS. O'Flaherty, who was in the lead, raised a warning hand. They stood close to the angle of the wall and looked across at Muldoon's house. A yellow light was on upstairs, gleaming behind a lace curtain. O'Flaherty nodded to the Shoeman. They walked softly across the cobbles to the front door. The Shoeman tiptoed over to the garage door but it was fastened with a heavy steel padlock. He came back and took a quick look down the mews. He touched O'Flaherty on the arm and the big man leaned heavily on the door bell. The Shoeman sidestepped and stood out of sight to the left of the porch. A window opened upstairs and Muldoon's voice rang out: "Who's there?"

"A friend of Jimmy's from Dublin," O'Flaherty replied.

"It's a hell of a time to come visiting," Muldoon shouted down.

"I know, but I didn't have your telephone number and it's urgent . . . I'm going back early tomorrow morning."

"It's that now . . . All right, I'm coming down."

The head disappeared from the window. There was the sound of heavy footsteps on the stairs and then a bolt being drawn. Muldoon stood framed in the doorway, the yellow light around his shoulders and head like a halo.

"What might your name be, friend?" he said.

"O'Flaherty, Paddy O'Flaherty . . . it won't take long . . . especially if you show a little sensible co-operation."

"What do you mean . . . ?" Muldoon found himself staring at a long-barrelled pistol with a silencer around the muzzle.

"Turn round, nice and easy," O'Flaherty said softly. "Who else is in the house . . . wife, kids?"

"They're in Dublin . . . won't be back for another week . . . what do you want . . . who are you?"

"I'm just on a friendly visit from the old country. Now, up the stairs." O'Flaherty prodded Muldoon.

He followed him up the narrow staircase, leaving the front door open. When they reached the living room where Muldoon and Grogan had talked the night away less than a fortnight ago, O'Flaherty searched the tall Kerryman thoroughly. He pushed him roughly into an armchair and went across the room to close the window. Then he sat down opposite him, straddling a high-backed chair. He pointed the pistol at Muldoon's stomach.

"Where's Grogan?"

"I don't know."

"You know . . . and you'll tell me," O'Flaherty said menacingly. His face was flushed. Small beads of sweat stood out like blisters on his broad forehead. "You were thick as thieves back home, and you've seen him since he came over this time, haven't you?"

"Get stuffed . . . and get out of my house," Muldoon yelled, suddenly losing his temper and lunging out of his chair. O'Flaherty was on his feet in a flash, kicking his chair straight at Muldoon and stepping swiftly to one side. The chair caught Muldoon in the stomach as he came forward, O'Flaherty's massive fist crunched into his face. Muldoon gasped and recoiled. O'Flaherty whipped the pistol barrel across his face, now a mask of blood, two, three, four times. There was a crackle of steel and bone. Muldoon screamed with pain. He sank to his knees groaning, blood gushing on to the dusty carpet. O'Flaherty, eyes flaming, kicked the fallen man hard in the belly. Muldoon screamed again and writhed on the floor, his long thin legs pressed up hard against his chest like some great wounded insect.

"You've seen him, you bastard," O'Flaherty breathed. He lifted his foot again. "Where is he now?"

Muldoon's breath was coming in great rasping sighs . . . "I don't know . . . I saw him but . . ." He choked and retched.

"But what?"

Muldoon groaned again. The pain in his stomach was worse than anything he'd ever known.

"But what?" The voice seemed different.

Muldoon wiped some of the blood out of his eyes and looked up. A thin, putty-faced man stood above him, his face expressionless.

"But what?" he said a third time with the same quiet insistence.

"He said he would contact me . . . that he would be out of reach until he contacted me."

"Where is he hiding?"

"I don't know . . . it's the truth, I don't know," Muldoon whispered, the pain ebbing and flowing in irrepressible waves. The slim man's hand moved fractionally. Muldoong, throuh a veil of blood, saw the light flash on steel. The man's other hand moved, swooping downwards like a bird of prey, and ripped Muldoon's shirt from collar to waist. The knife followed, its point coming to rest gently, almost tenderly, just below Muldoon's left breast.

"Talk, Muldoon," said the Shoeman. "This is it. I don't bluff."

Muldoon felt the knife prick his skin. He tried to put his hand across his eyes but couldn't move. He closed his eyes and when he opened them again, O'Flaherty was up there in the circle of light. He was muttering something about the garage.

"Keys, keys, Muldoon," the pale man said.

"In the desk, top drawer . . ." Muldoon's voice faded away as a fiery darkness overwhelmed him.

O'Flaherty raced down the stairs while the Shoeman went into the kitchen to find some water. A few minutes later, he heard a shout of surprise from O'Flaherty who had reappeared at the foot of the stairs.

"Come and look at this . . . bloody fantastic!"

The Shoeman went back into the living room and put the pitcher of water down on the table. He cast a quick glance at Muldoon, who was still unconscious and breathing heavily on the floor, and went down to join O'Flaherty. The big Irishman had the doors of the garage and workshop open. In the far corner stood the gleaming outline of Muldoon's Citroën. Beside it was a workbench covered with scraps of wood, chisels, handsaws, hammers and scattered nails. But it was an unobtrusive trap-door in the ceiling that had caught O'Flaherty's attention. With the help of a ladder he had climbed up and opened it. A few dozen small packets wrapped in oilproof paper, identical in size, lay on the stone floor of the garage. He took the Shoeman over to the loft and shone a powerful torch up into it. On all sides, stretching away as far as they could see, were neatly-stacked sticks of gelignite.

"Enough to blow up the Europa three times over," breathed O'Flaherty, awe in his voice.

"The lying bastard . . ." The Shoeman spat the words out and turned back to the house. As he did so there was a creak on the stairs and the next second, the gangling and bloodied figure of Muldoon lurched out onto the streets, an apparition from a nightmare with his torn shirt billowing out behind him.

"Jesus Christ, come back!" O'Flaherty yelled. He turned to the workbench, picked up a heavy adjustable spanner and bounded off after the fleeing Muldoon like a huge leopard about to sink his teeth into his prey. Within a few paces he was up to him. Muldoon tried desperately to put on a spurt. He seemed to gain ground then his knees buckled and he slowed. From where the Shoeman was standing it was difficult to see what happened next. O'Flaherty's right arm swung in a high arc, then disappeared in the blackness of the night. But the sickening impact of the blow was clearly audible and the crash of Muldoon's body onto the cobbles echoed down the mews. When Shoeman reached his side, Muldoon was dead. O'Flaherty was breathing heavily, the bloodstained spanner still in his hand, poised over the dead man as if challenging him to try to rise.

The gunmen dragged the body back to the garage. They cleared the gelignite out of the loft and stowed it away in the boot and back of the Citroën, together with the primers, safety fuse and time-pencils. Then they heaved Muldoon's body up through the house to the back bedroom, where O'Flaherty dumped it into a cupboard. Downstairs the Shoeman was busy cleaning up the bloodstains in the living room and on the cobbles. The cul-de-sac seemed to have insulated them from the rest of the mews. They saw no one as they went about their work. When they finished they locked up the garage and workshop and went upstairs. The Shoeman telephoned their Kilburn IRA contact and gave him a terse account of what had happened. They had the gelignite and they would sit tight and wait for Grogan. He asked Frank to pass the news on to Kelly in Dublin. O'Flaherty found a bottle of whisky. He poured two stiff drinks and gave one to the Shoeman. He switched off the light and the two men sat in the darkness drinking slowly. They did not talk. There was nothing left to say.

22

GROGAN KNEW NOW THAT HE MUST MOVE FAST. Back in Southwark the first thing to do was to change his appearance. He cut his dark hair very short and dyed it a sandy colour. Already there was a difference: in the mirror his ears were prominent, standing out from his head. He put on a pair of spectacles that he's bought a few days before with thick tortoise-shell frames. They had plain glass lenses. Using the kit he'd bought at the theatrical outfitter's near the Charing Cross Road, he fitted small pads into his nose and cheeks, fattening his face. Skilfully applied, they changed the whole contour of the face, giving it a subtly different silhouette.

He went to the wardrobe and pulled on some casual clothes, different in style from the neat suit or dark blue blazer he usually wore. He put on a flowered shirt under a loose-fitting Shetland sweater and a pair of brushed denim Levi's. With a heavy leather belt and suede desert boots, the transformation was almost complete. As a last touch, he practised a new walk—looser, slouching and slightly round-shouldered.

By nine o'clock he had finished. He rang Muldoon but there

was no reply. Perhaps he'd gone round the corner to the pub. This was a good moment to pick up his papers. He'd kept in touch with Avakian on the telephone and tonight he was to go to an address in the East End, an apartment over a Chinese restaurant near the East India Dock Road. He went out into the street and hailed a taxi. It was all very simple, nothing to it. He gave his false name at the door. The nondescript man in the flat, who looked like some kind of clerk, made him wait in the small entrance-hall. He came back with a large brown envelope which he passed over without a word. Grogan checked quickly through the contents and that was it. No money changed hands here, the man was on Avakian's regular payroll. The papers confirmed what Avakian had already told him on the phone—the next day he was to be in Hull to sign on a boat destined for a number of Scandinavian ports. He'd already checked the timetable and chosen a train that left early the next morning. When he got back to Southwark Grogan packed his gear and did a final check through all his papers. Then he rang Muldoon. Still no reply. He decided to try again very early the next morning. Perhaps he'd have to do a breaking and entering job on the mews workshop. He was going to need the gelignite. He slept, lightly but easily.

He was awake just before dawn. He rang Muldoon. No reply. He made coffee, then rang Muldoon again. Still nothing. He put on a blue lightweight overcoat and slipped his Colt ·45 into the outside pocket. He left the flat, walking quickly down the long staircase, just after four thirty. A taxi dropped him near the mews in Kilburn half an hour later. It was a cold morning. At the bottom of the mews a man in pyjamas and dressing-gown was letting his dog out. He looked up at Grogan, nodded, and disappeared into the house. Grogan walked along the mews towards Muldoon's place. He could see the big Citroën parked directly opposite Muldoon's front door. From this angle he could see that the heavy wooden sliding doors of the workshop were wide open. Why wasn't Muldoon answering his phone? Grogan looked again at the Citroën. He remembered Muldoon usually parked it in the mews when he wanted some space to work inside, but he always left it alongside the sitting room window of his house, next door to the workshop.

The reason for it, Grogan remembered, was something to do

with the man opposite getting his car out. Today the Citroën was parked on the other side of the mews.

Grogan walked straight past the open door of the workshop. He glanced out of the corner of his eye as he passed, but could see nobody. He continued to the end of the mews, turned casually and headed back again. This time he walked, hands in pockets, straight in through the open door. There was no sound inside. He moved past a pile of empty crates, towards the back of the workshop where the staircase linked it with the house. He heard a noise from the house beyond that sounded like someone in the kitchen. At the same moment a cold voice spoke from behind him.

"Hold it there. Don't make a move or you're in bad trouble." Grogan threw himself sideways, twisting around at the moment he hit the ground. It was a pure reflex action, practised to perfection in the SAS. The Shoeman fired but missed. Grogan's hand was already on the Colt and he fired twice through his overcoat pocket. The Shoeman, jerked back by the impact of the bullets, crashed into the pile of wooden crates which toppled and fell with him. Grogan's glasses had fallen off and lay broken on the floor beside him. The disguise had worked. The Shoeman hadn't recognised him and had hesitated, otherwise Grogan would have had a bullet through the back. His body twitched in a series of sharp convulsions, but he made no sound. Then he lay still on the floor.

Grogan moved fast up the staircase leading to the house. He reached the top as the connecting door at the end of the corridor burst open and a stocky, shaven-headed man in shirt sleeves came through, a gun in his fist. This time Grogan had the Colt in his hand and the other man had no chance. Grogan fired once, aiming a fraction below the heavy belt buckle. The man went down, dropping his gun, and rolled sideways several times before hitting the wall of the corridor with a heavy thwack. He clutched at the wound in his stomach.

The house seemed suddenly very quiet. The wounded man's breath came in uneven rasps. He tried to move but Grogan waved his gun at him and he lay still.

"Who are you?" he croaked.

"The man you were sent to kill," Grogan replied coolly. He picked up the man's gun and put it in his overcoat pocket.

Grogan thought he heard footsteps in the street outside. He went to the window and looked out but could see no one. He turned back to the man on the floor and pointed the Colt at his head.

"Where's Muldoon?"

"Fuck off!"

The wounded man gasped as a spasm of pain passed across his face.

"Where is he?" Grogan snapped.

"In the bedroom . . . he tried to run for it . . ." There was fear now in the man's bloodshot eyes. "It was an accident, believe me . . . it was an accident." His voice tailed off.

Grogan moved the barrel of his gun a fraction closer to the man's face. "You killed him, you bastard!"

"For Christ's sake . . . get me a doctor." The wounded man's face had turned the colour of dirty wax.

Grogan looked at him closely. "You've got a fair chance I would say . . . providing something's done about that . . ." He waved his pistol at the man's stomach. "But I'm going to drill a hole through your head anyway if you don't talk . . . right?"

The man's head sagged and his eyes closed for a moment.

"Where's the gelignite?"

"In the car."

"Who sent you?"

"Kelly."

Grogan's mouth tightened. "I recognised that piece of carrion down below. But who are you?"

The man seemed to have become unconscious. Grogan prodded him in the chest with his gun. He opened his eyes and licked his lips. "O'Flaherty," he said.

Grogan let the name sink in. "I've been looking for you, you bastard. You were with my father when he died, weren't you?"

O'Flaherty nodded and looked down at his stomach. The blood had seeped out between his fingers and was spreading in an ever-widening stain over his trousers and shirt.

"How was he killed? . . . I want the truth, O'Flaherty."

The gunman tried to pull himself up against the wall as Grogan watched him. But the effort was too much and he slumped back.

"It wasn't my fault," he said with difficulty, his voice almost a whisper now. "Your father was hit and we panicked. We left him and ran ... all of us ... For Christ's sake get me a doctor!"

"Who was closest to him?"

"I was ... but the others weren't far away."

"How long did you leave him lying there?"

"About three hours ... He was dead when we went back ... it wasn't our fault, I tell you."

"But he died from loss of blood, you fucking coward!" Grogan burst out. His face showed uncontrollable fury. His left hand shot out and cracked O'Flaherty twice hard across the mouth. Then he was himself again. He sucked in his breath and stepped back.

"You know who planned that border crossing?" he said slowly.

O'Flaherty shook his head.

"Kelly," said Grogan softly.

O'Flaherty cursed under his breath. He looked dully at Grogan. "It was your father's fault ... he was too feckin' old for the game ... Get me a doctor for Jesus' sake ..." He groaned. Blood trickled out of the corner of his mouth as he haemorrhaged.

Grogan looked at him in silence and started to move away.

"What are you going to do?" O'Flaherty cried out, his voice cracking with the effort.

Grogan, his hand on the door handle, glanced back. "Leave you," he said simply.

"No, no, no come back ... I'll die ... I'll die ..."

Grogan slammed the door and raced down the stairs. He looked at his watch as he stepped cautiously out into the mews: 5.15 a.m. He could hear voices further down the street and windows opened opposite as he jumped into the Citroën. Thank Christ the ignition key was there! He turned it and pulled the starter. The engine turned over protestingly and then burst into life. He crunched the gear-lever into first and the heavy car leapt forward. Bundles of gelignite wrapped under a blanket slid across the back seat as Grogan hurtled out of the mews into the open street. A man in a bottle-green dressing-gown shouted at him to stop. People were leaning out of their windows. He put a safe distance between himself and the mews and turned into a deserted car park off Kilburn High Road. He stopped the car, jumped out, and hurriedly began to move the rest of the gelignite from the boot into the back of the car. The primers, detonators, safety fuse and, most important of all, the time-pencils were all there. He carefully stacked the greaseproof packets of gelignite on the floor and back seat, binding them tightly together with some gardener's twine in the boot. He took out the primers and embedded four of them in the gelignite. He cut off four lengths of instantaneous fuse, took out four small silver-coloured detonators from a box and fitted one end of the plastic-covered fuse into the hollow section of each detonator. He crimped them on firmly with his teeth. It was broad daylight now. Grogan checked an impulse to rush the job; it had to be done well or not at all. He placed the capped ends of the lengths of fuse into the primers. Each one had a hole in the middle and was about the size of a nightlight. He made sure they wouldn't slip out. He then linked up the four loose ends with a mainline fuse and ran it under the passenger seat into the front of the car, being careful not to bend it at right angles. He'd seen the best-laid charges fail because a sharp turn or twist had resulted in the fuse cutting itself in two before reached the explosive.

Back in the driver's seat, Grogan opened the box containing the time-pencils. Roughly the size of a fountain pen and made of copper, a time-pencil is the crucial initiating agent. Its hollow end fits onto the fuse. The other end contains a small phial of acid which, when broken by being crushed between finger and thumb, eats away at a protective covering and releases a plunger which ignites the fuse. The delay is governed by the thickness of the covering and can range from less than a minute to several hours. Grogan looked at the colour code inside the lid of the box and selected a time-pencil which had a delay of a minute and a half. The noise of a car close by startled him and he looked up to see a baker's van coming into the car park. Five forty-five. Grogan started the engine and a few minutes later was moving fast in a southerly direction towards the Harrow Road.

The big police Jaguar hummed along the motorway. Barnes and Franks were slumped in the back seat, exhausted.

They had managed to snatch a couple of hours' sleep in Cheltenham but it hadn't been enough. The Concorde alert had ended in the early hours of the morning. Although they had been tempted to stay on a little longer in case Grogan decided to look for Mairin after all, Barnes had really wanted to get back to London. He felt he had to be at the centre of things and his boss was on his back again. Fitchett's death had changed things. A general alert had been put out for the Shoeman and the other man but they seemed to have gone to ground. The IRA contact man in Kilburn, had been hauled in and his house searched from top to bottom. There was also the unsolved Figgis murder. Grogan seemed to have the knack of leading them up blind alleys wherever they turned. Barnes yawned. Well, there was nothing much he could do until he got to the office. He looked at his watch: 5.20 a.m. They were on the outskirts of the city. Franks was snoring gently. Barnes settled down more comfortably in the leather seat and closed his eyes.

The car's radio suddenly crackled into life. The police driver gave his call-sign and the message came through. There'd been a big shoot-up reported in Kilburn. Barnes was awake in a flash. The mews address was given and Barnes told the driver to put his foot down. Franks was also awake now, rubbing his eyes. The driver knew his London and twenty-five minutes later the Jaguar was turning off Westway with a squeal of tyres and heading northwards to Kensal Town. Heavy lorries were already pounding into the city but there were only a few cars about. Barnes was sitting on the edge of his seat, tension and fatigue showing on his face but his mind clear. They had just crossed the Harrow Road when he saw it. The long black Citroën came slowly out of a side turning ahead of them and, gathering speed quickly, flashed past, its yellow wheels twinkling in the morning light. Barnes caught a fleeting glimpse of a sandy-haired man at the wheel. Then the car was gone.

"Turn round!" he yelled at the driver. "The black car . . ."

Grogan had seen the police car. He thought it had slowed down after he passed it. But he couldn't be sure. He pushed the Citroën up to seventy miles an hour. He had turned into Maida Vale High Street and the traffic was building up. A pale gold sun had appeared which did nothing to take the chill out of the air. The dashboard clock said it was five minutes to six. He kept a wary eye on the driving mirror but could see nothing suspicious behind him. As he swung round Marble Arch into Park Lane, he checked over in his mind once again his preparation of the charges. He reached out and tucked the mainline fuse a little more firmly in the crevice between the two front seats. Looking up again he saw another police car coming in the opposite direction along Constitution Hill. He slowed down as it went past. As he swung round the Queen Victoria Memorial outside Buckingham Palace he looked in the mirror and his heart missed a beat. The patrol car was at right-angles, across the road, completing a three-point turn. Bloody hell! The Citroën bounded forward as Grogan threw it round the memorial and roared down Birdcage Walk. He gave a long blast on the horn to clear an early morning walker out of the way and a couple of minutes later he was speeding along the Embankment. He could hear a police siren wailing now somewhere behind him. Through the early morning haze over the City, Millennium House loomed up ugly and strangely menacing . . . he could feel the gelignite shift on the floor behind him as he hurled the car through the Blackfriars underpass . . . now he was on familiar ground . . . but another siren followed by a bell, clanging furiously, rose above the noise of the traffic . . . did it come from ahead or some way south? Impossible to tell.

Grogan cast a swift glance at the dashboard clock: six five. His eyes were gleaming now. He slowed the car into Cannon Street and thundered across a set of red lights. He was almost there. He saw the dun-coloured building glowing dully in the morning sun! Grogan braked hard as he swung into the open courtyard. There were a few cars parked near the building but no pedestrians. He cruised past the entrance and saw two uniformed men sitting behind the reception desk, drinking tea and reading the morning papers. He turned sharply and drove slowly round to the back of Millennium House. The wooden boom, blocking access to the underground garage, was down and padlocked. Grogan saw another uniformed guard peering out at him through the fogged window of the checkpoint box. . . . He pointed the Citroën at the boom, put the car in first gear and trod on the accelerator . . . the car shot forward . . . As Grogan jumped clear and began to run he saw a police car, its blue light spinning and its siren howling, tear out of a side street into the square . . . there was a crash of splintering wood as the Citroën burst through the boom. . . .

Barnes and Franks were hurled on top of each other as their car spun crazily into the forecourt of Millennium House, and over to the ramp.

The police car shuddered to a halt and the two Special Branch men tumbled out. Franks was about to break into a run but Barnes caught his arm. "Hold it!"

They stood transfixed watching the Citroën. Its long bonnet dipped and it began to roll slowly forward, gradually gathering speed . . . There was a squeal of tyres and tearing of metal as it bounced off the side walls . . . but its forward momentum continued . . .

Barnes and Franks, yelling to their driver, raced back across the square to take cover . . . they turned to look back and saw the tail end of the Citroën disappearing down the ramp . . .

Barnes sucked in his breath. "The bugger's done it!"

Epilogue

"Less is more." *Mies van der Rohe.*

IT WAS MIDSUMMER'S NIGHT in Stockholm. The moonlight glittered on the water and stone of the city as the Swedes celebrated the pagan festival. Grogan had found Sweden a friendly place for political refugees. But even so, it had taken him several weeks to unwind. He had put on a little weight though his face remained lean and rather pale. His new friends regarded him as disillusioned but not embittered.

Tonight Eva had persuaded him to go with her to a party in the old section of the city. The room was noisy, dark and hot. The men with their beards, scruffy jeans and overheated political theories contrasted unpleasantly, Grogan thought, with the clean-limbed and suntanned Swedish girls. The talk was still about Ireland and Vietnam. The acrid smell of marijuana caught in Grogan's nostrils and he abruptly turned and went out onto the balcony. A few minutes later Eva followed. She looked up at him with an open smile, full of the summer sun, and shook her long blonde hair.

"Don't sulk," she said with only a trace of a Swedish accent. "I want you to meet a couple of visiting British journalists."

Grogan scowled but shook the two men by the hand. He told

them bluntly who he was and said he didn't want to talk about Ireland. Eva left them alone but when she returned half an hour later the three men were deep in conversation. She had never seen Grogan so animated.

"That's fantastic!" one of the Englishmen was saying. He paused for a moment. "But tell us one thing."

"What?" Grogan asked.

"Millennium House. It's still there. What happened?"

Grogan grinned. He reached inside his jacket and pulled out a small copper tube, about the size of a pen.

"The time-pencil," he explained simply.

"But why?"

"Why not carry it through?" Grogan smiled. "Because I'd proved the point to myself. And I'd decided that no one, but no one, would gain from what I'd planned."

"So you blew their minds instead."